THE MARK

A Novel of Dinka In the Time of War

By

JEFFERY L. DEAL

ISBN-13: 978-1495211553
ISBN-10: 149521155X

"The Mark is a harrowing and beautiful story of a young man in the Sudan, a Dinka tribesman set in the midst of unimaginable turmoil; it is genuinely frightening and genuinely revelatory. Jeffery Deal has caught a true voice here, and the book's tone and texture make his hero, and the whole of his culture, matter to us immensely. I recommend everyone read this book."
Bret Lott

Bret Lott is the bestselling author of fourteen books, most recently the nonfiction collection *Letters and Life*: *On Being a Writer, On Being a Christian* (Crossway 2013) and the novel *Dead Low Tide* (Random House 2012.

Dedication

I would like to dedicate *The Mark* to my lovely wife, Hart, and my remarkable and patient children, Russell, Nancy Hart, Grace and Andrew. All of these loved ones shared in the amazing adventures which made this book possible. This is my third book about the Dinka Agaar of South Sudan. To my Dinka friends, I thank you and continue to pray that you will someday live in a free and prosperous South Sudan.

Table of Contents

Chapter One

The war with the Laraap threatened our lives. The Evil Thing threatened our souls. Both would force me onto a path not of my own choosing, a path I had already begun on the day I got the mark. It was a day before the war we called *Anyanya* spread across the land, leaving devastation in its wake like its name which means "venom of the snake." It was a day before we awoke to find the world in chaos, before the people of the North sent death in waves like summer clouds, before great men sat in great houses and wrote on papers about how we Dinka should live. It was at the beginning of a time when the Evil Thing would gorge itself upon the leavings of war and spread across this hard land of ours, a place so vast that whole tribes are swallowed up in its belly and invaders expend themselves in the fruitless pursuit of vapors.

My home is a land where there is no stone, an endless expanse, level and dry with no features except the plants that struggle their way from it and a few muddy rivers. The land is flat, with a distant sea to the east and poor mountains, in truth only slight hills, to the west. A place at the center of the world—or so think those who live there.

In most years the rains come in early summer and for a couple of months they drench the land with more water than it can absorb. The land is so flat and level that the rain does not run off as in other places but stays where it has fallen until the sun bakes it away. In the short months when the land is wet, walking is difficult for the hard clay becomes soft and slippery. Roads, that are barely passable when dry, become a trap for anything with wheels. Cattle and men move slowly. Goats move hardly at all. Plants burst out of the ground as if there was a mad rush to cover the earth while it is wet. The rains last but a short while, then the clouds leave with the abruptness of the tropical dusk and the land is hard again.

Within weeks after the rains leave the crops are dry as if they had never seen water. The trees and brush stay green for some months afterwards, however, reminding the people that at one time it had indeed rained in their land. As the months pass, the plants turn brown and dry. Before the rains begin again, the land looks dead as if no amount of water could revive it.

In some years the rains do not come until very late in the summer. The people grow hungry and cattle die. After the cattle start to die, children follow them as their mothers' milk fails and food becomes scarce. Wells dry up and the people begin to drink water that should not be drunk. In those dry years, sickness and fear spread with the thirst. The people move toward the distant and shrinking rivers. The land becomes dotted by abandoned mud huts with clean swept yards where you can tell that at one time a family lived. But eventually, the rains come again and the people move slowly back into the land as they have done since men began to mark time, or so think those who live there. They believe the center of the world is their hard, dry land where there is no stone.

The people have a sorghum that thrives in the hard land. They plant it one seed at a time and it grows almost twice the height of a man. A month or so after the rains, the tops of the sorghum plants grow heavy with seeds and bend the shafts toward the earth. When they have grown to the right size, the people cut them down one by one, carry them home, and thresh them by hand. They then place the grain in upright hollow logs and rhythmically pound it into flour with heavy sticks. The sounds of this pounding can almost always be heard echoing across the flat land and from a distance one could mistake the work as an eternal dance. However, such labor is hard, painful on the back, and done almost exclusively by women grown themselves as hard as the land.

On a day when the harvest was done and the land smoked of grass fires, I, Thon Bol, sat on the hard ground that was without stone. I am Thon named after the bull which was the most prized of the cattle my grandfather gave for my grandmother, a bull that would never be castrated. I am also Bol because I was born after my mother birthed twins, though they both died in less than a month and I am now their oldest.

I sat third in line where the *Beny Bith* had pointed. The Master of the Fishing spear carried the tool that created this name, *"Beny"* for Master and *"Bith"* which is the fishing spear. Such a tool has been the symbol of this holy class of prophets for so long that no one knows how it came to be so. Forty others who would also bear the knife that day sat with me and faced the rising sun. I was so tired that I struggled to keep from falling forward into the dirt. An ant stung my ankle. I thought that the sting would hurt for several days, but I did not move to brush off the ant or rub the place where it had stung me. I could not move on this special day. The sun glared at me, an angry color of white-yellow as it rose across the bushy horizon. Dust covered all the boys and our legs hurt from three days of almost constant dancing. My eyes were gritty from the dust and lack of sleep. But I did not dare wipe them or act as if anything mattered except the business at hand.

Today was the day, I thought. It was a good day to become a man, a good day to get a name. Later in life when I remembered the day, the thought of it would be clouded by time and expectations. Most clearly I would remember the feeling of newness and hope. I remembered feeling rich though I owned nothing of consequence, strong though my body still looked like a boy's, and secure though death surrounded me. I knew, as few knew, exactly who I was and what I was to become, and that it was on this day that I would become it. Not even the day of my birth was more important than this day and I would remember forever the day I got the mark.

Matak Mabor sat at my right. He is called Matak which means "Nhialic Thought About Me" after the long, barren time his mother was without child before he was born. He is Mabor after the color of the best cow his father gave for his mother. He was older by a year than me, but smaller and shorter—a trait from his mother's side of the family. Wrapped in a red blanket against the morning chill, she sat off to the edge of the clearing and joined the singing. I watched her sing and saw the decorative scars on her face move as if they had a life of their own. She was beautiful, Matak Mabor's mother. Small, delicate, with bright eyes that sparkled now in the growing light. Even a month from having her fifth child, she was beautiful. A woman worth many cows, though rumor in the village was that her husband paid for her with promises that were never made good. Matak and I did not speak of it for one does not speak lightly of such things. It was the speaking of such shame that causes friends to fight and be friends no more. Others gossiped and laughed about the bride price that was never paid, but not me, his best friend, age mate, and defender for life.

Matak's father was a good man who took care of his family and his in-laws, so there was no sense among their clan of any disgrace. On her hip, Matak's youngest brother clung to his mother fast asleep. I could not find Matak's father, though I knew he was there among the crowd. It was not good to show too much concern over the rite that his son would go through that day. Too much concern suggested you worried that he would shame the family when it came his time to endure the knife. Matak's father could ill afford more scandal, so he melted into the crowd as one unconcerned that his son would fail him on this day. Matak's uncle would do the worrying for the family. His uncle would carry the spear that in moments could end Matak's short life, a life that would not be celebrated, not be mourned if it ended in that way.

I looked for my own father, though I knew he was at war and would not be there. I hoped perhaps that word of my day under the knife had somehow made it back to my father. I dared to hope that somehow when he had heard that his oldest son by his favorite wife would become a man that he would travel the long distance to see for himself. I could hope, but it was not so. My father was nowhere to be seen. Possibly others would tell him of the day I became a man and got my scars. Others would tell him how brave I was, how the elder used an extra slow hand with the knife and yet I did not cry out or shame him with any show of pain or fear. I would not speak of it for that would be bragging. Others would brag for me and my father would be proud. His name would continue as it had since Nhialic made Garang and Abuk, the first man and the first woman. My father's name, my name, would not end in an untimely death filled with shame or fear. My father, I thought with a warmth in my belly, would indeed be proud of his boy who was now a man. I let the fantasy of my father's pride spread like a cloak over me, pretending it would happen and refusing to think otherwise.

My mother sat on a grey tarp under the strangling fig tree surrounded by many children. They lay on her, tugged at her hair and clothes. Some were of her own family. Others were, well who could know such things when children are so common. My mother was tall and straight, her great stature evident even as she sat with her legs stretched across the tarp. One of my young brothers tugged at her left breast with both hands and latched on to it with his mouth. She did not seem to notice, but sat still and quiet amid the commotion around her and the tiny assaults on her body. Her skin was shiny and smooth, dark as if made from the night sky. Her eyes were small ovals set deep over prominent cheeks. She too was beautiful. As I watched her I hoped to someday find such a woman at a price I could afford. I only hoped she had five fingers on each hand and five toes on each foot, not the six fingers and six toes my mother carried.

We boys to become men could not see the Beny Bith dancing and singing behind us. We could hear the shuffling of feet, hear the singing of old songs in an older language, most of which we could barely comprehend. The Beny Bith of this clan was older than most, chosen when my father's father was yet a child. No one remembered how the Beny Bith was selected since no one else was alive who had done the selecting. This Beny Bith was unlike any that had been or any that would be. Unlike the Beny Bith who served the other clans, this Beny Bith was a woman—a woman who had never bled as other women do each month. This Beny Bith was not distracted by the desire for men or the drive to bear children. For these traits Nhialic gave this Beny Bith powers, the elders of the clan say. The Beny Bith of my clan is one that has never failed to make the rains come when they must or to protect the village when raiders threaten. Such was the Beny Bith that danced behind the boys as we sat facing the rising sun. We could not see her, but could imagine her toothless smile and sagging flesh bouncing as she danced. We all thought we could hear her bones creaking. I could feel her power radiating on my back making the hairs of my neck stand on end. She raised her voice, a sound that did not seem to come from her at all, and we heard a song of the *Dheeng*, Marks of the Dinka Agar.

"My marks shocked the Laraap to hold his head.
My marks shocked the Laraap to bite his lip.
My marks shocked the Laraap to close his eyes.

'This thing is death,' he cried.

No, it is our ancient honor, it is our Dheeng."

As the elders directed us, we dug depressions half as deep as our heads in front of us to receive our blood. "Not too deep," one would say. "That would be too much blood." Or, "make it wider so all of it goes into the hole." We scraped at the dirt with our fingers, leaning back and forth in rhythm to the songs.

A girl moved slowly in front of us, stopping occasionally to jump and shout. I pretended not to see her, but my eyes darted toward the girl when I thought she would not notice. Her hair was clipped close about her head. A string with blue beads hung from each ear and they swayed back and forth as she danced. When her dress fell forward I could see the slightest hint of breasts forming around a slim, skinny and almost boy-like body. I had seen this girl before, watched her from the bush as she worked her family's gardens and pounded grain. I could tell in the way she danced that the girl was graceful. I could tell in the way she dug in her gardens that she could work the ground with ease, felt comfortable and familiar with the feel of it in her hands. She wore a necklace of cowry shells. Her dress, little more than a long scarf supported on one shoulder by a simple knot, was clean with trimmed edges. She joined a group of girls that sang and danced, jumping into the air with their arms extended behind them. I thought I noticed her looking my way as she bounced high in the air amid the dust and confusion of songs.

This was a good girl who would make someone a good wife, I thought that day. She stopped briefly and looked straight at me, catching me looking at her. She lowered her eyes and smiled, bright teeth gleamed with her smile and a dimple formed on her right cheek. I felt blood rush to my face and I quickly averted my eyes hoping no one noticed me looking at the girl. This was not a day for looking at girls or anything else. This was the day to put away childish things and become a man. This was the day I would get the marks that show people I was a man among men, a *Muonyjang*. I must remember the purpose of this day, the day I was to take the mark while facing the rising sun in the land without stone.

I turned from the girl and forced myself to think of who I would become that day. I would become one of the men who show others what men should be. All things would center around me and those like me, I thought that morning. Children would quake and women lower their eyes when I passed. The enemies of the people would fear me and I would cook no more for myself or others. Only certain work would be acceptable any more. I would have a voice at the Counsel of the Clan, a small voice, but a voice that is heard, must be heard for I would be one of the men of men. All this will come for I was chosen to make the change, chosen earlier in years than others.

I must pass the test without flinching, without tears or any sound—I thought. I will answer their questions while the knife is still in my flesh. I will act as if there is no blood in my eyes and mouth. I will show the Clan that I am one who would face death for them, thrust and receive the spear for them. The Second Anyanya was still a small thing and had not yet spread to our lands, but as I think back to this time I think a deep part of us knew it was coming, knew we had to brace ourselves to be strong against it. No words formed in my mind or came to my ears of the time of devastation to come, but somewhere inside of us I think we all felt it looming across the horizon. I would look back at that day as if it were a day on which I had drunk too much beer or taken some root that blunts the mind, my memories full of hope and warning. I would remember things as if the whole world had shrunk to the size of the clearing in which I sat. People spoke, but only later in bits and pieces did I recall their words.

Fear flashed into my mind and I heard my heart beating in my ears so loudly that I thought surely the others could hear it as well. Was it fear of the knife or fear of failing? I could not tell. I thought of the knife for it was the one thing I could picture and fight in my mind. I struggled to push the fear of the knife back into my chest and let it be swallowed by my pride—fought so hard that I felt something break in me that day. Whatever broke killed the child in me so that it would never speak or laugh again. The man may speak. The man may laugh. But not the child, for it had died for fear of the knife. The rising sun burned the back of my eyes and I thought I could feel it scorch to cinders all traces of the child within me and with it the thing that made fear.

People danced. Many songs were sung. Some together as one, many sung heedless of the songs of others as if sung only for the singers themselves. The songs praised the cattle, the Personality Oxen, the sun, Deng, the divinity of clouds and sky. They sang of the greatness of Nhialic, God and Creator of all. The songs praised the strong women. Songs and songs for we are a people of songs where a poetic voice is valued greatly and men have no more shyness of singing than the women. Such are the Muonyjang, the people of this hard land where there is no stone.

The crowd grew quiet as the Beny Bith slowly and with great reverence placed the knife in the hand of an elder, a specialist of sorts. I did not know how such a man obtained the skills to make the scars. I did know that my family paid the man two goats to do this thing. The Beny Bith handed the man the knife, then danced before us four boys who would be first among the others. She then turned her back on us and faced the sun. She would not look at the cuts, only the healed scars, for to do so would curse the boys. I did not understand such things, but they are told to me by those whose words I had learned to trust so I believed it to be true.

Just before she turned, her eyes swept across the group of us, the initiates waiting for the knife. For the briefest of moments her eyes met mine and in that instant my heart froze. A flicker of surprise flashed across her face then quickly left. In that instant I knew she saw something of me or my future, something that she did not see in the others, maybe something of the part I would play in the battle against the creeping darkness that even then shrouded our land. All of this I saw and thought in the heartbeat of time when our eyes locked across the dust and noise of the celebration. She then turned away and looked at us no more and the coldness left me. I had no time to dwell upon the strange look or the feeling it created in my heart as the dancing and singing started back again even louder than before and I heard heavy footsteps.

I sensed the man approach behind us. Elders stood in front of the first of the four. They watched carefully for any sign of fear in us. They saw none. They began to talk to the first boy, having him repeat praises and songs to the totem of his clan.

"*Wen Anyuon*, Son or Grass" an elder said.

"Wen Anyuon," the boy replied.

They sang songs of praise to the Grass Totem, the Crocodile Totem, and to Deng, the Divinity of Clouds and Rain and the boy-becoming-a-man sang the words back to them, his voice growing stronger even as they cut his flesh.

"Do you sing praises to Nhialic on this day?" they asked him.

"I sing praises to Nhialic," he replied.

The boy continued to answer them in turn, his voice steady and clear. He could easily have been watching a herd of goats for no sign of pain showed in his voice or face.

"Is your heart crying?" an elder asked the boy.

"My heart is full of joy today, *Babba Dia*, my father,"

And indeed you could hear the joy in his voice even as the blood bubbled around his lips. I looked straight ahead but could see the movement as the man made the seven cuts of our people. His clan, the Clan of the Crocodile and of the White Grass was strong with many members and elders. Without them, our section would have long ago been overrun by the Atuot and Nuer raiders. Theirs was a proud clan and his strong voice spoke of that pride.

At last it was done and the elders and the specialist moved to the next boy. The first boy, now a man, leaned forward so the blood would drain into the hole that he had dug and the earth could drink of it. It ran in a steady stream down his face and dripped from his chin. I turned my eyes and face just enough to see it, then looked ahead as the fear flashed in my gut again—the dying child in me crying out one last time.

The men moved to the next boy. Again, the elders asked their questions, had him repeat the songs of praise for his clan's totem. This boy answered but a bit too fast. I could hear tension in his voice, but not quivering. He did not cry out. I looked forward, but at the edges of my vision I could see the boy-to-become-a-man wavering as the specialist cut his forehead. I could hear the slicing sound the knife made, even above the voices of the elders. I prayed for him that he would not faint, for that weakness would be almost as bad as showing fear. The boy-now-man stayed upright and answered all their questions. His heart did not cry through his voice. He too then leaned forward to let the earth drink his blood.

They then came to me. My heart beat fast and strong within my chest. I was sure the elders could see it move my ribs. My eyes seemed to bulge from their sockets, but I kept them on the rising sun behind the elders, kept listening to the sounds of the morning.

"Can you be a brave man?" the elder asked me. He had asked no such question of the others.

"I can be a brave man, *Babba Dia.*"

"Will you be a man of men? Will you be Muonyjang?" his voice bellowed so deep and strong the sound of it seemed to come from the earth itself. Fear pushed out of my chest again. Not fear of the knife, but fear that this elder knew of some reason that I should not be a man. Fear that he was asking things not asked of the others to trick me into saying something that would stop the ritual and shame my family. I pushed the fear back and replaced it with anger.

"I will be a man, Babba Dia. I will be a Muonyjang, Babba Dia," I answered not trying to hide the anger that had been fear.

"Then who is your mother?" he asked. As I opened my mouth to answer, the knife made contact with the skin of my forehead.

"My mother is Athen Ayokoi Laat, daughter of a great family by the river." I was sure my mother felt pride from hearing my answer. Hers is a good name. Athen meaning she was born as the day was ending, Ayokoi meaning putting oil on water, and Laat for the day of the week her mother birthed her. It was a name that could only be spoken with pride.

The specialist grasped my head firmly and then pressed the knife into my flesh. In one swift motion he twisted my head as he held the knife straight. The blade cut deeply into my forehead. I felt the scrape of its edge as it moved across bone. I fought to keep my breathing steady and to concentrate on the elders and the rising sun, to make the pain something felt by someone else.

Nhialic made me for days such as this, I said to myself in a mumble that made the elders lean forward to hear. Blood poured into my eyes and I could not see for a while. I resisted wiping the blood for that would show those around me that the cut was noticed.

"And where is your father?"

Not the best question to ask, I thought. Someone was taking advantage of this time to ask a question they knew I must answer when such a question should be asked in private.

"My father fights in the great war," I answered and tried to sound proud. "My father fights in the place of many who would not fight but stayed at home with the women and children."

Perhaps it was too much to have said, but it was said and there was no taking it back. I did not quiver as the second cut scraped across the bone of my forehead. It seemed the pressure from the knife would squeeze out my brain. I worried briefly that perhaps the specialist wielding the knife was offended by my answer and was trying to kill me.

"Will you fight for the people?" he shouted angrily.

Again, more questions not asked of the others.

"I will fight for the people, Babba Dia."

"Will you die for the people?"

"If the Beny Bith sees it, it will be as you say. If Nhialic wills that I should be protected, it will not be as you say. I will fight for the people when the people need me to fight."

Perhaps my answer was too proud, I thought. But I heard grunts of approval from the elders and was assured. Women broke out in new song that sounded so distant that they could have been singing from across the river.

The specialist made another cut, this one I barely felt. More questions that I could never recall. More cuts I did not feel. The knife made cuts and more cuts as if the man intended to remove my face. Finally, the men moved to the next boy and I leaned forward. I felt the warm blood run from my face and into the earth. I felt the child in me bleed out of the marks I would forever bear. Marks of the Dinka Agar. Marks of the Muonyjang. I knew that I could never go back into childhood and become anything else. I could not become another people for the marks cannot be removed on this side of the grave. I heard women trill and children cry out in fear. I heard the words of the Beny Bith as she spoke toward the rising sun—words that I could not understand that sounded important and holy. I felt the attention of Nhialic turn toward me as she spoke the strange words and danced before Him. God saw me at that moment and marked the path I would take and the days left of my life, I thought.

I am a Man of Men, Husband and Father, Protector and Guide to the people. I am Muonyjang, I thought as I sat before all the people facing the rising sun in the land without stone that now drank of my blood.

Chapter Two

At the edge of her vision the Beny Bith saw a slight movement in the tall grass. She forced herself to keep her head turned toward the rising sun. Above the turmoil and noise, her mind crept across the field and slid easily into the brush where she had seen the movement. She felt a darkness push against the morning light that now poured into the land. She prayed that Nhialic would protect those whom He had put in her charge and revealed to her the source of the evil she sensed. She prayed and sang as she shifted her body back and forth in time with a drumbeat that barely penetrated her trance. She felt the first light of morning strike her face and felt the radiance of the Creator push against the dark power that lurked nearby. She knew that whatever evil prowled outside of the confines of their village would not feed on them this day and she relaxed slightly.

She had heard the rumors of war, another Anyaya, which would rumble across the land as it has done since the beginning of time. They used new names with each generation, but she knew that it was only one war with many faces—a war without end for this land that lies at the center of all things. She could sense a gathering of dark clouds to the north that would sweep the land clean of those too weak or too noble to kneel to the latest conqueror or those too unwise to wait for their inevitable departure. This war would be terrible, she knew, but it was not the darkness to the north that frightened her this day. The evil thing was here.

A man watched the celebration from within a strip of grass that the fires had passed by. The entire village had converged on the line of boys who would receive the mark and left their belongings and their animals at his mercy, a mercy that he did not possess. Already he had bludgeoned one dog and tossed its carcass into an open well. Within days, the water would be putrid and men would have to climb into the dark abyss and clean out the rot. Hundreds of people would be forced to walk hours longer to get their water elsewhere and he smiled to think of the chaos his one small act would create.

He thought of how he could have been there among them, receiving the honor of the marks and having women sing and dance for him. It was his right to be there. He hated those that had withheld their support for him and had let others less deserving than him become men of the Jeeng. He had known this day was coming and weeks earlier he had left to be alone in the bush so that others would not see him in his disgrace. He crouched low when the Beny Bith turned toward him, fearful that she would sense his presence even if her aged eyes could not see him. He watched her dance and gesture over the boys as the sun rose and sent shafts of yellow among the crowd.

Some of them knew of the coming darkness, he thought. They knew of the First Anyanya and how the wave of destruction it brought with it had never abated and that it would soon expend itself once more upon this land. The second Anyanya served his dark and hidden purposes and he alone welcomed it and its power. He loved the darkness, loved the chaos of war that fed his desires. He drank of it as the earth now drank of the blood of the Initiates and he felt it burn within him and feed his hate.

He felt satisfaction that those who now sang with joy would someday know of the power he wielded. Soon they would all know that he was to be feared even more than the insignificant insects that they now honored with the marks. He watched the tall woman sitting on a tarp among a hoard of children. He hated her and all of her foul brood most of all. He would take this woman someday, he knew. He would take her even though she fought him with her great strength. As he thought of it he felt a slight arousing in his loins and he crouched further into the grass.

The celebration ended by midday and people slowly walked back to their own compounds. They talked and joked with one another and even the dourest of souls smiled at the new men who walked in small groups and adjusted the leaves that covered their wounds.

No one noticed the missing dog but they did note the many food pots that had mysteriously emptied themselves during the celebration and that several articles of clothing had disappeared. A few old men looked anxiously into the empty bush for a mischievous spirit or jok and some of the women shouted accusations at their neighbors. The Beny Bith made motions of protection with her spear that others noted, though they did not know why she felt the need of it, and a wave of anxiety swept across the village. Men counted their cows, women counted their children, and children counted their goats. Without a command from anyone, men with spears ringed the village and cast brave faces toward an unseen enemy. Many prayed that the thing which stalked them was of flesh and blood as they shook their spears in the air and searched the grass and brush for a foe and searched their hearts for courage.

He saw them form their puny line of warriors, already too late, always too late. Soon, he thought. Soon they would know the cause of their fears and they would grovel to him for protection and justice. He could be patient when patience served him. He shouldered a bundle of blankets wrapped tightly with ropes and left them in their confusion and fear.

He moved swiftly northward. Even in the full light of the noonday sun he was visible only to the sharpest of eyes. He laughed out loud as he moved and his voice carried to the Beny Bith's ears. She sniffed the wind and made more protective gestures with her spear as the sense of danger slowly receded.

Chapter Three

I sat up slowly and blinked into the darkness. Outside the mud hut I could hear echo of bird calls as they began to rouse. The faintest light filtered through gaps around the oval wood door of the hut in which I had slept. Around me I heard the sounds of others breathing the breath of sleep. The pain on my forehead reminded me of what had happened yesterday as I wiped sticky lumps of dried blood from my face and eyes. This would be my first full day as a man of men and I was anxious to cross the threshold of a new day and a new life.

I pulled my blanket over my shoulder and rose. The door, half my height, gave way on leather hinges to let me out. I had to duck to get under the low overhang of the grass thatching of the roof. As I stood upright, the banana leaf that covered the wounds on my forehead slipped to one side and I quickly replaced it. A *Tiet* can show up at any time, I thought. One look at the open wounds and all my pain and suffering would turn to a curse.

I knelt next to the glowing coals of last night's fire. I carefully placed a few sticks on the coals and blew. Within seconds a small flame grew from the coals and began to consume the wood. The ring of ground around me glowed in the golden light as I sat on a crooked log to warm myself against the morning chill. I reached into a clay pot by the fire and brought water to my face to wash away some of the blood. Later, I planned to go to the borehole to bathe and possibly show myself as a man to some of the girls who were always there. I would stand aloof from them and casually rinse myself in the water that they would bring me, must bring me, for I was now a man.

In the distance, I could hear the chant of a man and his family as they sang songs of praise and encouragement to their ox. In my mind, I could see the family as they ploughed the field in near darkness. I knew them, could recognize them by the direction of the sounds and the words of their song. They were a wealthy family with a father who worked all day in the fields with his wife and children and the metal plough. I did not know where the man got the great plough that added to the family's wealth in such a way. I heard that a group of people from across the seas had given him the plough, but I knew of no such people near where we lived. But it was a great blessing, this plough. While others worked with small, metal-tipped hoes and wooden adzes, this father could turn the soil as fast as a man could walk. This and the fact that he and his family worked together as one for as long as the day had light, created the wealth his family enjoyed. It was a wealth so well earned that no one need envy it. They did, however, envy his possession of the plough.

A slight twinge of hunger rose in my belly as I sat by the fire. I looked at the bowl of pounded millet my mother had set by the door last night. Yesterday, I would have considered mixing it with water and heating it over the fire. But it is not proper for men to cook, and I was now a man. Better hunger than even a small disgrace. I knew my mother would rise from her hut shortly and cook for me.

More birds called as the eastern horizon began to glow a deep orange. Piak piak settled into the trees over my head, watching for the movement of cattle that they could follow in order to snatch up the insects that they disturbed. Small swifts, with their sleek wings stretched behind them as if they had been molded by the wind, darted in and out of the tree tops. In the far distance, a hyena gave the last whooping cry of night as it settled into its den. I marked the direction and distance of the call with no more thought than I would give to breathing. The cattle of my family began to bellow to one another. I listened intently, hearing and identifying each voice as surely as I would the voice of a sibling.

Across the swept dirt yard, I heard a door slide open. I could see only a shape emerge, but knew it was my mother. I heard the sound of pottery clinking on hard ground. My mother began to sing softly to herself through closed lips, the words heard only in her head but the lilting melody spread across the compound like a welcoming blanket. I smiled and turned my head to stare into the fire.

In all of the three round huts scattered about the compound, I heard the stirrings of people rousing themselves from sleep. The largest house sat on stilts above a stick fence where goats slept. Like my hut, the others rested on the hard ground.

"I would eat before I go to care for the cattle," I said across the dark yard.

No answer.

"Did you hear me, Athen?" I said slightly louder. "I would eat now."

"Athen is the name I would use for men of the village and for my husband," my mother replied sharply. "I am still Mama Dia, to you."

I looked back at the fire again.

"Did you hear me, my son?"

"I heard you, Mama Dia," I replied, hoping vainly that no one else heard my rebuke. I heard only silence from the huts.

"Make sure the cattle have not wandered into the ground nut field again. Then you shall eat, my son."

I did not reply.

She is testing me, I thought. Should I refuse her and demand she obey me as I know Father would? Or should I go after the cattle? What I do now will be reflected in the way I deal with Mother for the rest of my life. I made my decision swiftly and was about to reply to her when she spoke again, her words so soft I could barely hear them.

"It would please me greatly if you would make sure the cattle have not ruined my many days of work in the ground nut field, my son. When you return I shall have food ready for you."

Athen was a good mother and never harsh when gentleness would do as well and again I thought of how I hoped to someday marry a girl like her, or almost like her. Some said the extra toes and fingers were a sign that Nhialic had looked down from heaven and marked my mother as one of His favorites. She did not seem to mind the extra fingers as she worked. Her strong walk and stately stride did not seem hampered by the extra toes. I therefore chose to believe them. Others, mostly women jealous of her family and the produce of her gardens, said the oddities were a sign of ill intent from God and that only bad luck could come of her deformity. I chose to ignore these foolish women. My mother gave birth to many children including three sets of twins. Her sorghum grew tall. Her millet bent under the weight of fat seeds. I did not believe my mother was cursed in any way that mattered. But when she was a young child herself no one could have foreseen the fine woman that she would become. Perhaps that is why her family accepted my father's offer of twenty-eight cows and seven goats, meager as it was for such a woman. Perhaps her father feared seeing the first sign that she was indeed cursed, a sign that would make her worthless so that no bride wealth would come to the family. Perhaps it is the extra fingers and toes that made her my mother after all. I could not say. But

I did know that she was a good mother. A woman that other women envied and men coveted.

Forgetting the harsh words that had welled up in my chest, I rose and headed toward the sounds of our cattle. I found them at the edge of a brushy field and moving south. I picked up a thin switch and walked swiftly around them. They would be in the newly planted field within minutes if I did not stop them. When I was between them and the field, I struck the largest bull across its shoulder. The bull turned away from the ground nut field and back toward the empty bush. The herd followed. Even in the dim light I could match the sounds of the cattle to their color names, malith, ajak, adol, mabor, magok, malual, all the names of cow colors and therefore the names of people as well. Each cow stepped slightly different from the other, bellowed and even breathed a different sound. I knew them all and could know if any were missing or sick just from the sounds of the herd. On that morning, all was well with them and their pace and collective murmurings were peaceful and healthy.

We of the Dinka love our cows too much, the Laraap will often say of us. My uncle once told me why it is so for he says that in the olden times, even the Dinka would kill the wild cow. He told me that our love of cattle was both a blessing and a curse brought on us by our own sin. He said that one time a warrior killed the calf of a cow and the calf of the mighty buffalo. The buffalo decided that she would take vengeance on man by attacking man any time he is seen in the forest or grasslands. For this reason, to this day when a buffalo sees a man in the forest it will attack him and they are feared everywhere. But the cow was more clever. She decided to endear herself to man, make man care for her, groom and feed her, and even risk his life to protect her. My uncle told me that this is why we care so much for them and will risk our lives for them. We never eat them just for food but only in celebrations where Nhialic is praised or where great power is needed. On those days, we will send the spirit of a cow to tell Nhialic of the occasion why we are so happy. On days such as these, I feel the love of the cows tug at my heart across endless time and could feel the grief of the ancient mother for her calf.

I walked slowly with them, careful to step only where the cattle had walked to avoid snakes in the dim light. My bare feet moved silently and I could feel the cool grass slip around my ankles. Whenever I got close enough, I struck the bull with the switch to keep them moving.

The sun had just peeked over the distant trees when I returned to the family compound. The children were already up and packing their mouths with a porridge of pounded millet topped with a slurry of crushed okra leaves. They paused and watched me as I approached.

This was the first day of my life as a man. The children would not know how to react, I thought. I will be kind, but strong and noble. I will be what Father would be if he was here.

I sat on the crooked log apart from the children. Athen scooped some of the food into a bowl made from a dried gourd and brought it to me. She laid the bowl within my reach then returned to the children. I did not acknowledge the act for it was as it should be. A Dinka man does not cook for himself or serve himself. I sat on the log and with as much of a carefree air attitude as possible, I brought the bowl into my lap. Over the sounds of the children whispering to one another, I could still hear the family with the plough as they chanted and worked the distant field.

Perhaps I should ask them to borrow the plough, I thought. Surely they will have turned enough of the ground for many families by now. I thought how they would likely turn me down, not trusting anyone else with such a prized possession. They would probably offer to plow our fields themselves for a price—a cow, a couple of goats, maybe money. I tried to figure how much the work was worth, how much more we could reap if we ploughed a larger field than we could do by hand. But I could not imagine why I would do such a thing. We needed nothing and we should be content with the knowledge that good rains always brought us enough to eat. If the rains were bad, the size of your field meant nothing. Still, the man with the plough was rich with many cattle and enough money to buy clothes and tools from the Laraap traders. Perhaps the *pan*, my family, should speak of it together.

When I had eaten enough, I walked over to the children. My mother had already wiped the clay dishes with a tattered rag and stacked them under the shea nut tree that shaded all three of the huts. It was the season for the nuts and their green husked fruit lay by the scores around the compound. Some had already had the yellow outer fruit chewed off by the children revealing the brown kernel beneath. Athen had begun to gather them in a pile near the trunk of the tree. Later she would crush and boil them to extract the oil.

"Will you go to the cattle camp today, Thon?" asked my younger brother, Gum.

I answered with an affirmative grunt and a slight lifting of my chin.

"I should go with you," Gum said.

I knew that our mother would be nervous about the way the village reacted after the celebration the day before. A collective shiver had run across the community and the people would still be talking of it. Even though no one knew the cause of the fear, rumors and distrust would spread. She was a wife without a husband to protect her and I knew she would want the younger children to stay close to the compound.

"You have not yet seen five seasons here," I replied. "You would be a burden to me, a target for the older boys to tease, and of no real help. You should stay here and tend the fields and goats."

"The others can tend the goats," Gum replied. He stood as tall as he could with his shoulders back. In his mind he thought the pose made him look strong, but in reality it only exacerbated the bulge in his abdomen and created a silly image. The string of beads around his waist, the only thing he wore, stretched tight and threatened to break.

"Besides," I said. "Mother would never let you go."

I sat my bowl on the ground and lunged at Gum. The child stood his ground. I then tried to pick him up but Gum fought me off.

"I am too old to be picked up like a child."

I laughed.

"Then we will fight like men," I said.

With that I lunged for Gum again, pretending to be slow to allow Gum to dodge out of my grasp. Gum kicked at me and struck me in the knee. The blow was too weak to be meaningful, but I grimaced and limped. The other children laughed and shouted. I then pretended to attack with short punches and fierce gesturing. Gum replied in kind and the play-fight went on for several minutes.

When we stopped and leaned against tree panting, Athen approached us.

"The grass is drying and the cattle keep trying to graze in our gardens. You should take them to the camps," she said.

Gum started to speak.

"You must stay with the goats from sunup to sundown now or they will destroy our fields," she said before Gum could speak. He slumped against the tree.

"Others have already gone," Athen continued. "Your grandfather's half-brother is the Pied Bull of the camp by the river and he sent word that he expects you to come today."

I wanted to argue, to make plain that the decision was mine to make. Instead, I nodded.

"One more thing," my mother said after Gum had slunk away from us. She spoke in a whisper and leaned into me.

"Some men from Rumbek came yesterday while you were getting the marks," she whispered. "They said there have been raids from the north as far as Aweil, mostly following the river. They have killed many Dinka and taken many others as slaves. Speak to no strangers and tell no one where you go, my son. The men who came here are looking for soldiers to fight against the Laraap warriors. They take some even before they have gotten the mark." She glanced toward Gum as she spoke.

"Did any of them know of Father?" I asked.

Athen shook her head. A look of sadness fell across her face as it did every time she spoke of father. She cocked her head slightly and glanced to the north, lowered her head, and walked back to where the children played.

The sun was hours over the horizon when I set out for the cattle camp. I walked slowly with a spear in one hand and a small bundle of food and camp items slung over my shoulder. The cattle moved along the trail with little prodding, seeming to know the path they had all taken many times. To the east, I heard a familiar bell.

Shortly, I saw the favorite oxen of Matak Mabor move from the bush. The ox looked at my bull briefly as if to take stock of who would be the leader. Both blinked sleepily toward the other. My bull shook his great horns. The hump on his shoulders quivered and the skin of his neck twitched. Matak's ox stood rigid, and then lowered his head to graze. The battle of wills ended and my bull continued in the lead up the trail toward the cattle camp. I loved my great bull with its deep black, almost purple color in the front and back and brilliant white in the middle. Majok, the color of this bull, is a name that any man would take as his own--a rare combination of the colors of Deng, dark and white clouds, carriers of good rains. It is a name that I would give to one of my children if I live long enough and Nhialic so blesses me.

As the two herds merged, Matak stepped from the brush and joined me. He too sported a broad leaf across his forehead. For a long while neither of us spoke.

"We will not make the cattle camp before night," Matak said.

I stepped closer to Matak. He nodded and grunted, then reached out and interlocked his fingers with mine. The two of us walked hand-in-hand for a long while in silence.

"I am in no hurry," I said.

"Nor am I," Matak replied. "But you should not worry."

I tried to pull his hand away but Matak held it tightly.

Matak laughed as I pulled harder to remove his hand.

"He is with his uncle, Matur," Matak said. "Matur is not interested in a fight between the families that no one can win."

"I am not afraid," I replied, letting my hand lie limp in my friend's.

"I did not say you were," Matak replied. "But you would be foolish to not worry that you would have to deal with him. After all, it is because of you that he did not get the marks with the rest of us."

"It is not because of me," I said. "He is the one who was hurting the girl. I just stopped him."

"Yes," Matak said. "But when the girl told the others what you did, the Beny Bith told your family you should get the mark early and that Chol should not. He will blame you. You can expect him to challenge you at the camp."

"I am not afraid of Chol," I said, this time succeeding at pulling his hand free.

"You should be a little afraid," said Matak. "His father has flown the wrestling championship flag over their hut for two years. He is very strong and not very smart."

"I am not even a little afraid," I said proudly.

"Of course. For you have the bravest of friends at your side," Matak thumped his chest and said.

I laughed and pushed Matak almost to the ground. We continued to walk and again our hands found one another. His was smaller than mine as was the rest of his body. Both of us walked naked in the dappled light, clothed only in stringed beads around our necks, the soles of our bare feet as thick as a Larap's sandals. Matak seemed thinner and taller than he had appeared just last week. The Feasts of the Mark added nothing to his frame. But I also knew him to be fast and quick. No one could catch or even touch him if he did not want it. Speed, I thought as I watch him stroll at my side, speed is as good as strength.

"Yes, my friend is brave, small, and with an ugly ox," I said to break the silence.

Matak stopped walking. The cattle continued, but I stopped and looked back. Matak appeared to be thinking. Without warning he launched himself at me and looped his arm around my neck. I responded by picking Matak up by the waist and throwing him to the ground. As he fell, Matak grabbed my wrist and dragged me down with him. We struggled in the dirt and laughed the laugh that only the best of friends can share. Within minutes we stopped and lay beside each other on the ground with our possessions scattered in the grass about us. The burnt red color of clay smudged our bodies and both of us bled from small scratches. We lay looking into the sky for a long while before speaking, both of us content to be in the best place with the best friends and most beautiful cattle in all the world.

"I don't think I will ever marry," Matak said as he laid his head back in the grass.

"Why would you say such a thing?" I asked. I glanced at his genitals, knowing already that they were normal and that he did not bear the mark of one who could not father children.

"My family does not have the wealth of cows that yours does, Thon. No one will give me a daughter to marry without all the payment."

I did not reply. His father's debt would follow Matak, I thought.

"And besides," Matak continued. "The Beny Bith has told me I would never have the company of wives. What else can it mean?"

I turned toward Matak who lay staring into the late afternoon clouds. I could hear the cattle still moving away from us, still content and still safe.

"Our Beny Bith said that to you?" I asked.

"She did," Matak replied. "She said that I would do well enough without a wife. She told me that in order to be happy that I should follow the path of Deng."

"I do not know that path, Matak," I said.

"Nor do I," Matak replied. "But she said that Deng, divinity of the clouds and sky, a great manifestation of Nhialic Himself, would lead me to peace and happiness. She said the path would lead me to her."

"To her?" I asked.

Matak continued to stare at the sky.

"To her. She said that I carried the gift to be a Beny Bith. She said that she would not live long and that I should let Deng guide me to replace her."

"You, a Beny Bith?" I said. I lay back and looked at the sky with Matak. "I can see you as a Beny Bith. But I cannot see you without wife and child. Other Beny Bith have wives. Why not you?

"I cannot say. I only know what she told me."

"Have you told your mother and father?" I asked.

"I have not. I am not sure I believe her," Matak said. "And to die without children? That is something that my father would not let happen."

"He has others to carry his name," I said. "He will live on through his children without you. And your brothers can bear children in your name. We both have uncles with ghost wives, levirate wives, wives of all types. Your clan can manage another in your name even if you choose never to marry."

"That is so," Matak said. "But he still wants more. Even with the debt for my mother unpaid he is talking about marrying some girl of the Atuot."

"Maybe Deng will speak to you," I said.

I stared hard at the sky. Perhaps Deng would show Himself to us in the clouds. Perhaps Nhialic would speak to us, I thought, though I have never heard his voice.

"If it was another Beny Bith I would ignore him," I said. "But this one? This one is not one to be taken lightly. This one has power. Even my mother says so and she has little love for any holy person, man or woman."

Matak stared silently into the sky. After a few minutes we rose wordlessly, brushed off as much dirt as possible, and gathered our belongings.

We moved the cattle slowly toward the river and the cattle camp. The path was well known to us and our cattle. Each tree we knew. Each homestead we passed brought forth family members who spoke to us in familiar terms. When we were far enough from any of the planted fields, we stopped the cattle. I put a tether around the forefoot of my bull and staked him in an area with thick grass. The other cattle browsed around the bull, but stayed within sight of him.

A small depression in the ground held enough water for us to bathe. When we had dried, Matak pulled a straight stick from the bundle of goods he carried. He took a knife and drilled a small hole into a dry piece of wood. He then took a pinch of sand and sprinkled it in the hole. Matak and I then took turns whirling the stick in the hole until a small curl of smoke formed. Matak continued to whirl the stick in his hands while I took a clump of dry grass and dung and placed it on the ground at his side. Matak flicked a tiny ember onto the grass, then blew gently. Within minutes a flame began to consume the grass. As Matak built the fire, I pulled bundles of sorghum flour from my pack. I poured milk from a gourd into the flour and stirred the mixture with a stick. I then spread the thick paste onto a flat piece of metal. By that time, Matak had a substantial fire going and had moved clods of dirt around it. I placed the metal on the dirt and over the fire. In a few moments, the paste began to sizzle on its edges. With the edge of my knife, I lifted the flat cake at its edge, then flipped it.

"Here we are," Matak laughed. "Men for a day and still cooking for ourselves."

"There is no one here, so it is allowed." I said.

Mosquitoes buzzed around us as we ate.

"Do you believe the government man about the mosquitoes?" Matak asked.

"You mean about fever?" I asked.

Matak nodded. By this time darkness had come and the fire cast dancing shards of light in a small circle around us.

"My mother said it is true," I replied. "She learned it from her mother as well."

"Then why do the cattle not get the fever from them?" Matak asked.

"This fever is a disease of men, not cows," I said. "Just like there are diseases of cows that we do not catch either."

Matak nodded.

"But that is the sort of thing a Beny Bith should want to know," I said.

Matak did not reply. I could tell that there was something else in his mind that he was not telling me. I think it was something in his encounter with the Beny Bith that troubled him in a way that he could not share even with me, his closest friend. I knew the dark thought was there but I did not press him for it. Later, I wondered if she had told him of the evil that stalked us even then.

We spent the night under cloth held up by sticks pushed into the hard earth. The cattle bellowed occasionally. In my sleep, I counted them by their voices. When morning came, I already knew that I would have to look for one of the heifers before we could continue. We found it in the forest nearby, grazing on a short bush with yellow and orange flowers.

It was just past midday when we came to the river. The cattle moved into the shallows to drink. Both Matak and I stopped at the grass to watch them. We then leaned forward to put our noses to a bundle of grass. We then blew mucous into the bundle and tied it into a knot. Similar knots of grass dotted the riverbank.

"If mosquitoes carry the fever, then how does this protect us from it?" Matak asked.

"Another question befitting a Beny Bith," I replied. "But it is easy enough to do and the whole clan believes it will keep us from getting the fever when we ford the waters."

We crossed the river and immediately encountered a third herd. My bull bellowed a challenge that again was not met. Two boys ran toward us waving their hands and jumping through the grass.

"Do you know them?" Matak asked.

"I am not sure," I said. "They look familiar, but boys that age change so fast."

The boys ran up and began talking rapidly.

"You are Thon," the taller boy said. They wore nothing except thick necklaces of beads around their necks. Their hair and skin were covered with a layer of grey dung ash. Thin mucous ran from their noses leaving a dark trail in the ash between their nostrils and their mouths.

"Yes," I replied.

"I am the oldest son of Maker."

"I am John Deng," the shorter boy said.

"John is a Kawaja name," Matak said. "Are you not Dinka?"

"I am Dinka," the boy replied. "And I don't need a cow name to be Dinka. It is a good name, found in the book of God."

"Boy with a name from the book of God," said Matak. "Have you seen this book of God?"

The boy kicked a stump and looked away.

"Dinka have no book of God, John Deng," Matak said.

"There is no need to chide the boy," I said. "He did not choose his name."

"It is a good name," John Deng said proudly. "I would choose it if I had a chance."

I laughed. I hoped it was the laugh a man would make when amused by a small and unimportant boy.

"And why would you choose a Kawaja name?" I asked.

"It is the name of a good man from the book of God. And it is the name of a good man who is helping my father go to school," the boy answered.

"School is for children, John Deng," I replied.

"Perhaps the schools of the Dinka are for children, Thon," the boy answered. He no longer looked at the ground but in my eyes. The other boy had walked to the river's edge. "But the school my father attends is in Uganda. He is learning to be a great man, perhaps the greatest in all of Sudan."

I laughed again. A look of shame flashed across John Deng's face. I immediately regretted the laugh.

"It is good that men learn of the world outside of Dinkaland, John Deng," I said. "Your father does a good thing. And your name is a good name."

John Deng broke out in a wide smile and ran after the oldest son of Maker who was now splashing about in the grassy shallows of the river. Already the river had washed the grey ash from him and his small body appeared as a dark slash across the green.

The combined herd had turned of its own accord toward the cattle camp, but stopped to graze in the lush riverside grass. Matak and I left them and headed for the camp. John Deng and the son of Maker left the river and raced to join us.

We smelled the camp before we saw it. The odor of dung fires wafted across the low expanse of river grass. The boys led the way as if Matak and I did not know the trail. We followed a path past several bamboo sleeping platforms and a small garden. I turned to check on the cattle once more before losing sight of them, but they were still grazing on the thick river grass. I saw a man sitting partially hidden in the trees holding a spear. He appeared to be watching another group of cattle further down the river, but I knew that he would keep an eye on ours as well for that is the way of men of the cattle camp.

John Deng and the son of Maker talked quickly and loudly while they walked. I was annoyed, but Matak simply laughed. We entered the camp and quickly surveyed the ground for the best place to stay. The ground was swept clean of leaves and branches. An old man worked on his knees, spreading dung to dry as small boys carried it from a central pile. Scattered across the camp, conical piles of crumbled, dry dung smoldered, covering the whole area with a pungent white smoke. The small boys and the man had covered themselves with white dung ash against the insects. John Deng and the son of Maker found a pile of ash and were again quickly dusted to the pale grey color that they had when we met.

An old woman tended a wood fire near a grass hut at one end. Scores of stakes marked the places where cattle had been tethered for the night.

"We should take the area closest to the forest," I said. Matak nodded.

Without speaking, we moved to the edge of the camp and laid our spears and bags on the ground. I pulled out a large knife and went into the bush while Matak began to pull up clumps of grass. By the time the area had been cleaned of anything green, I had returned with an arm load of sharpened sticks.

John Deng came to stand where we worked. He looked at the ground as if too embarrassed to speak.

"Mama Dia said you should use her mallet," he said as he held out a wooden club with a flat head at one end.

"Thank your mother for us," I said. "Would you ask her if she would be willing to cook the millet we brought, for we are men?"

"She told me that she could see by your covering of your marks that you were men. She already asked if you would like her to add your food to the pot," John Deng replied.

I grunted a response. Matak took the stakes that I had made and, using the mallet, drove them in the ground across the cleared area.

"It is getting late," I said while Matak pounded the stakes into the hard ground. "I will go to the cattle while you finish."

Matak nodded without looking up. John Deng turned on his heels and ran away toward his mother's fire.

I walked back down the trail toward the river and the cattle. I heard them from a distance and recognized their sound. As I approached them I heard voices coming from the riverbank. I turned and followed the sounds. I heard a girl laughing, several men's voices, and someone clapping. This part of the river held a steep bank two or three times the height of a man. On its edge sat someone I did not know. The man held a brass and wood pipe in his teeth as smoke trickled up the side of his face. As I approached, I saw his hand move to one of the spears that lay at his side but the man did not turn his head or give any other sign that he was aware of my presence.

"*Kudual*," I said as I approached.

The man turned and looked up and down at me. He took another puff from the pipe before answering.

"*Kudual*," he replied. "*Yiin apuol?* Are you well?"

"*Heen apuol guop*, I am very well," I replied.

The man took his hand from the spear and turned back toward the river. I moved to sit beside him. In the water, two adolescent girls splashed and swam. They laughed and pointed at an older boy who kept ducking under water and trying to catch them. The muddy water swirled around them. The boy never completely submerged and the girls easily eluded his underwater approaches. I laughed as the boy rose from the water and roared at the girls. They feigned terror and high-stepped across the shallows into deeper water, screaming and laughing as they went.

I longed to join the game as I had in the past. But men did not participate in such things. I touched the leaf over my forehead and felt the soreness beneath.

"*Col e di*? What is your name?" the man asked. He kept his eyes on the river.

"*Ana chol*, Thon. *Chol edi*?"

"*Ana chol*, Jurkuc," the man replied. When he turned his head to face me squarely, I noticed his scars. Instead of being parallel to the ground, this man's forehead sported scars that angled into the space between his eyebrows. They gave me a fierce look that belied the serenity in his eyes and carriage.

Atuot, I thought with alarm. What is an Atuot man doing here?

I wished I had brought my fighting club with me and remembered leaving it at the camp bundled with my other supplies. As if sensing my discomfort the man turned and smiled.

"I am passing this way and stopped to rest by the river," he said. "I heard these young ones playing. The sight and sound of it restores me."

"They play as if there has never been work to do," I said. I could not think of the questions I should ask, could not think of what a warrior should say to an Atuot man in Dinka Agar territory.

"The Atuot are not at war with the Agar," Jurkuc said to the unasked question. "You need not worry. Besides, I am alone against a cattle camp filled with fierce warriors such as yourself. What could I do?"

I relaxed a bit, took a deep breath.

"But there have been men killed and cattle taken," I said.

"That was months ago," Jurkuc replied. "Soldiers came and took away the men who did these things. The worst of them were killed. The rest waste away in the Rumbek prison. There is no war between the Agar and the Atuot."

"I do not know if all of the people of the cattle camp will know this," I said.

"You can tell them," Jurkuc said. "Right now, I would hear the river and these children."

Jurkuc and I sat in silence. A malachite kingfisher flew over the river before us, looked about for fish, and then moved upstream. It flashed blue and red colors as it hovered looking down into the water. The children continued their playing. After a time, several other children joined them. The stream churned with their splashing.

Across the river, a long line of white cattle slowly made their way upstream along the bank. The lead bull had horns so wide I would not be able to touch both of their tips no matter how far I stretched. A red band held a bell to his neck and it clanked with each step. A tall figure, so black as to obscure any features in the late afternoon sun, walked with them and absentmindedly swatted them with a stick. The man was naked except for an armband of brass he wore just above his left elbow. He carried a spear in one hand and the switch in the other. The cattle disappeared around the bend of the river. I could hear them as they splashed across and headed toward the camp. I rose and eased down the steep bank to the water's edge. I waded out to waist deep, and then began to wash myself. Jurkuc stayed at the edge of the water. He appeared to be watching the children, but something about the way he sat and moved his eyes told me that the Atuot warrior was attentive to more than the children.

While I was still washing, Matak joined me.

"I thought you were watching the cattle," Matak said as he too washed.

"The cattle are fine," I replied. "They will not cross the river on their own and if they move at all they will move toward the camp."

Matak looked at the children playing.

"I would like to swim," Matak said.

"It is not becoming of a man to play with children," I replied.

Matak nodded. The children continued playing in the river. In the distance I heard the sounds of other cattle herds returning to camp. When he finished washing, Matak and I climbed the bank and again sat next to Jurkuc. The Atuot warrior stayed motionless as if he were an idol of wood and not a man of flesh. Only his eyes moved as they scanned up and down the river in both directions. The muscles of his arms flexed and I could feel his tension.

"Is this part of the river safe?" Jurkuc asked.

"It is called Wath Kawaja," I said.

"An odd name for a river," Jurkuc replied. "Why name this part of the river after a white man?"

"Many years ago, while my father was small, a kawaja, a white man drowned here," I said. "He was British."

Jurkuc grunted.

"Is it safe now?" he asked.

"I know of no one who has died here since that time," I replied. Matak nodded and hummed in agreement.

Suddenly Jurkuc leapt to his feet with both of his spears in his hands.

"Get the children out of the water," he shouted as he ran along the bank.

For a brief second, Matak and I looked at one another. We then jumped to our feet and ran down the bank. Matak fell forward into the water and came up coughing. The leaf that had covered his cuts floated down stream.

"Get out of the river," Matak shouted at the children. The sound of laughter drowned his words and at first none of the children reacted.

"Get out of the river, now," he shouted again. This time he grabbed a small girl near me and dragged her to the edge of the water. I picked up another child and headed toward the bank. Both of us continued to shout for the children to leave the water. Laughter turned to cries of panic as the children began to scramble toward the banks.

Upstream, closer to where Jurkuc ran, an older child stood in waist deep water and watched as the others scrambled up the banks. Jurkuc shouted at him, but he stood motionless. Behind him, the water swirled and surged. He stared at Jurkuc as the Atuot warrior ran toward him and then the boy stepped back toward the river's center. Suddenly, the boy rose part of the way from the water and screamed. A long head and jaws appeared from the muddy river, already clamped around the boy's chest. When he was near the boy, Jurkuc turned and launched himself toward the river. While still in the air, he hurled a spear toward the river and it embedded itself within the white throat of the beast. The boy's scream ended abruptly as the boy and the beast disappeared and the water churned and turned dark.

Jurkuc landed at the river's edge and ran through the water with his other spear held high. He stopped where the boy had been and searched the waters. A few steps ahead, in the deeper part of the river, the crocodile rose with the struggling boy clamped in its jaws. Jurkuc lunged toward it as the crocodile began to spin its body in the water. The boy's head went under as his feet appeared. Then the feet went under and his head appeared, his face contorted in a breathless scream. Jurkuc's first spear spun into view, now broken where the shaft met the metal tip.

Jurkuc waited until the white underbelly of the crocodile appeared again. Then he jumped into the air with his spear clutched tightly in both hands. As he came down, he plunged the spear deep into the center of the crocodile's abdomen. The creature continued rolling and this spear too broke away. Jurkuc then pulled a long knife from his belt and fell onto the beast. He drove the knife repeatedly into the neck and face of the crocodile, aiming for its eyes. The rolling stopped, but the creature's jaws stayed clamped tightly across the boy's chest. The boy weakly pushed against the jaws as Jurkuc continued to stab it.

Matak and I ran toward the battle.

"I have no weapon," Matak shouted. I did not reply.

As we approached, the crocodile suddenly released the boy and disappeared into the muddy water dragging with it Jurkuc who still held the knife he had driven into its throat. Swirls of blood marked where it sank with the Atuot warrior still holding fast. The boy floated on his back and gasped for air. He continued to flail his arms as if still fighting the crocodile. I reached him first. As I picked him up, I heard the sound of ribs crunching against ribs. Blood mixed with spit trailed from the boy's mouth. Matak took his legs as we pulled him toward the bank. Jurkuc rose from the water with the knife in one hand and one of his spear tips in the other, still looking at the place where the crocodile had sunk. Blood ran freely down his right leg from a puncture he did not appear to notice. He slowly backed out of the river toward us.

Most of the younger children had run back to the camp. The older ones moved to the high bank and looked down as Matak and I carried the boy to the river's edge. After a moment, Jurkuc came out of the river to join us.

As we laid him ground, the boy stopped flailing his arms. He wheezed and coughed weakly.

"Go and get this boy's family," I shouted to the children on the bank above us. A boy turned and ran toward the camp. The others stood dripping water and staring at us.

Jurkuc knelt in the mud beside boy. He laid his hand gently on the boy's chest, and then leaned forward to listen to his breathing.

"He is hurt badly," Jurkuc said. "But if the bleeding stops soon, he may yet live."

Blood poured from puncture wounds in his chest and left shoulder. His left arm hung limply with an abnormal angle at his elbow.

"The arm will heal," Jurkuc said.

Minutes later, the boy's mother arrived and scrambled down the bank. She gasped as she saw the blood and injuries, but did not cry out. She took off her wrap and laid it on the ground. Matak and I helped her roll the boy on the wrap, and then we lifted him from the ground and carried him to the camp.

When we had reached their place in the camp, I watched as the boy's mother took some ash of a dung fire and pushed it into the bleeding wounds. Moments later the bleeding stopped. She called for other family members to help. Soon a crowd formed as people began to shout advice and warnings to the boy's mother.

Matak and I walked back to the river to gather the herd as the light began to fail. Already, the other herds were tethered around the smoldering dung fires. The old men attended their favorite oxen as if unaware of the commotion and our battle with the great crocodile. The sounds of their songs rose above the din of men and beast settling in for the night. They sang songs of praise to the oxen as they patted and stroked them, arranged the decorations that hung from their great horns and powdered them with dung ash. One was close enough that Matak and I could hear his words as he patted and stroked the great ox.

"My bull is a great bull

The only bull in my eyes

If we are away, there is no bull in the camp.

The Pagong Wut of the big camp has not come.

If we are away, there is no bull in the camp.

When we have come, the bull of the camp has come."

The man looked lovingly at the ox as he sang, the passion of his voice filling the air. The ox stretched over a smoldering pile of dung as smoke engulfed him and the man. It was deep into the night before Matak and I had tethered our cattle and set out our nets. The old man was still singing to his ox when we fell asleep hungry and exhausted.

Chapter Four

The cattle became restless well before the first light of dawn appeared over the river. I sat up and lifted the netting. Already I could see fires rising beside a few of the grass huts as women prepared food for the day. Black and grey birds with long tails called from atop great palm trees, anticipating the movement of cattle and the insects they would roust from the grass. A goat bleated at the far side of the camp. Cattle began to bellow. I heard Matak stir.

"I must eat this morning," Matak said as he stood.

"John Deng's mother should still have food from last night," I said. "She will make it for us."

We rolled and stored our nets, then made our way toward John Deng's family's gathering. A young woman, wearing only a tattered short cloth around her thighs, leaned forward over a blackened pot. I noted that the small fire burned beneath it with almost no smoke, a sign of a good fire maker.

"Have you food for us?" I asked.

"I have food from last night that you did not eat," she said without looking up. "I am mixing it with more."

Matak and I sat on logs near the fire. An old man came out of a net, led by the hand by a young boy. The man sat on a log near us and lit a pipe while the boy stood and stared into the fire. Neither of them spoke to us.

The woman tended the fire while watching the nearby cattle. As one of the closest cows stretched its legs, she walked quickly toward it. She held her hands under the cow as yellow fluid gushed from it. When she had finished washing in the cow's urine, she returned to the fire.

When she was done, the women brought us a thick, grey mass of cooked millet on large leaves. We acknowledged her with a nod and she returned to the fire. We ate with our fingers as John Deng's family slowly emerged and congregated around the fire. She cast me with an appreciative gaze as we made sufficient noise with our eating to acknowledge her cooking skills.

A woman from another family group approached and spoke in whispers. She then knelt by the fire and pulled out one of the hot coals with her calloused fingers. Shifting it back and forth with her bare hands, she scuttled off to start her own cooking fire.

"You fought the crocodile," the old man said without preface as I watched the woman leave. The boy continued to stare into the fire.

"We pulled the boy from the river," I said. "Someone else killed the beast."

The man grunted and nodded.

"That is not what I heard," another said.

"That is what happened," I replied. "An Atuot man killed the crocodile."

"Atuot men do not fight crocodiles to save Agar children," the man said.

"This one did," Matak said. More of John Deng's family stood around the fire and listened.

"That is not what I heard," the old man said.

"*Monydit*, Old Man," Matak said. "You are respected because of the grey in your head, and it should be so. But someone told you wrong. The Atuot man killed the crocodile. We only pulled the boy from the river."

"Whatever you say is what you say," the monydit replied. "But that is not what the people are saying. It appears the boy will live. They say you killed the beast and saved him. They say nothing good of the Atuot man."

"Then the people are stupid. Stupid people of the cattle camp, just as the people of the towns say," Matak said, his voice loud and insistent. "It is no wonder that you are as poor as a dog without a tail."

"Some of the young men have given chase to the Atuot man. They would kill him for coming here," the monydit said.

"Why would they do such a thing?" I asked.

"One of the men here had a brother who went fishing on the lake by Atiaba. It is not a thing that I would do as I do not like fish and most men would not stoop so low as to catch them. But these are changing times and the brother had no such concerns. One part of the lake is in Atuot territory. While he placed his nets, he may have stepped into their lands. Some Atuot men caught him and beat him with canes. It has annoyed his family. Since then they have not yet taken their revenge for the beating."

"I know that story," Matak said. "It happened over seven years ago. The brother of the Agar man who was beaten is Akec of the Pyang Clan. He went to prison for cutting off an Atuot girl's ears. He started a great war with the Atuot by doing this thing. The Chiefs already made peace from those things that happened. The Beny Bith has sacrificed many bulls in the making of this peace. I myself stepped across the bull. Why would they still make war over it?"

"I cannot say," the monydit answered. "Perhaps they have another wrong they feel the Atuot must answer for. Or perhaps someone forgot to invite them to the peace ceremony. I cannot say. But they left with the rising sun to track the man down. They believe he is following the river and will be easy to find."

Matak and I stood, thanked the mother for cooking for us, and then returned to our cattle. I thought of the man, Jurkuc and of how he walked fearlessly by the river and of how he defeated the crocodile. I did not think he would be easy to find if he did not want to be found. I also believed that he would be a formidable adversary and that those who followed him would be wise to abandon the chase. We continued to walk while I considered these things, Matak beside me, silent within his own thoughts. Other families watched us move through the cluster of camps and tethered animals. I felt their eyes.

When we had released the cattle, we moved them a few miles into fresh grass where it appeared that no cattle had been. We sat in the shade of a shea nut tree and watched the cattle feed and for a long while neither of us spoke. Matak sucked the yellow meat off of some of the nuts hulls, but I only watched.

"I do not believe these men can find Jurkuc," I said. "You saw him in the river. I think he is strong and fast. He does not wish to be found, they will not find him."

"But he does not know that some still fight with the Atuot," Matak said. "He may not avoid them as he should. And I think he lost his spear within the crocodile. He will have only his knife with him."

"Perhaps," I said. "I recall him having two spears when he went into the river. He came out with one tip. By now he will have made another shaft for it."

We sat for a long while without speaking.

"Why do you think Jurkuc saved the boy?" Matak asked just before he popped another nut into his mouth.

"Why would he not save a child's life," I answered. "Is it not the duty of every warrior to protect the people?"

"The people, yes," Matak replied. "But we are not his people. He is Atuot."

"Would you do what he did for an Atuot child?" I asked.

Matak sat munching loudly and thought. After a moment he replied, "I do not know. Things like this happen so fast, I think you act from the character of the man you are rather than the man you like to think you are. I would hope I would save the child, but I do not know."

"I think you would save the child," I said. "You are a man of courage and character."

"It is good that you say such things," Matak said. "But I do not know. I do not think I would if I knew it was an Atuot. But if I saw the child in danger and did not think, perhaps I would try to save him."

"A good answer," I said. "But you would save him— Atuot, Nuer, even Laraap. I am sure of it."

Matak smiled and continued to eat. I too began to chew the soft hull off of the shea fruit. Just before midday, we walked to the river to drink. The cattle stayed together, following the lead of the large bull ox. We drank from the river, then stepped in to bathe and cool ourselves. We sat on the clay bank with our legs hanging over the edge and our feet in the muddy water. It was my favorite place in the world, a world that made sense to me in a way that would not last. Matak leaned his shoulder against mine and grasped my hand. I felt a shiver pass through him and he sighed deeply.

From a distance we watched him coming, walking slowly, stopping periodically to touch a place on his leg. He did not speak or wave or in any way acknowledge us, but came straight to us. The boy was young, half my age at least, I noted as he sat on the ground near us. He was doing something to one of his ankles. I watched him for a moment, then nudged Matak to look also.

I walked over and stood by the boy. The child never looked up. In his right hand he held the end of a grey worm that protruded from his skin just above the ankle. He was trying to wrap the end of the worm around a short stick, but it kept slipping from his grasp. The boy winced occasionally. Matak stood beside me as we watched him toy with it.

"There are people here who say this worm comes from the water," Matak said as he watched the boy. He knelt beside the child and took the stick from him. Gently, so as not to break the worm off at the skin, he wrapped the protruding end of the worm around the stick, then he tied a strip bark around the boy's ankle and the worm to keep it from unraveling.

"But we must drink the water," the boy said. "Does that mean we will all get this worm?"

"Perhaps," Matak answered. "I saw a man wearing a shirt last month that showed a picture of the worm. They call it a 'guinea worm.' The shirt had a message. It said to pour the water through cloth to keep from getting the worm."

"Is this magic?" he asked.

Matak thought for a moment. "Perhaps magic of a sort. I don't know how the worm can be in river water. I've never seen it there. Perhaps the spirit of the worm is afraid of the cloth and leaves the water. Perhaps the message on the shirt is wrong, just a bad joke. I don't know."

"But it is the sort of thing a Beny Bith should know," I said.

Matak grunted.

"*Apath areet*, thank you," the boy said.

Matak nodded. The boy stood and stepped lightly with his injured leg. I noticed then that he had only two toes on the leg without the worm. There were no wounds suggesting a recent injury and the boy stepped on it normally.

"Walking does not make it hurt more," the boy said. "That is good for I have much walking to do today."

"That is good," Matak said. "But it may take several weeks for you to pull the whole worm out. Do not pull too hard or it may break inside you. Pull only a little each day. It will come out."

The boy nodded. "It is just what my grandmother said."

"And where is it that you must walk today?" I asked.

The boy did not answer, but instead started walking along the river bank.

"I asked you where you were going," I shouted after him.

"I heard you," the boy said. "But I have no time to talk. There is a great war coming and my mother has sent me to search for my father. He travels along this river to the lake to fish."

Matak and I ran after the boy and walked with him.

"A great war? What do you know about a great war?" I asked.

"I do not know much," the boy answered. "But the Laraap are coming again. Mother heard it from a soldier who had deserted the army and was going back to Juba to live."

"The Laraap are far from here," Matak said.

"Perhaps you are right," the boy said. "But my mother wants me to find my father and ask him to return home. She is packing our things to flee if they come."

Matak and I exchanged glances.

"Has anyone else spoken of the Laraap coming?" I asked.

"None that I know," answered the boy.

"Do they come by footing?" I asked.

"I have told you all I know," the boy answered. "Have you seen a man traveling this river bank on the way to the lake?"

"We have seen only people of the cattle camp," I answered.

"You would have seen him yesterday or today for he left our home only two days ahead of me," the boy said. "He must have already passed. My father is a great warrior and can move fast when he wants and move without being seen when he wants."

"Why would he not want us to see him?" I asked.

"Sometimes Atuot men are not welcomed in Agar territories," the boy said.

"If you father is Atuot, I think we saw him," I said.

The boy stopped and looked up excitedly.

"Where? When?" he said rapidly.

"He was here yesterday," Matak answered. "Right by this river. He saved a boy's life by killing a crocodile that had attacked him."

"That would be my father. If he gave it, his name is Jurkuc," the boy said. "A great warrior and hunter. Do you know where is?"

"He gave his name to be Jurkuc. He cannot have gone far," Matak said. "I lost sight of him when we brought the injured boy to the camp. But surely the boy's family fed him as thanks for his bravery."

"Perhaps," the boy said, looking at his injured ankle. "But my father says that sometimes the Agar will not treat Atuot with honor."

"I am Agar. So is my friend," Matak said. "We are men of honor. We bear the mark." I touched the leaf covering my scar. Anyone would know that I bore the marks beneath it to show that I was a man now.

The boy did not answer, but continued to walk.

"Would you want us to help you find your father?" I said.

"It is good to have help," the boy said. "But there is nothing to the finding of him except to walk the river to the lake. If you see him again, perhaps you can tell him that I am looking for him and tell him to find me on the river. Mother said for me not to come home without him. I am hungry. If the shea nuts had not been out, I might have starved already."

"We will watch for him," I said. "We do not know your name."

"I am Matueny," the boy said.

"That is not an Atuot name," Matak said.

"My mother is Agar," Matueny answered. "My father married her when there was peace between the Atuot and Agar."

"There has never been peace between the Atuot and Agar," Matak said.

"There is no war now," Matueny answered.

"For a brief time there is no war, but that is not peace," Matak replied.

I nodded. Spoken like a Beny Bith, I thought.

"Perhaps," Matueny said. "But my father is Atuot and my mother is Agar. He has no other wife than her. I live with the Atuot. My mother says that we are one people, the Agar and Atuot. There is no river between us."

"There is no river between us," I answered. "Go in peace and find your father. If we see him we will send him after you."

We gave the boy some ground nuts and a bit of dried goat meat and he continued down the river. Matak and I returned to our herd. The day grew late and the cattle moved to the river to drink. They moved of their own accord, the old bull familiar with the routine of the camp and the lay of the land. Soon Matak and I were sitting on the bank watching for more crocodiles while the cattle drank. To lose a cow to crocodiles would be a disgrace that as newly made men we did not want.

"There is no river between us," I heard Matak say to himself.

I watched the sky turn to fire as Nhialic pulled the sun below the horizon.

Later, I sat alone in the camp while the men around me sang to their oxen and tended the cattle. Matak had gone to collect cow urine to use to color his hair.

A young boy walked up to me wearing a mask over his face that bristled with long thorns. He stood in front of me silent, waiting for a response. His abdomen bulged on legs so thin they looked as if they may break. While he waited, he placed one heel on the opposite knee in the way of Dinka who want to rest while standing.

I raised my eyes toward the boy.

"Is your mother having trouble weaning you?" I said.

The boy took off the mask and sat on the log beside me. "Must you sit on a dirty log instead of the *thoch* that other men make for themselves?" the boy replied. I did not take the bait but looked down at my feet.

"I am Dol," the boy said.

"I did not know you, Dol," I said. "And now I do. Is there a reason that you would bother a man who is thinking important thoughts?"

."I was sent to put the spiked mask on a calf that will not stop nursing," Dol said. "I saw you here, the man who fought the great crocodile. I wanted to speak to you."

I started to correct the boy regarding the story of the crocodile but stopped myself. I had credited Jurkuc with killing the crocodile many times and the people refused to believe it. "No Atuot would do such a thing for the Agar," they kept saying.

"You have spoken to me," I said sullenly. "Do you have work to do?" I did not feel like talking, especially to a silly boy.

"It is funny," Dol continued as if he did not understand my words. "This calf will not quit nursing, so I put the spiked mask on it to make its mother refuse it. Another cow will not nurse a calf whose mother has died so we have to tie her up."

"What is so funny about that?" I asked, still looking at my feet.

Dol laughed the small laugh of boys who make jokes to themselves. "When we cannot get the mothers to do what they should, we also hurt them. When we cannot get the calves to do what they should, we make them hurt their mothers too. Is that not funny?"

"I do not see how that is funny," I said. I looked at the boy who now stared back at me. His eyes were small slits set in a round face covered with white ash. He wore no clothing and no ornaments.

The boy sat silent for a time and twirled the mask on its string.

"We make the mothers suffer for everything," Dol said. "It is a funny way, do you not think?"

I did not answer him. Suddenly, the boy bolted to his feet and trotted toward the center of the camp. I stood to look after him but he was soon lost in the crowd of cattle. I walked toward the sound of Matak's laughter. I found him sitting in a crowd of old men, all of them smoking pipes. Matak was trying to talk an old man into letting him use his pipe. The old man refused Matak's pleadings with a shrug.

There was a commotion behind the men that caught my attention. Some older boys had tied a cow's front and back legs together and were trying to get it to hold still while a young calf nursed. Every time the calf latched its mouth to the cow's teat, the cow began to thrash about wildly. I knew that the calf was orphaned and the men wanted the cow to nurse it or else it would die. After a time, one of the men with a pipe stood and approached the cow.

"It is time," he said. The boys held the cow down while the man pulled a pouch of dried herbs from his belt. He carefully packed some of the herbs into his pipe, and then leaned down to get a burning stick from a nearby fire with which to light it. He puffed hard on the pipe and the smoke from it grew more dense. When he was satisfied, he approached the cow. The boys held it tightly as the man knelt behind it. He then inhaled deeply from the his pipe, leaned forward to put his mouth on the cow's vaginal opening, and blew hard. I could hear the sound of wind passing into the cow. Smoke curled from the cow's backside as it lay panting on the ground.

The man tapped the remaining herbs from his pipe, refilled it with tobacco, and sat down with the other men with his back to the cow.

"Try her again later in the morning," he said. "She will nurse the orphaned calf then."

The boys released the cow. It stood slowly as if exhausted, shook its head toward the boys, and then walked away. One of the boys followed it, towing the calf on a rope behind him. At the edge of the camp, I thought I saw the boy, Dol, looking at me through gaps in the herd. Then a bull stepped between them. When I looked again, Dol was gone.

"Great crocodile killers," a man said through the pipe in his teeth.

I turned to walk away.

"It is not polite to walk away from an elder who has spoken to you," the man said.

I stopped and turned. The men all sat on thoch. Most of the short, wooden, stools bore the image of an erect penis. The man who spoke sat on one that was little more than a simple curved piece of wood with short knobs that held it no higher than the length of a finger off of the ground.

"I have told the camp so many times I grow weary of it," I said. "Matak and I did not kill the crocodile. An Atuot man killed it. We only pulled the boy from the river."

"It is a brave thing to go into the river when a crocodile is nearby," the man said. "Is it a much greater thing to then put your knife into it?"

The other men nodded and clucked in agreement. Smoke curled from each of their pipes. They sat with their knees almost touching their chests.

"Perhaps," I replied. "But when a tale is said of a man who killed a crocodile, is it a much greater thing to say the man's real name?"

The elders nodded and looked up at me through the haze of smoke.

"Perhaps it is not such a great thing if the man is Atuot," the man said.

Some of the men nodded agreement. Others looked at the ground.

"People of the cattle camp have need of Dinka Agar heroes," the man spoke. "The Beny Wut has also spoken and he too sees that the two of you deserve honor. He makes no mention of the Atuot man."

The man was a distant relative and I had to be careful to show proper respect. I turned away. I had taken only a couple of steps when I heard someone laugh with a familiar voice. I froze.

"Perhaps the child saved these two from an Atuot man who appeared as a crocodile," said someone hidden behind two cows near the group of men. "Or perhaps the Atuot man came here just to kill the crocodile, our clan identity, our clan divinity. Perhaps the boy got in the way."

The old men sat motionless, waiting to see if I would take the bait.

"Chol is a maker of lies and a child who hurts girls," I said. "What would he know of a battle against the great crocodile?"

A young man stepped from behind the cattle. He stood tall, taller than any of us, with strong arms ringed with brass. The red scarf on his head fluttered in the breeze as he stared at me and Matak. A red blanket hung by a single knot at one shoulder, covering most of his body.

"Perhaps Thon and his little friend will prove to us here and now who is a man," Chol said.

I turned to face the larger boy.

"It is not proper for one without the scars to speak thus to a man," I said.

Chol spat in the ground at my feet.

A large man rose and stepped between us.

"I am Matur, Chol's *Wallen*, his uncle," he said. "Chol should not speak like this to a man. I am sure that he will apologize to you." He put his hand on Chol's arm.

Chol pulled his arm from his uncle's grip and stepped back. He raised his spear over his shoulder and pointed it at my chest. As a man should, I stood rigid and did not flinch. Chol took a deep breath and seemed ready to thrust his spear when Matur again stepped in front of me.

"The Beny Wut has spoken that there will be no fighting in his camp," Matur said. "You will obey or we will send you home to your mother."

Chol stepped backwards with his spear still raised. After a few more steps he turned and ran through the cattle. I watched him as he turned one last time before he disappeared among the animals.

"You would do well to avoid Chol," Matur said to me. "He blames you for keeping him a boy for another year."

"You would do well to keep him away from me, Matur," I said.

The older uncle took a step toward me, raised his club, but did not strike me. Another elder cleared his throat loudly and Matur lowered the club.

"Chol is humiliated," he said. "He blames you. He blames me. Everyone but himself. Be careful you do not antagonize him. And you would do well to speak respectfully to an elder, particularly one who could kill you before you can think to cry out."

I nodded that I understood him. I felt ashamed to have been corrected in front of other men, but I knew Matur was correct to do so. My heart still raced from the encounter with Chol.

"He goes with some others after the Atuot man," Matur said. "He thinks killing him will restore his honor."

"The girl was only ten," I said. "He has no honor."

"I know," Matur replied.

"He would have... taken her."

"I suspect he would have."

"What else could I do?" I asked.

"You did what you should have done, Thon," Matur said. The other elders nodded agreement.

The things that Matur said were what I would expect of a man of honor, but something in the way he looked at me made me think he did not believe his own words. I suspected that he would have sided with Chol against me if the other elders had not been present. Both of them were powerful men and formidable enemies and I thought then that I should take great care when I was alone. Had I known of the depths of the evil that Chol carried even then I would have fought him to the death.

I grunted and turned to leave. Some of the elders murmured something I could not understand. I left them talking.

"Thon," Matak said as he trotted up behind me. "It is not good to arouse the elders against us."

"They would have us lie to the people," I said. "I will not start my manhood with lies. I would have killed the crocodile if I had to. But I did not. He can make his own stories. I will have none of it."

"The girls like the stories," Matak said, nudging my side.

"The girls like men of character," I said. "Let's speak no more of it this day. I would move the cattle further up the river. I think the grass is sweeter there."

We released our big bulls and herded them a small distance from the camp. The cows followed them. When they were moving steadily and together, I walked beside Matak. My hand sought his and I leaned against his smaller frame as we walked.

"Did you see a boy named Dol in the camp?" I asked.

"I know no such boy," Matak answered. "Whose family is he?"

"I do not know," I said. We settled ourselves under the boughs of a great mahogany tree while the cattle grazed nearby. We both slept for a few minutes, and then moved to another tree as the shadows moved with the sun. When the day ended, we returned to camp.

Chapter Five

He found the girl alone and making water. Her naked form appeared little more than a faint denseness of shadows in the night, her presence announced by the faint sound of the fluid that flowed from between her legs. She crouched on the barren ground, oblivious to his presence as he crept behind her. Surrounded by men of the cattle camp, she would not suspect the danger that stalked her.

He waited for her to finish and make the first step toward her camp before he took her. His movements were so swift that she had no chance to cry out before she was pinned to the ground and a powerful hand had been clamped across her mouth. His weight crushed the wind from her. She felt his hands on her body and she fought against what she knew he intended for her. She felt a sharp pain and the crack of bones in her right hand as the darkness of night became the darkness of death.

He did not try to hide the girl's body or the signs of what he had done to her but left her in the short grass within sight of her family's camp. He could already picture the terror that would sweep the camp when they found her and he craved it. This small death would herald the Anyanya that would establish his power and the dread of his wrath. He tucked the trophy of his kill into a small pouch and stashed it in a bundle of his other belongings before slipping into the night. Already he heard dogs barking at the strange scents of others who did not belong with the camp. He could put miles of trail behind him before any alarm could sound. He felt the comfort of darkness envelope him as the light of the campfires faded.

He chuckled softly as he thought of the enemy of the cattle camp that now waited in the forest. The men of the camp would fight the invaders. He knew it was likely that they would win the day and keep most of their cattle and children. He thought of how the size and strength of the camp would surprise the attackers and wondered if they would know he had betrayed them with false knowledge. He did not care for they were neither his most important nor most powerful alliance and the death of men from either side would only add to his own power.

He tossed a stick at a large bull tethered at the edge of the camp. As he knew it would, the bull shuffled and grunted a warning to his herd that cascaded across the camp like the wind rippling over the tall grass. As he slipped deeper into the forest, he could already see a few campfires being enlarged as the collective consciousness of the camp roused to look for a threat. He chuckled again as he thought of the battle that would soon take place and leave him as its only true victor.

Chapter Six

I bolted upright, sleep suddenly gone from me. I listened to the sounds of night. Something had changed and that change had alerted me. I lifted the net and stepped forth into darkness so deep I could feel it. Clouds covered the moon and I could see only faint shapes near me. Across the camp, the cattle had stopped shuffling in their sleep and stood still. A great ox bellowed suddenly, causing me to jump. I felt Matak's presence at my side.

"I heard it too," he said.

I knew that other men of the cattle camp were finding their spears and listening as we did. A cow at the north edge of the camp shook herself and rattled the metal bell around her neck. I could hear the sounds of the cattle breathing as one. A few night birds called in the distance and a jackal gave his unearthly bark from across the river.

"Hyena?" Matak asked.

"Not in camp," I said.

"Lion?"

"There have been no lions here since my father was a child," I replied.

"Raiders," Matak stated.

I nodded, though I knew Matak could not see me.

The Beny Wut of the cattle camp lit a fire of palm fronds that blazed a circle of light around him, a signal that the men should gather. Matak and I worked our way through the crowd of tethered cattle. The older bulls had started to bellow and the cows shifted and pulled at their ropes. A few calves that had wandered during the night called for their mothers.

At least two dozen men moved into the firelight, all holding spears or clubs. The Beny Wut sat on a bamboo chair holding a staff tipped with steel. Firelight blazed in his eyes. When he stood, he seemed twice the size of the other men and his shadow danced across the ground.

"Foreign scouts sit within the edge of the forest near the river," he said, his voice as deep as a bull ox.

"Who?" a warrior asked.

"We cannot tell," the great man answered. "We heard a dog bark once, then the sound of it being killed. I sent my oldest son to see who or what had done this thing and he discovered them."

"How many?" another man asked.

"No more than three or four," a young man answered. I recognized him as the Beny Wut's son.

"I can circle them and we can kill them where they sit," another warrior said.

"Perhaps," the Beny Wut continued. "But I think they wait on others. The scouts could not hope to hide in the daylight so the others likely will come tonight. They may be close or even here now. I would face them in our own camp where we know the land best."

A few of the men nodded and clucked in agreement.

"They watch from the river side only," the Beny Wut said. "They cannot see this end of the camp, though they will have heard our talking and seen the glow of the fire. We need the women to come and sit by the fire and pretend to be men. I want the rest of the women to move with the children to the forest away from the river. Take no cattle and be silent. The rest of us will form a line between us and them. When they attack, we will surprise them. If dawn approaches and they have not attacked, we will attack them instead."

The men again grunted their approval.

"Go now," the Beny Wut said. "I will make three calls of the hornbill to signal an attack. Two calls to warn of one coming."

The men disappeared in the darkness. The sound of cattle shuffling moved in a wave across the camp as the men slipped into huts to arouse their families. A few children cried.

Matak and I crouched in the dark near our nets. Both of us held the *leec,* the war club, and a spear. Neither of us had made a shield yet and we both regretted it at that moment. As the women and children moved away from the river, the men shuffled on their knees toward the waiting enemy. Matak and I joined them but stayed close to one another.

"I will watch for you," I whispered.

"And I you," Matak whispered back. An elderly warrior rapped Matak on the back with his spear.

"Silence," he whispered and Matak nodded.

We moved only a few paces into the grass that abruptly marked the edge of the camp site, and then settled to the ground as one. I did not know how many men stood to face the unnamed enemy. For the second time that week I hoped that my courage would not fail me. We waited in silence. Night birds swooped overhead and insects chirped. I resisted swatting at the mosquitoes that buzzed around my ears. I could not see the others or even hear their breathing. It was as if I was alone.

I had just moved to relieve a numbness in my left leg when I heard shuffling and murmurs from the trees ahead of us. I saw the shadows of the trees appear to move, then detach themselves from the forest and glide toward us. I caught the slightest glint of metal as dim moonlight glanced off of a spear. The enemy line approached within twenty paces of us, then halted. I counted at least thirty of them—too many of them to win the battle without losing many of our own men. I worried that perhaps they had guns.

I heard a bird call that did not sound right coming from the river bank. An identical call came from the line of shadows. The line wavered, then moved slowly back into the trees. Then there was silence for a long time.

A grey dawn crept into the bush. The grass, wet from dew, hung heavy and silent as we Dinka warriors, protectors of the People lay in wait. From behind us, we could hear the cattle bellow and strain at their ropes, anxious to begin grazing. We neither heard nor saw movement from the forest where we assumed the unknown raiders still hid. None of us knew why the raiders had stopped their advance. Perhaps one of them saw us and knew that they could not surprise the camp. None of us knew. We only knew that the dawn came and there was no attack.

Toward the back of the line of men, the Beny Wut made the call of a hornbill three times. As one, the men rose with their spears lifted and rushed the line of trees. We shook our spears and shouted threats as we ran. When we reached the trees, we found nothing but some areas where the grass had been flattened. We searched about and found a trail leading away from the camp toward the southwest. The old men clustered together to talk while the rest of us stood staring into the forest. After a long while, the Beny Wut came to where we all stood and tapped his walking stick on the ground for us to listen.

"They detected our ambush," the Beny Wut said. "I will send scouts to track them and know where they are. The rest of you keep your cattle close to the camp."

The men nodded, then walked slowly back toward the clearing and the fires. I found Matak and the two of us walked hand-in-hand.

"I wish we could have killed them," Matak said. "They may be back with more men or even guns."

"Only the Laraap have guns," I answered, not wanting to admit that I had the same worry. "These were not Laraap."

"Perhaps," Matak said. "But we are now Dinka men. It would have been good to have proven ourselves in battle early."

"This may have been the best of all types of battles, Matak," I said. An elder walking nearby grunted his agreement.

"I did not see Chol in the line," Matak noted.

"Neither did I," I said. "But there were many men hiding in the grass and we could have missed him. He surely would have been with us."

We returned to the camp and unfettered the cattle. As we left, John Deng's mother gave us food to take into the fields. Though we were hungry, we resisted the temptation to eat any of the food while walking as such a thing is unseemly for any Dinka, much less a warrior.

While we walked, we heard a mother call for her daughter. Girls do not often go to the cattle camp, but this family had no other children and the father needed to bring their cattle here himself. The girl I had seen with them, just showing the first signs of womanhood in her body, was very quiet and largely stayed to herself. Her mother called her name and searched desperately. I stumbled onto a young goat. I pushed it away and noticed that it did not run but stood searching the grass with its lips. I picked it up and it lay limp in my arms and did not struggle as other goats would. Then I noticed the glazed grayness that covered the goat's eyes and I knew that no light could enter those eyes. The goat bleated once, so soft that I felt it was meant for my ears only. A soft sound that seemed to plead with me to release it or kill it swiftly. I remember that goat, but do not know why. Perhaps the Tiet can tell me sometime. But on that day, I simply lowered it to the ground as softly as I could, turned it so its face touched fresh grass, and walked away.

I had only taken a few steps when I saw her. She lay in the grass, naked, blood pooled around her head and between her legs. I heard the mother calling for this girl who would never reply. She was small, almost as small as the blind goat. If not for the goat, I would likely have walked past her without even seeing her small form. Her face, frozen in a silent scream, looked past me with blank and glassy eyes. One hand lay across her chest. In the briefest of seconds before I looked away, I noted that the smallest finger of her right hand was half gone. A trail of blood marked where the mangled stump had slid across her body. I then remembered the girl's name. Nyeriak, which means seed. It is a name given to one who is the last survivor of a family. This was the seed of this man and woman, the one hope that their name would continue. The hope of this seed died with the girl I now saw.

I looked for the goat, but it had wandered off toward the sound of others of its kind. I looked toward the girl's mother, saw in her stride a nervous step, heard concern in her voice. From across the camp I saw her and even from such distance I could feel her gaze when she looked toward me. I waved both hands over my head and motioned for her to come toward me. She walked swiftly to me, but kept calling the girl's name. She almost stepped on her daughter's limp form before she saw her. She stood looking at her daughter for a long time, her face contorted as if frozen in the middle of calling out, but unable to make a sound.

I stepped away to find Matak just as her wailing started. The sound of her voice at my back seeming to propel me away. Others came running toward the mother as I left her. Perhaps a man would have stayed, offered comfort, sought an answer to the girl's death. Perhaps only a boy would leave such a place. The mother's wailing drove through my chest like a knife, sharing her grief with my body, breaking my kidneys, sapping my strength. Who would hurt a child of such a young age, I wondered. Even as I asked the question, the answer came to me.

Chapter Seven

I sat beneath a tree watching our cattle graze. The great lead ox never strayed far from the camp, seeming to sense the tensions of the people and our own uneasiness. I heard the wailing of many voices, could make out the mother's voice among them though she grew weaker as the day progressed. I could hear the sounds of others trying to comfort the girl's family. I knew that they were telling stories of the girl, what a fine woman she would have been, how she helped them with this thing or that chore. How beautiful she was. Through their wailings, the girl's family would hear praise for the girl and words of comfort of how she is not dead but will live on in the children born in her name.

I thought of how the girl's aunts would wash her from head to toe, trim or shave her hair and arrange a red sash about her. I knew they would rub her down with lulu oil until she shone like polished wood. This they would do quickly for the sun would not set before she was buried. I heard sounds of mourning echoing along the river and it seemed that all the birds and beasts stood silent and listened also.

Matak glanced toward me as if he wanted to say something that would not come to his lips. I knew the horrible truth that he would say and we both knew it did not bear saying. We both knew what had happened to the girl. We did not speak the whole morning.

As the sounds of wailing weakened and moved across the camp, we left the cattle and joined the mourners. One of the girl's uncles pulled a tuft of grass from a nearby shelter. He walked solemnly to the grave and knelt with the grass in his hand.

We stood by the small hole in the ground made just steps from where the girl would have slept. A fresh goatskin had already been placed in the bottom of the grave. It was the color of the blind goat that I had seen earlier and I wondered if it had survived by the kindness of the now dead girl.

Her mother and father eased the naked form into the grave on her right side with her head facing away from the Tree of Life that grows still somewhere a long way to the east. Her father curled her with her knees to her chest and placed one of her hands under her face as if she was sleeping. He pulled himself from the hole and barely caught his wife as she wailed loudly again and tried to fling herself into the grave.

The girl's uncles had made four piles of earth from the hole. If it had been a man or a boy, he would have made three piles. I do not know why it is so. Someone draped a white cloth over the girl and again the family and friends began wailing. Where in the cattle camp they got a piece cloth that stayed white and clean, I could not say. Perhaps from a Larap trader nearby. But the cloth was a wise choice for we believe that the soul of the dead may take on the color of the burial cloth. It should be clean and white for this girl.

The girl's uncle then stepped into the grave and straddled the girl, pressing his feet into the sides of the grave. He then took four pieces of grass and held them in his hand. He took one of the blades of grass, leaned into the grave, and carefully placed it in the dead girl's hand.

"You, you call his name," he said as he straightened himself. "You call the name of the man who killed you if it was a man."

He again leaned down and placed another piece of grass in the girl's hand and spoke again, this time looking into the crowd of mourners. Everyone stood silent.

"I give you this. If a person was looking for the way to kill you by a magic word, you will look for that person. You shall bring death to that person."

Even the girl's mother kept quiet while the old man spoke. Again, he took a piece of grass placed it in the girl's hand with the others.

"If this death of you has come from a family member among us, you check the person among us that killed you. Make it known to us."

He took the fourth piece of grass and laid it to the side of the grave.

"If the death of you has come from God, no one can do anything." The old man stepped out of the grave and again the wailing resumed.

It took all of my courage to keep from running away from the sound. Several family members knelt around the grave facing away from it. They took soil from the three piles and threw it backward into the grave. Slowly, the white cloth disappeared beneath the soft dirt. The crowd gradually scattered and people returned to their lives. I had seen the burial of many children, heard the sounds of many mothers wail, including my own. I hated the sound of it.

Two days later there was still no further sign of the raiders. The Beny Wut told the elders that they were likely Nuer fighters who had been working as of late with the Laraap. Rumors had spread that they were taking advantage of their status with the government to raid Dinka villages.

Matak and I looked after the cattle, built a small grass enclosure against an unlikely rain, and took our food from John Deng's mother. A dark mood had descended upon the cattle camp. Old men still sung to their oxen, but no one danced or joked, and the Beny Wut commanded men to stand guard deep in the forest surrounding us.

One day, several weeks after the aborted raid on our camp and the girl's death, Matak and I were sitting by the river with a fishing spear between us watching for any movement in the water. Across from us on the opposite bank, John Deng sat with a string on a small stick. On the string we had seen him tie a metal hook of some sort on which he had impaled an earthworm. John Deng pulled several small, smooth fish from the water while we watched, an art we assume he learned from the Kawajas who gave his family such names as his.

"Do you think he caught the Atuot man?" Matak spoke suddenly, keeping his eyes on the boy across the river.

I did not answer and I think Matak knew I had no answer for him.

"No one has seen him since the night the Nuer came to raid us," he said.

I grunted in reply. I did not want to think of Chol, him given the name that means he was born after the firstborn died. He was not worthy of the respect an oldest son should have and thinking of him gave me a pain deep in my chest. We both knew that Chol had killed the girl, likely to keep her quiet after he took her. I had seen the blood between her legs, seen the way her head had been crushed. I also had seen Chol attempt such a thing before.

A dance of youth had been staged the previous year. Hundreds of people close to my age came. Drummers filled the forest with complex rhythms, women and girls trilled, and everyone danced. Chol was there with some of his age mates, all wearing bright red strips of cloth around their necks. They pushed younger boys to the ground and laughed at them. Some girls slipped into the darkness toward home when they saw them for they were known to start fights and take girls who had not known men before. Most of us kept dancing and ignored them. We jumped in time with the drums, sometimes bumping heads and chests. Chol carried a small branch in his hand. All of the girls knew he meant to choose a partner tonight and none of them wanted his attention. They melted away from him as he worked his way through the crowd.

One girl, tall for her age but likely two to three years before her time of monthly bleeding stood frozen in fear as the crowd fell away, leaving her alone as Chol approached. It was unseemly for him to dance with one so young, but still, he placed the stick on the girls shoulder. It must have been the first time she had been chosen by a boy to dance. She lowered her eyes to the ground and at first did not acknowledge Chol's invitation. Chol tapped her again on the shoulder, then without waiting, he started to writhe with the drum beat and jump around the girl. I did not know this girl's name, though I had seen her around the village many times. Her mother made mandazies in the market area and her father was an elder. She made a few half-hearted gestures at dancing. Chol continued to dance around her. The girl glanced up and saw that most of the people were staring at her. She put her hand to her mouth and ran from the crowd into the darkness.

Chol stopped dancing and watched her flee. His age mates burst out laughing and pointed to him. Chol shouted curses at them, and then he too fled into the night.

I had lost my taste for dancing and was walking back to our compound when I heard a girl scream. I had my leec with me and I brought it up as I ran toward what I thought would be the scene of a hyena attack. Moonlight confused my vision for a few seconds, but in that time I could see that Chol had caught the girl from the dance and was attempting to mount her. The girl squirmed and fought him, but Chol was stronger and much bigger. The struggle would be over soon.

Without a sound, I brought my leec down hard against the bone of Chol's left forearm as he rose to strike the girl. I was rewarded with the sound of bone splintering and Chol's cry of pain. He instantly rolled off of the girl and lay writhing in the grass.

The girl sprang to her feet and raced into the bush, sobbing as she went, dragging her torn cover behind her. I looked down at Chol and he froze. I could see only the light of his eyes in the darkness, but they blazed hatred toward me. He rose slowly to his feet while cradling his broken arm. I could hear murmured curses coming from him as he carefully backed away from me. When he was within the high grass, Chol turned and ran away. I could hear him as he made his way north toward his family's compound.

Two days later, the girl's mother brought me a gift of honey and ground nuts crushed into a sweet paste. She thanked me for saving her daughter. She told me Chol had spread rumors among the village that I had ambushed him without cause and he was seeking revenge. She told me the Paramount Chief was thinking of calling for my capture.

"A chief always sleeps with his hand outside the net," she said to me. Bribes are common among the chiefs. This paramount chief was cheap and Chol's family was wealthy.

I thanked her for her gift and the information. I did not hear from the Chief, but rumors of Chol's intent for revenge continued and his age mates always cast angry glances toward me when we walked through the market.

Matak knew of Chol's attack on the young girl. He told me his mother knew of other girls, even younger than this that Chol had attacked. Most of the girls were too afraid to go to the chief with their complaints and Chol's reputation for such things grew. It was not hard for us to assume that Chol had attacked and killed the girl at the camp. We knew of no one else who would do such things. I told Matak of the girl's severed finger and he clucked and shook his head at the news.

"I thought Chol was chasing the Atuot man," I said to Matak.

"So he told his uncle," Matak responded. "But do you think Chol has the courage to hunt the man we saw kill the great crocodile?"

I did not answer him.

"Perhaps it was Chol who guided the Nuer to us," Matak said. Again, I did not answer that which needed no response. John Deng pulled another fish from the river. We waved at him and he raised his pole in reply.

"Perhaps we can ask the Beny Bith to give us wisdom," said Matak. "I can ask one of my relatives for a goat. It may be enough."

I nodded. It was a good plan.

Later that night when the cattle were put to rest, Matak found the Beny Bith. He was not of our clan, but people of the camp said that his power is sure and he does not charge for services he cannot do. The old man draped with wooden beads and wearing a green robe sat before a hut of woven grass. His grey hair and clouded eyes spoke of great age. He clutched his fishing spear to his chest as he sat silent and unmoving. A gentle breeze ruffled the feather he had tied to the end of the spear.

"Babba Dia," Matak said to him as we squatted to his side. "I am Matak and this is Thon."

The man nodded toward us. I could not tell if he could see us, though the light was still strong in the western sky.

"You are the killers of the great crocodile," the man said, chuckling to himself with a private joke.

"I am Thon," I said. "A man."

The *monydit*, old man, turned toward us and stared. "Yes, I see that you are men. But for not too long."

I touched the leaf over my forehead.

"And now you would ask me to give you wisdom for some great task," he said, turning back to stare across the camp again.

"Yes, we would," said Matak. "How did you know such a thing?"

"All new men wish for wisdom, though they rarely use the mind that they already have," the old man replied. "What would you give me for this work?"

"One full grown goat, a male. A black male," said Matak.

"Black, like the color of the cape buffalo," said the old man. "It is a good gift for that is the totem of my clan."

Matak and I smiled toward one another at this piece of luck.

"It will be enough," the man said.

He made no movement to get up or start his work. Matak believed the man was waiting to see the goat, so we hurried to retrieve it. We had traded an old knife and a bit of cloth for the goat. We tied it to a palm tree near the old man. He looked at it and nodded. The man stood and stretched his back. He was much shorter than either of us with bowed legs and a bent back. His fingers looked like sticks of wood.

He held his fishing spear over his head for a moment, then spit on the ground. He blew on the spear twice, then moved it in circles over our heads.

"You should shave your heads," the man said after a few minutes of prayer. "It will give you wisdom."

"We will do it, Monydit," I said. "But we paid you a goat. Can you give us directions?"

The man nodded. "Of course," he said.

The man lifted his robe over his knees, stood with his legs apart, and motioned for us. We knew what to do as we had seen the ritual performed many times as men went to war.

We got on our hands and knees and crawled through the man's legs as he chanted and waved his arms.

"You will go this way, but your enemies will not find you for they will go that way," he said, motioning first between his legs where we had gone and then to his side. "You will go this way," he said again, motioning to us. "But they cannot find you for they will go that way."

We repeated our trip through his legs three times before the old man seemed pleased. "You will have wisdom to stay away from your enemies," he said. "You must also do what you know to be right in your hearts for the other things. And shave your head."

We walked back to our sleeping area holding hands and thinking in silence. "Do what is right in your hearts," the old man had told us. That was easy to say. I knew what I must do and before I could say it, Matak voiced it for me.

"We have to accuse Chol before the judge," he said. I felt his hand relax as if the burden of the decision had been lifted.

"We will tell the Dungoor Bai," I said. "It will be between me and Chol."

Later that night, I sat on a log by the light of John Deng's fire as Matak shaved my head with the sharpened side of his spear. He took a long while before my already short hair was gone. The night breeze brushed my bare scalp and cooled the places where he had nicked my skin. When he was done, I shaved his head in the same way. We went to sleep hoping that wisdom would find its way into our bare heads and show itself to us in our dreams.

Chapter Eight

The man walked down a road of broken pavement and deep pits. Cars carefully picked their way through the potholes, almost all of them driven by Indian merchants. Men on motorcycles flew past him at impossible speeds, some carrying terrified passengers who bounced in the air and clung desperately to their drivers. Marabou storks with their neck pouches bulging from the day's feast picked through piles of garbage amid noisy flocks of crows, their squawking briefly interrupted when he walked close by. In the distance, he could see the narrow section of Lake Victoria where less than a kilometer to the north it would give birth to the Nile River.

He turned past a hotel at the edge of the town of Jinja and walked down a steep dirt road that led to the lakeside. Children hawking trinkets and fried bread ran to him but turned away when they saw the scowl on his face. Ahead, an unofficial market with broken signs and ramshackle shops sprawled along the water's edge. Dogs barked at him briefly as he passed and women watched silently. A small ramp led to an ancient dock where fishermen sat and worked on their nets. He made his way to a man who sat smoking a cigarette and watching the water. The man looked up and nodded, then without a word he began to untie a wooden boat covered with peeling blue paint. Inside the boat, the man sat on a wooden bench and lowered his eyes to stare at the water. The boatman gave two pulls on the starting rope and the outboard engine came to life, sputtering white smoke that drifted back to shore. A few fishermen briefly looked up at them, and then returned their attention to the nets.

They crossed the lake against a light wind. In the two-hour trip to the far shore they passed many fishermen casting nets into the murky waters. The boatman waved at a couple of the other boats and men waved back at him. He sang to himself in Arabic until his passenger cast him a dark look. Otherwise, they did not communicate.

The village of Walumbe rose up in front of them as they approached the far shore. Place of Death, as the name meant in the local dialect, was little more than a few hundred mud huts and a borehole. Dozens of children carried yellow jerry cans of water from the beach and they parted to create a space for the new boat. The driver cut the engine and they drifted until the point of the hull embedded itself in the sandy shore. The passenger got out and walked immediately up the bank past women who raked drying piles of minnows across large tarps stretched on the grass. White egrets walked unmolested among the women and picked at the minnows. No one spoke to him and only a few turned to watch him pass.

He made his way up a road that wound among the huts and shops. A woman beckoned him to enter her hut, calling to him that she had beer for sale while shaking her hips to suggest that she could offer more. The man ignored her and she spat a curse at him as he hurried by with his head lowered. He walked swiftly through the village toward a rocky hill. There he found a small trail that wound around boulders and abandoned fields, following the base of the hill. He took several more turns and twists until he came to a swept yard shaded by two large jackfruit trees. Set against a steep, rock cliff sat several mud huts with roofs of bundled grass. In front of one of the huts a naked infant sat playing with sticks and pebbles while a woman watched it. She turned to glance at the man and quickly averted her eyes.

The man walked through the compound to another, slightly larger hut hidden behind a wall of thick brush and grass. The hut had a single door made of thick mahogany on rusty hinges. The man pulled back an iron bolt and entered to the sounds of metal scraping on metal. He then pushed the door closed behind him and turned.

Only a few small slivers of light from the grass roof penetrated the dusty air and it took him a couple of minutes for his eyes to adjust to the darkness. As he stood looking around, he heard whimpering from every corner of the single room.

"I have a new one," a woman's voice came from the dark behind him and he started at the sound.

"Where?" he asked without turning to her.

"Against the far wall," the woman said.

He looked into the darkness and saw a small form curled up on the floor. He walked slowly to it, his eyes darting around the room. Something was different here and he needed to know what.

He came to stand over the small girl who was either unconscious or asleep, he could not tell. He nudged her with his bare foot. She did not move.

"I have given her a strong drink," the woman's voice told him. "She cried all day and I did not wish to hear more of it. You are half a day early. If you had come when you told me, she would be awake by now."

The man knelt and turned the girl on her back and carefully inspected her face and arms.

"Where did you get her?" the man asked, still staring at the girl. She could not be more than nine years old, close cropped hair, ragged dress of some nondescript color, bare feet. Most importantly, she did not have a single defect. No pierced ears or nose. No scars on her face.

"Someone, her stepmother I think, brought her to me," the woman answered. "The woman brought her here and told me she is from somewhere across the lake. She is Acholi. Not from here."

The man nodded and smiled to himself. He stood, still looking at the girl and considering how he would use her. He could feel the power from her innocence and youth, could almost smell it.

"You have done well," the man said. He could hear the woman behind her catch her breath at the rare compliment. He was still troubled and he looked about the room for something amiss. In the darkest far corner, behind him and to his left something stirred. He whirled about and pulled his long knife from his belt.

"You are being a fool," a male voice came from the corner.

The man dropped the knife. Bright light poured into the room briefly as the woman slipped out the door. In that instance the man could see another man sitting on a wooden chair. He wore a black leather hat with a broad rim, military green uniform, and boots.

"Lord Kony," the man said as he dropped to his knees in front of the seated man. He then crawled across the dirt floor, pressed his forehead to the ground, and lifted the other's boot to hold it to his own head.

Kony pressed his boot into the man's head and ground his face into the dirt. The man made no effort to protect himself but instead put his hands flat to the ground and accepted his humiliation. After a moment, Kony lifted his boot from the man, and then stood over him. He felt the gun at his waist pulling at his belt and the temptation to use it was almost more than he could resist.

"Stand up," Kony said to the man. "I was traveling to my pilgrimage to the Ato Hills. The Spirit told me that I must come here first because one of my flock is straying. I did not expect it to be you."

The other rose quickly, saluted, and then stood straight and rigid in front of his superior.

"You expend yourself on these girls to satisfy your lust when you should preserve them for the power they can bring us," Kony said. His voice was deep and seemed to come from all around the room at once.

The man stood rigid and looked ahead. He did not dare look directly into the eyes of Joseph Kony, Prophet of the Lord's Resistance Army, and a powerful wizard.

"I will be in Sudan soon," Kony continued. "I will need people there who I can trust, who understand where we get our power and can feed that need."

"Sir, there is another," the man replied.

"Of course, there is another," Kony replied. "There is always another."

Kony walked around the rigid man, ignoring the hushed whimpering of girls crying at the angry sound of his voice.

"If you would have this girl, take her now," Kony said. "When you are done, bury her. She will be of no use to us."

The man started to reply, but Kony cut him off.

"I have told you that for the magic to work, the child we use must be without blemish, like the lamb that Moses used," he said angrily. "When you take these girls, you ruin them for me."

Kony's shout set off a new round of crying from the girls. Kony pulled a pistol out of his belt, walked to the loudest one, and shot her through the forehead. The screams of the girls died immediately into soft whimpering and snuffling.

Kony walked to the door, still holding the pistol. The man followed him into the bright sunlight and was surprised when half a dozen soldiers appeared from the bushes, all carrying rifles and belts of grenades. The soldiers ran to form a line and stood at attention as Kony walked past them.

Kony never travels without his guards, the man thought, and he wondered that he had missed the signs of them.

"The Dinka you sent to me has a great talent for the work of God," Kony said.

The man stood at attention and waited. Kony took off his hat and wiped his brow with the sleeve of his uniform. He then walked over to where the man stood and looked directly into his eyes. Bright light now showed on his face and Kony noted again the seven parallel scars on his forehead.

"You cannot manage the magic that we use," Kony said to him. "But do not fear. I will not forsake you. You will have magic made from the hands of another. I will see to it. In the meantime, cover yourself with yao oil every evening. It will protect you."

The man relaxed slightly. Kony took a few slow steps away before turning back to the man.

"I am told that you warrant some congratulations," Kony said.

"Sir?" the man asked, still looking straight ahead.

"It is not every day that a Dinka warrior is so honored with your new rank," Kony said.

Chapter Nine

I found a distant uncle in the cattle camp and asked him to watch both of our herds. He readily agreed and thanked me for the honor. We hurried back to the village, stopping only to eat once. When Matak and I want to move long distances, we can move faster than almost anyone. We arrived in the market place late in the day. We went immediately to the Dungoor Bai's compound which lay a stone's throw from the northern edge of the market. A bamboo fence surrounded his place which was kept clean and orderly by several young girls. As we approached the gate, Matak hesitated. "Are you not sure we should tell the Executive Chief first?" he asked.

"You know as well as I that this crime is of too high a level. Only a chief of the Dungoor Bai's rank can hear such a case," I replied. I kept walking but Matak fell back.

"Stay here if you'd like," I said over my shoulder. "I will do as the Beny Bith commands."

Matak hurried to catch up with me and we reached the gate together. We saw a cluster of men sitting on wooden chairs under a large strangling fig tree. Smoke rose from among them, but none of them seemed to be speaking. A couple of them looked in our direction.

We walked over to them and exchanged greetings. We were fortunate that the elders were here as it would make it harder for the Dungoor Bai to ignore our case.

"He is coming," said one of the elders.

We turned and saw a round man with a protruding belly, fat thighs, and thin calves waddle toward us. He bore the scars of the Agar across his forehead. The lowest scar curved abruptly upward near his right ear. I thought briefly that perhaps he flinched during the first cut and his uncle had mercy on him and did not kill him on the spot, as would be the custom. The thought flashed across my mind then I put it down so that it would not come up again. Such thoughts that turn to words can be dangerous, especially if you're talking about the Dungoor Bai.

We bowed slightly and touched our bellies with our palms in acknowledgement of the Dungoor Bai. He fixed us in his stare with eyes with yellow edges. He did not smile, but briefly lifted his chin to us. One of the elders rose to give him his chair. The Dungoor Bai did not thank him, but sat down and splayed his fat legs.

"Why are you here?" he asked. There was contempt in his voice that I could not explain. I wondered if he had a vendetta against my family which I did not recall.

"There was a murder in the cattle camp," I said. The other elders leaned forward. The Dungoor Bai continued his yellow stare. A grey kite swooped down and snatched at a strip of goat skin while a woman at the far side of the compound worked to clean the hide. The commotion distracted us and we all turned to the woman. She kept working and I turned again to the Dungoor Bai.

"I know of the girl's death," he said through a clenched jaw. "Were you involved?"

The elders leaned again toward us.

"We have knowledge of who we believe did this thing," I replied. Now that the time of accusing was here, I realized we had no reason to suspect him other than Chol's previous attack on another girl and his mysterious absence from the cattle camp during the raid and the girl's murder.

Looking into the Dungoor Bai's eyes, this now seemed not enough.

"Tell us," an old man said. The Dungoor Bai shot him a harsh look, and then turned back to us. I could not read his face or know what he thought. He could have been made of stone.

"Chol, son of Mabor, was missing when the girl was killed. He has attacked young girls before and we think he would kill again," I blurted out. Even as the words passed my lips I thought how silly they sounded to come from a man of men, bearer of the marks.

The elders sat back in their seats and the Dungoor Bai spit in the dust.

"Did you see him attack the girl?" he asked.

I shook my head.

"Did anyone see him attack the girl?" he asked.

Again I shook my head.

"Were any of his weapons bloodied? Did you find his knife in her? Were his tracks found near her?" he asked in rapid succession.

I shook my head.

"Will you swear by the spear?" he asked. The elders leaned in again. It was a question not often asked of men.

Matak spoke up before I could reply.

"I too accuse Chol," he said. "I will swear by the spear."

The Dungoor Bai laughed, showing us his rotten teeth. He leaned in to me, so close that no one else could hear us.

"Will he swear on the spear for you, boy?" he said. I felt his breath on my cheek and smelled the decay of his mouth and fought the urge to vomit.

"I speak for myself and will swear on the spear myself," I said pulling myself as straight as I could.

"I can swear by it," Matak said loudly. "I do not fear the spear or anything."

We argued for a few minutes while an elder went for the spear. We all knew of this piece of magic, knew its history. All of us knew of the crazed man who killed his Larap boss with the spear and how the spear came to have the power of the marked man. We knew it had been in the tribe for many generations, forcing justice and truth on us when witnesses failed. Other judges use a knife or even a stone. Near us, a small, insignificant tribe uses a coin. It is said that if you put the coin on your forehead and then lied to the judge, the coin would stay on your head and cause you great pain until you died. Our spear was simpler. If you swore something false to it—it killed you.

"I will swear on the spear," I said loudly. Matak backed away and stood with the elders.

A few minutes later, the Dungoor Bai stood before me holding the polished wooden shaft with a flat, double bladed tip. The spear's blade flashed in the sunlight as he twirled it and stared at me.

"You know what to do," the Dungoor Bai said.

I took the spear and knelt in the dirt. With the tip of the spear, I scraped out a small hole, smaller than my hand. It was my grave, too small for my body but big enough for my soul. I put the soil from the dirt in three piles, like the grave of a man would be. I then held the spear above my head and stepped over the grave three times. I then took the spear and held the point to my heart and said the words I knew the Dungoor Bai expected of me.

"May this spear, the one I hold now, kill me if I am not telling the truth," I said loudly. "May this spear kill me if the thing I accuse Chol of doing is not truth."

The Dungoor Bai chuckled, and then took the spear from me. I knelt again and filled the small grave from the three piles of dirt. The elders spoke in hushed voices to one another and pointed toward me. Matak came to stand beside me.

"The last man who spoke lies to me and this spear died only a few steps from my gate," the Dungoor Bai said, again with an evil chuckle. "He did not even make it to his home."

"I spoke the truth, Dungoor Bai," I said, standing as straight as I could. "Will you hold court?"

"Is the *Makongo* here?" he replied angrily. An elder stood.

"Go to the Beny Wut of this cattle camp and tell him to send Chol to me," he told the man. "Tell him that this man with new marks on his face makes a claim against him. Tell him Chol must come immediately." The Dungoor Bai kept looking at me as he spoke.

The old man turned and walked swiftly away. It was not seemly for an old man to run, but I knew that this man would eat the miles to obey the Dungoor Bai's words. The Makongo was just that, a messenger from the court to the cattle camp. He could bring cattle from a man's herd if so instructed. Even to his own family, Chol would not be held as tightly as would their cattle.

I turned to walk away and Matak moved with me. We came to the gate of the Dungoor Bai's compound and stopped to look back. The elders had resumed whatever discussion that would consume their day. I could not see the Dungoor Bai. It was as if he had vanished. I had the sensation that something watched us, something that I could not see. Not until we had entered my family compound did the feeling that something followed us go away and the hairs on the back of our necks relax.

I spent the night haunted by dreams filled with images of the dead girl and of the spear, of Chol lurking in the shadows ready to kill me. In one dream, I saw the dead girl now standing, draped in the white cloth that covered her in her grave. She pointed across the river to a dark mist that rumbled with thunder and flashed lightening as it moved across the grasslands leaving the ground scorched and smoldering. The front of the dark mist held the shape of a man's face I could not clearly discern. At times it looked like Chol, scowling and spitting hatred. Other times it was the face of a Larap with his head covered. Mostly, the face in the mist looked like an old man who had eaten well all of his life with his cheeks puffed up and round and his eyes mere slits. It was a face that I thought I knew but could not name. As I watched the mist stream across the land I heard the sound of thousands of feet shuffling and the unmistakable thud of bodies hitting the ground. I heard screaming, but from such a distance I had trouble telling it apart from the call of birds. The mist grew in size and blackness until it came to the river, a river I knew well, the River of the Ostrich, the Bahr Naam. There the mist broke upon the river shores and began to fade, leaving broken and bloodied bodies in its wake, all of which looked like the dead girl. I woke from the dream while it was still dark with my heart pounding in my chest as if trying to escape. Sleep did not come to me again until many hours passed and I heard the sounds of animals and birds announcing the early dawn.

Chapter Ten

He waited in the darkness amid a stand of blue gum trees planted by a British administrator two generations ago. Strips of bark swayed in the gentle breeze and made a ghostly whisper. He stood in the mass of shadows and absorbed the feel of the darkness that he loved so dearly. A hyena whooped nearby and he noted its location, though he had no fear of the other creatures of the night. He watched a snake as thick as his wrist slither onto the road, a black slash across the hard, packed clay. Half way across, the snake stopped and raised its head a handbreadth off of the ground and waited. Bats fluttered overhead and somewhere in the forest behind him, an owl called. The man turned his head to briefly gaze into the forest, then turned back to the road. When he looked again, the snake was gone. He did not like the sound of the owl and what it could mean. He liked even less the disappearing snake.

Somewhere far away, he heard the engine of a truck. Gradually, the sound grew louder and he edged back further into the shadows. He was anxious to be away from the road for soon the moon would rise and cast a steely light across the land. The sound of the engine came to an abrupt stop. He strained to hear doors closing and the murmur of men's voices somewhere north around a sharp bend in the road. The wind died and took the whisper of the trees with it.

He heard the newcomer coming long before he saw him, heard the squeak of stiff leather boots and the jingle of metal against metal. He tightened his grip on his spear with one hand and with the other he fingered the leather pouch around his neck. Soon, he saw the figure of a man trying unsuccessfully to walk in silence as he crept along the far side of the road. Clumps of dried clay crunched with each of his steps. Twice he stumbled and mumbled curses heard clearly by the one who waited for him.

He let the clumsy man walk past him, and then stepped out onto the road. Even then, the newcomer did not see him or hear him. Only when he laughed out loud, a deep rumble that could have been an elephant's stomach, did the man stop and turn around. For a moment they stared at each other across the darkness.

"Do you have it?" the newcomer asked.

He grunted an affirmative. He waited while the man made his way back to him and stood within arm's reach.

"The men will do as you command," the newcomer said. "They will be there within a week."

"Three days," the man replied.

"They need a week," the newcomer said sternly.

"Three days," he replied again. There was no malice in his voice, but there was also no hint of retreat.

The newcomer let his hand wander to the pistol at his belt. The man noted the action and he lifted the butt of his spear from the ground. He knew he could plant the spear in the man's chest long before the other could pull his gun. The newcomer hesitated, moved his hand away from the pistol, and then reached into his shirt for a small bundle.

"Your money," the newcomer said as he held it out toward the man who did not reach for it.

"Three days," he said again.

"Three days," the newcomer said with resignation in his voice. "Now give it to me."

The man broke the leather string from his neck and handed him a pouch. The newcomer snatched it from him and started back toward the waiting truck. He looked over his shoulder once, but the man had already faded into the shadows.

Chapter Eleven

Later the next morning, word came to us that the Makongo could not find Chol and no one of the cattle camp had seen him since the night the Nuer scouts came to us and the girl had died. His family insisted that he was on a mission to find and kill the Atuot man, the same one that we knew had saved the boy from the crocodile. My dread of the spear greatly decreased with the news that Chol appeared to have fled. However, my mother searched me for signs of sickness, worrying that the spear would still work its magic and kill me anyway.

"I have seen with my own eyes a man who swore by the spear that he did not have relations with a neighbor's daughter," Mother said. "He died before he made it home. His bowels began to pour water and he vomited so violently that he could not stand. His wife called the Tiet but he was dead before half a day had passed."

"I did not lie," I protested as she finally sat back to rest.

"Perhaps not," she replied. "But you spoke of things that you could not be certain were true. You did not see Chol kill the girl."

I made no reply. At that moment I saw Matak working his way up the trail. He seemed to be moving slower than usual and casting anxious looks into the tall grass. When he stepped into our compound he greeted Athen respectfully, as any

Dinka of good character would do. I already knew that my mother had hopes that Matak would marry one of my sisters and she always smiled at him and treated him well. My father was not there to represent his interests, but I knew he would wish for a son-in-law who would pay more cows than Matak's family ever could. My sisters were all tall and stately, not likely to be as tall as my mother, but at least they had the usual numbers of fingers and toes. My oldest sister, the one Athen was likely to try to pair with Matak always stayed near the compound when Matak visited. She would be a fine wife for him, if his family chose her, for she spoke rarely and always with respect, worked hard, and could even read some of the Arabic pamphlets that the Laraap left lying around when they passed through our village. How she learned this, I could not be sure, but I suspected that my mother taught her in the evenings.

"Chol has fled," Matak said after my mother walked off to tend her garden.

"I heard," I replied. "Is that not what we would expect of a guilty one?"

Matak nodded, and then added, "Is it not possible that Chol was killed in the forest by the Nuer? And is it not also possible that the girl stumbled upon a Nuer scout creeping into our camp and the scout killed the girl to keep her quiet?"

"The girl had blood between her legs," I replied. "I do not think any scout would risk detection in order to have his way with a girl."

Matak again nodded.

"It seems an unlikely thing that the girl should be killed and the Nuer attack us on the same night," he said.

I agreed, though I did not tell him this.

"Does Chol's family do business with the Nuer?" Matak asked. He knew I would not have such knowledge and

I did not answer. The question was his way of suggesting such a thing.

"Perhaps it was Chol who led the Nuer to the camp," Matak finally said directly. "Perhaps he wanted the girl and knew the Nuer were planning to attack us that night. Perhaps he took the girl, killed her, and then fled thinking that the girl's death would not be noticed among the other signs of battle."

Again, I did not answer, but again I recalled the girl's amputated finger. We sat and watched as one of my younger brothers scattered a few grains of millet on the hard ground. He then took string and made a series of slip knots, leaving the open loops the size of a man's thumb. He then attached the other end to a stick. He left the loops among the millet and walked into the grass and crouched out of sight. Matak and I had done the same thing hundreds of times. We knew that if the boy was patient and if his knots were good, a dove or pigeon would fly down to take of the millet. The bird's feet would tangle in the string and the knots would grow tighter the more the bird pulled. When the bird tried to fly it would find itself attached to the stick. It would flutter and bounce about until it was exhausted or the boy killed it. In this area, the boy would have to move in fast or the grey kites would swoop down and snatch the bird away. We watched, noting with satisfaction that the string was set properly and the loops appeared to have good knots. Already we could see green pigeons moving lower in the branches of the shea nut tree and spying the seeds.

"We should go on a journey, go to where we can prove we are men," Matak said, breaking the silence.

"You have listened to too many old men's stories," I replied with a laugh.

"Thon," he said. "I am serious. We need a journey, a great journey to find many things."

"Find what? Chol?" I asked.

"Yes, Chol. For information on the war and what the Nuer are doing so far into our territories. Perhaps even for your father."

My father, I thought. Matak is playing on the idea of finding my father and possibly sending news to my mother that he is alive. Already there was talk among the clan that she should take one of my uncles as the *Alohot*, or inherited wife so they may father children with her in his name. In honor of my father, my mother would comply, though I am not sure how many more children she could support. Even with her great strength and hard labors there are times of hunger in our compound. Finding my father was sufficient reason alone to go on this journey, and if I did not settle the matter about Chol's guilt regarding the girl's death, the threat of the oath I made to the spear would forever hang over me. I decided to go on the journey minutes before I told Matak, who continued to make up reasons for it. I loved to hear him talk, so I let him continue until I could stand no more.

I finally laughed and leaned into Matak. "We will have great stories to tell our children," I said. He laughed with me.

"When should we leave?" I ask.

"Perhaps a few days, four, maybe three," he replies. "It is the time of the Fat Man Contest. The judging begins tomorrow and I would like to stay for it."

We sat and talked of our journey, our families, how we will bring them news of our decision. My father is not here and my uncles will not attempt to dissuade me. Only my mother will object. But with the cattle in capable and safe hands, there is no need for me to remain here.

I thought of the Fat Man contest and how she had encouraged me to enter.

"We do not have enough food for me to compete," I had said after the fifth or sixth time she suggested that I enter the contest.

"Are you saying that I could not make my oldest living son fat with the product of my labor?" she had replied indignantly.

I had no reply. If I said we did not have the wealth for me to become fat, she would take it as an insult. If I entered the contest, she may take food and milk for my siblings that they needed much more than I did.

"I have no time," I finally replied. "Perhaps next year."

This seemed to please her and she had not brought it up again.

Later that day, competitors in the Fat Man contest began to arrive. I knew several of the participants, but could hardly recognize them. Their normally spindly legs were soft and no muscles showed from them. Their faces were swollen and most of them looked miserable from the volumes of milk they consumed hours earlier and for the months they had prepared. Fat stomachs bounced and I heard many of them emit gaseous sounds almost with every step. They all appeared to be in pain.

The next day, the judging of the contest began in earnest. People circled the participants and danced, calling the names of their favorites to the crowd, trilling and singing. There was no leader, no official council to name the winner who was as often as not the one whose supporters were the most persistent and loud. Gradually, a census seemed to emerge. The chanting of many names became the chanting of a few and then the one. "Mabor, Mabor," they shouted.

Mabor waddled up to a line of women, naked except for a string of beads around his neck. He had covered his face with white dung ash and put charcoal around his eyes.

"At the last village, near Atiaba, they picked a different Fat Man winner," Matak said to me over the noise of the crowd. "He drank so much milk that his stomach burst. They buried him yesterday, but not before declaring him the winner. I am surprised that he did not win here as well."

I continued to dance while Matak spoke. He knew as well as I that Mabor had many family and clan members here and they are the ones who gave him this honor.

When the crowd had spent itself and the fat men lay slumbering under trees, we started back to my compound. We walked past roofless brick and stone buildings that still showed the signs of bombing from the first Anyanya. Why the Laraap would want to bomb our small village, no one knew. Some of the old men had lived through the Anyanya One and had seen the bombs fall on our unsuspecting village. Most thought that the Laraap just flew in their machines and dropped bombs on anything they could see from the air. About us lay deep craters filled with vines where other bombs had missed their marks. People now tossed refuse into them and flies rose from their depths in great black waves.

We passed two Kawajas at the north end of the market, one tall girl with brown hair and a tall man that looked to be her father. He had a grey beard, dark glasses, and a hat the color of *agook*, or monkeys. They walked slowly, each chewing on a mandasi they bought from street vendors. I heard murmurs from some of the older ladies of how rude it was for them to walk and eat at the same time, something that no Dinka of good character would ever do. The man and girl walked on and greeted the people in short Dinka phrases, oblivious to the offense they were giving.

"He is a doctor who works here for a month each year," Matak said. "He brings his family along, sometimes just one or two. His son fights in a great war far from here."

"Why would he come here?" I ask. "We have nothing for him."

Matak shook his head and we kept walking, ignoring them as we passed. They did not seem to notice the rudeness we flaunted at them by not greeting them as would be proper.

The rare visit by white people excited the children and they called to the strangers, "Kawaja, Kawaja, Kawaja."

We passed the compound of a woman who had lost three of her children to a disease of the dry season. Her oldest son survived but has not acted normally since. He sat on a crooked log staring at a pot that boiled over a fire. When he saw us, he jumped to his feet and barked at us like a dog. We did not meet his eyes or acknowledge him in any way as we knew from experience that he would likely attack us if we did. On the ground near him his mother sat staring at her feet. She did not look up as we passed. She was thin, dirty, and her clothes were tattered. We both knew that they would all be dead by spring. No one from their own clan even bothered to bring them food.

When we turned off of the main road onto a smaller trail, we stepped around several small piles of sticks and leaves. Without thinking, we broke off twigs and added them to the pile. Somewhere near, a *jok*, or lesser spirit, lived and we did such things to protect ourselves. The jok could live in a termite mound or a special tree. Sometimes we saw its place and other times we trusted the people who started the small piles that they had found or sensed it. I have seen people who did not honor the jok in such ways. I have seen them drop to the ground, writhing, making odd sounds as spit smeared across their faces. I even saw one drop into a fire on which sorghum beer was cooking. Before anyone could act, she was burned across her face and chest. Her face now looks like a wooden mask, all because she failed to give the jok this small tribute.

Mother was surprisingly calm when we told her we would take a journey in search of Chol. She did not ask the obvious question. What would we do if we found him? Would we try to force him to return and face the judge over murdering the girl? Would we kill him? Fight him? She did not ask and we were grateful. She did not ask if we would search for my father and I thought she already knew that I would.

She cooked some food for us and brought out what little money she had. The paper bills were worn almost beyond recognition and all of them had small tears along the corners. We could not read the words, but knew their worth, knew how many of each kind would buy us beans or sorghum. We took the food, knowing as did she that we could not cook it, at least where there were others to do so for us. We were Dinka men now and it was improper for us to cook. We could use the money to buy food or pay someone to cook for us. Only in the direst situations or when we could be certain that no one would know of it would we ever cook again. We bundled the food and money within rolled up robes and blankets. We each took one knife and a spear for it is improper for men to journey with empty hands.

My spear was also my father's spear and his father's before him. Its shaft was dark, heavy wood. Someone had taken bullet casings from a long forgotten battle, cut them, and pressed them over the shaft so that my spear had brass rings that set it apart from others.

"The Dungoor Bai sent word that he knew of your journey," Mother said as we prepared. I cannot imagine how he knew such a thing. If he was not guessing, he was using powerful magic.

"You must be careful of messages he sends," Mother continued. "Do not trust them."

When I asked her to explain more, she simply shrugged and walked away. As we left, I looked back to see her watching us from her garden. Our eyes met for an instant. Later, when I recalled this moment, it seemed as if we looked at each other for a long while before she turned and started pulling weeds. I saw the heart of the Dinka reflected in her eyes-- pride, fear, and strength, all mingled in a look that had lasted less than a heartbeat. I knew that as long as women like her lived, worked the land, and held her family together, we Dinka would be eternal.

Matak and I walked for two days, stopping only to sleep and take brief meals from the food my mother had prepared for us. On the afternoon of the third day we entered a village where one of my uncles lived. We stayed with my Wallen for two nights while his primary wife prepared food for us and we rested. Twice I had the dream of the dark mist covering the land and both times I woke drenched in sweat and shaking. Matak knew I dreamt of bad things and did not ask me what I did not volunteer to tell.

On the next morning, my uncle and I sat under the shade of a mango tree while I told him the story of my fight with Chol, the dead girl, the Dungoor Bai and our journey. He nodded at the right times to indicate he heard and understood but did not speak until I had finished.

"My wives are fighting again," he said and I wondered if he had heard me at all. "They say that I should not let you stay to make more work for them."

I felt the blood rush to my face. We Dinka are known for our hospitality and I could not imagine that he was suggesting that I, a man of his own clan, was not welcome. Wallen laughed and I felt a bit better.

"They say that of each other too," he said grinning. "I have too many."

"Your pan, your family, is great among us," I replied. "You have how many, six, maybe five wives?"

"Yes, five," he replied. "Sixteen children. Six boys and the rest girls. The boys are brave, tall, and strong. The girls are beautiful. Men are already offering many cows for them, enough that I will have cows enough for many more wives. They will take care of me long into my old age."

"That is good," I said, still wondering why we were talking of this thing.

"Chol was born in the dust of the cattle camp," Wallen continued. "His mother had been forced to marry a weak young man of the clan in the name of a dead grandfather who had no children of his own, or at least none that carried forth his name. As a young man myself, I knew the grandfather Chol's mother had been forced to call her husband. This grandfather, the ghost husband of Chol's mother, did evil things. I believe it is this ghost that possesses Chol, has been in him since he was a child."

Wallen traced circles in the dust as he spoke. Matak slipped silently behind me and squatted to listen as Wallen spoke.

"Chol's grandfather, the man I knew, went to Uganda to buy cloth for his shop. When he was there, he met people who convinced him that great fortune could be gained by using charms of the most hideous things. It was in Uganda that he learned of this evil and brought it here."

I heard Matak swallow behind me.

"In Uganda magicians make charms of the fingers and ears of stolen children," Wallen said. "If it is a boy they steal, they cut parts from him before they kill him. If it is a girl, they take her before carving her up. They believe that relations with a virgin girl will cure all sorts of diseases."

Now I understood what Wallen wanted us to know.

"We caught Chol's grandfather cutting parts from a girl who was several years from menstruating. We killed him on the spot and left his body to the hyenas. Everyone knew what we had done, your father and me. Everyone knew and blessed us in secret for by then we all had known of the evil and had seen Chol's clan grow in great fortune from its magic.

Dark and rotten fortunes. We never spoke of it after that day and I tell you this now so you know what you face if you find Chol."

"We will find someone who wields strong magic and is a killer of children," Matak said, still crouching behind me.

"Yes," Wallen said. "But one who has learned dark things from his father's family and cares little for any life, perhaps even his own. You will face his magic. It will be strong and you must be of courage and uprightness to stand against it. You take great risks. He will not stop doing this evil thing for it has hold of him as it did his father and his grandfather before him."

"All the more reason to find him," I said. "Before he kills again."

"All the more reason," Wallen repeated. "Thoughts like this infect a people, pass from father to son and are as hard to eliminate as fleas."

Wallen rose as to leave, but instead put his foot to a knee and leaned against his walking stick.

"Has someone decided to marry in the name of the dead girl from the cattle camp?" he asked.

We both shook our heads.

"I think they should do so, and soon," Wallen said. I had almost forgotten that Wallen too was a Beny Bith, a Master of the Fishing Spear. "I think the spirit of a child killed in such a way will not wait long before she brings adversity to her family. She must become a brother to them and her brothers should marry a girl in her name."

Wallen picked up the small seat he carried with him and walked back to his hut. One of his wives pounded millet and smiled at him as he passed. He did not respond. She then cast a sharp look toward us.

We left my Wallen's compound that day, moved north toward the town of Rumbek. We crossed the river Bahr Naam over an old metal bridge that Matak's grandfather had supervised building. He was a great man, trained in Khartoum for such tasks. A sick dog bit him while he was working on a road in the Lake District several years ago. It had taken him weeks to die and in the end he had to be tied to a wooden frame as he convulsed and salivated. My *Neneer*, maternal uncle, who lived there, said that he screamed for almost two days without stopping before he died and that he seemed to have drowned in his own saliva. It was a terrible death.

We walked far into the night, singing at times to ward off animals. Occasionally we saw the eyes of bushbabies gleaming in the moonlight from the trees. Twice we frightened hyenas from the grass at the edge of the road. If I had been alone, I would not have dared walk this road. Matak, as always, told stories as we walked. He absorbed knowledge from elders like water on dry sand and shared it freely.

"This is the area of the twin lions of my father's time," he said. "They came all the way from Yirol, killing cattle, goats, and many people as they moved."

I had heard the story before but let him tell me again. His animated speech and gestures always brought me into the tale and I could even feel my heart race when he came to a particularly gruesome or tense part.

"The lions made a den of a burned out hut not far from where we are now," he continued, gesturing to into the darkness. "Two males. Great beasts as large as cows, I am told. They caught travelers coming down this very road and dragged them to their den, sometimes still alive. There they played with them, hitting them with their paws and nipping at their feet. Their tongues are rough and can lick the skin off of a man."

I looked into a dark night filled with shapes and the hint of movement. A few night birds called and in the distance I heard cattle from a camp deep in the forest.

"Forty men these beasts killed here. I heard they killed as many or more in Yirol before they came here. But here is where they met Maciek, a powerful hunter of the Sheep clan.

"Maciek liked to drink sorghum beer. Sometimes he would drink so much that it caused him to fall into a deep sleep, so deep he could not be roused. His wife made the beer for him to keep him from visiting the loose girls who also made beer and would give themselves to their customers.

"One night, also not far from here, Maciek drank heavily and fell asleep outside of his hut. As his wife tried to bring him inside, the two lions walked right up to her. She threw stones at them and called for their neighbors to help, but no one came to her aid. The lions killed her and ate her on the spot. They then dragged Maciek to their den while he was drunk with the beer. He was so drunk that he did not awake until the next morning. When had roused himself, he found himself inside the lions' den with the lions still so full from devouring his wife that they slept the night and did not kill him. He recognized his wife's necklace dangling from the mouth of one of the lions. Maciek always kept a knife strapped to his waist. With this, he slit the throat of one of the lions and turned just as the second one awoke and launched himself at him. By this time, Maciek's neighbors had discovered where the lions had raided his compound and tracked the lions to their den. They arrived to see Maciek and the lion engaged in a battle to the death. The lion lashed at him and snapped his great jaws while Maciek flung himself on the lion's back and stabbed him in the neck with his knife. The neighbors rushed in and drove their spears into the lion's chest and he fell on top of Maciek.

"When they gutted the lions, Maciek's wife came out in parts. They buried her wrapped in the lion's hide. Maciek lived many years and fathered over a hundred children by dozens of wives. When he died, they buried him under a teak tree and placed a carving over him. His family put his best bull and many cattle in the grave with him. Six of his wives leapt into the grave as they began to fill it. They were the last of the live burials to be done in this area. To this day, Maciek's relatives come each year when the rains end and sacrifice many cows to his name. Other people come and sacrifice cows to a special jok at the same place. No one knows why they do this. It is just done."

After this story, Matak was silent for a while. The night sky gave just enough light for us to stay on the road, but the trees lined on each side of us were dark and ominous. From a great distance we heard a gunshot. A few seconds later, more shooting and an occasional louder booming sound. We knew the sounds of gunfire as many returning soldiers came home with their weapons which they soon used to wipe out the game around them. These guns, the soldiers carried casually from cloth slings and ropes as if to carry a gun was not great thing for them. But they were quick to point it if an argument did not go their way or they simply wanted something the people did not want to give them. But the louder sound was preceded by a prolonged hiss as if a thousand angry snakes had been roused from their dens. This one was new to us but we both thought it was another weapon of the Laraap and could only mean that the war was near.

Sounds, especially gunshots, travel great distances in our flat land so we could be almost a half-day's walk to the place where the weapons were fired. We knew they were not close and that we were in no immediate danger. But the road meandered in the general direction of what sounded like a small battle. The sounds lasted for other hours or so, then dwindled slowly and quiet again fell across the forest. Most of the night spent itself before we stopped to sleep among the roots of a great mahogany tree.

Bright sunlight and the sounds of birds roused us late the next morning and we resumed walking. By midday we found another compound belonging to a man from Aluakluak, not far from our village. He was not at home, but his wife thought she knew my mother's family. She fed us ground nuts mixed with honey and boiled okra and gave us water to drink. We thanked her for her hospitality and resumed our walk, not anxious to repeat our experiences traveling in the darkness.

We passed several men and women, some carrying loads of household goods. One woman stopped and talked to us while we all three rested in a patch of shade. The woman seemed about my mother's age. She wore marriage beads about her neck and a simple yellow skirt. While we sat and talked, several groups of people passed us walking fast. They all had worried looks on their faces and some carried children. In the distance, we heard the deep echoes of gunfire.

"We are moving south to flee the war," the woman said. "Many Laraap with our own Nuer brothers are raiding and killing Dinka all around Rumbek."

Her face was hollow and her eyes slightly sunken in, the look of someone starving, and yet she did not ask us for food. Matak gave her a few groundnuts and she hid them in a pocket inside her skirt. When I handed her a piece of dried goat meat she stuffed it in her mouth and chewed loudly.

"Do the Laraap still control Rumbek?" Matak asked. She nodded. She spoke of the SPLA, a name I had heard mentioned only once before. I asked her who they were and she told me they were the Sudan People's Liberation Army. I thought it was a grand name and those who carried it must be great people to want to liberate Sudan with an army of this name.

"There is a place where airplanes come from the north bringing more guns and men," she said. "The SPLA has tried to take the place, but it is well guarded. After repeated attacks on their camps, the Laraap began to clear all of the Dinka from Rumbek. Those that do not flee, they kill. Some of the women and children are taken north. My own daughter, not yet seven years, fell behind. My aunt saw the Laraap kill her son and take my daughter with them. She is dead to me now."

"We are sorry for your daughter," I told her. "Where do we find the people of the SPLA?"

"I cannot say," she replied. "Most of them seem to be moving from the east area of Rumbek. I would go there to find them. But take care. They are not hospitable to strangers and may shoot you if you walk up to them unbidden."

We thanked her for her information and resumed walking. When we looked back, she had already put a great distance between us.

We encountered more people as we walked, all of them heading south away from Rumbek and almost all of them carrying great burdens. Some limped and many bled from fresh wounds. Children scurried to keep up with parents and young men herded cows ahead of them, swatting them viciously with sticks and whips when they slowed or tried to graze. More people told us the Laraap were taking the area around Rumbek and most told us we should flee with them.

Once we heard a roaring sound approaching from behind us and turned just in time to jump out of the pathway of a line of trucks speeding north. People scattered before them and dust choked the air. I saw many men packed in the backs of the trucks, most of them wearing green uniforms and berets, but some looking like naked boys of the cattle camp except for the guns slung across their shoulders. A small distance behind the trucks raced a white car with dark windows. I could not see inside the car but noticed a red flag attached to a stick someone had tied to it.

We kept walking as the crowds fleeing south grew thicker. Soon we had to push our way through the people and cows. When we came to a long straight part of the road, Matak climbed a tree to see what lay ahead.

"People crowd the road for as far as I can see," he shouted down at me. "It will be slow going this way."

Just as he was about to start climbing down, we heard gunfire ahead. People started to run, knocking over the slower ones ahead. I jumped behind the tree that Matak had climbed and let the crowd surge past me. More gunfire in a steady rattling sound echoed and people ran faster and began shouting.

"Soldiers, not far ahead," Matak shouted to me. "They are firing into the crowd. I think they are trying to clear the road. Many people are getting shot."

Just then a branch near Matak's feet exploded into splinters. He ducked just as another bullet tore a hole in the bark a hand's breadth from his head. Matak swung off of one limb, and then dropped to the ground at a crouch.

"They shot at me!" he shouted above the noise. "Why would they shoot at me?"

We did not have time to talk but pressed ourselves hard against the tree as people and animals flew past us. The bell of one great bull clanked loudly as it loped by us, crushing people in its path.

"Let's go into the bush," I shouted to Matak. He nodded. We glanced from behind the tree and waited until no cows were in our way, then we bolted across the short space from the tree to a line of brush beside the road. A few others did the same.

We ran through spiked bushes and thorns, stopping only when we fell or became entangled. We did not heed the direction of our flight except that it was directly away from the sounds of people, cows, and gunfire. We ran until we felt our hearts would burst within us, and then slowed to a quick walk. Already the sounds of people and cattle had faded and only the occasional gunshot told us where the road lay. Both of us sported scratches and scrapes from rough underbrush.

When we finally stopped, we could hear no further shots or shouting in any direction. I took out my water gourd and drank a small bit, saving it for later in case we could not find a well. Streams would be rare in this area, I knew. Matak did the same.

While we sat, we heard a humming sound from the air. We looked up just as an airplane flew over us. It was so high that we could see only that it had square tipped wings and was painted white. Neither of us had seen one before, but stories of them abounded. It was said that a man could mount one of these machines and fly to Khartoum in one day, Egypt in two. They also carried bombs that they could drop from the sky at any time they wanted, an idea that frightened all the people. We could hear the plane long after it disappeared from sight.

"Were those Laraap who were shooting people on the road?" I asked Matak when we had gotten our breaths.

"I could not tell," he replied. "They stood on trucks parked by the road watching the people pass. I saw no warning that they were going to shoot. They just started shooting." Matak shrugged.

"Their clothes?" I asked. "What were they wearing?"

"They wore clothes that looked like a patch of leaves," he replied. "The truck was green. I cannot tell these soldiers from one another. I wonder how they tell."

"Their uniforms are different," I said. "But you can only tell up close. My father had told my mother these things and she told me."

We heard more gunfire, but from a different direction. When the sounds appeared to be moving toward us, we started walking away from it.

We spent the night again on the ground by a mahogany tree. We wrapped ourselves against the cold and mosquitoes, not daring to make a fire.

Chapter Twelve

In the morning we headed north again, this time staying in the bushes. We walked most of the morning before we came to a small village that appeared deserted. Near the center of the cluster of compounds, we found a well with a hand pump. We drank as much water as we could hold, washed ourselves, and filled our water gourds. A few goats strolled past, but there were no people. We believed they must have fled.

We had just picked up our belongings to continue when the wind shifted slightly and we smelled it. Matak looked at me questioningly. Silently, we laid our packs by the well and took our spears. We crept forward toward the smell. We saw dogs lying about, all shot. Some goats lay on the ground, some shot and others with their throats slit. Many of the goats had been skinned and the choice meats removed. All of them lay rotting in the heat with great clouds of flies buzzing about them. We both knew that this was not the smell that assaulted us and brought the hairs of our necks up.

We reached a confluence of trails that ran through the village and made a clearing and found what we both feared. The bodies of people lay stacked upon one another. Hundreds of them, men, women, children. All bloated and reeking of decay. A few men were tied to the trees. Some of these bodies lacked arms or legs, their limbs laying bloodied and rotting from where they had been hacked away from the living. Here and there a vulture tore strips of flesh off the bodies and fought with other birds that hopped across the ground and across stacks of the dead. We ducked back behind a hut and leaned against its wall.

"Laraap!" Matak said.

I nodded. In truth, we could not say who did this thing but we could not believe that any Dinka could kill like this. As we leaned against the wall we saw motion from the dark doorway of the compound across from us. The leather curtain that fell across the door bulged and swayed from something inside. Then a patch of brown, scruffy fur poked through, followed by the rest of a hyena. It dragged a baby by its head. We were about to back away when we saw the baby's hand move, just so slightly.

Without thinking or speaking to one another, we rose with our spears held high and ran toward the hyena. It saw us, hesitated, and then adjusted its grip on the baby's head. It tried to run with its catch, but was slow and the baby's body caught on some brush. Matak hurled his spear at it as we ran but the spear glanced off the creature's back and buried itself into the ground. We kept running toward it and were within a few steps when it dropped the baby and sped away into the tall grass.

I followed the hyena to the edge of the grass and stood watching while Matak stooped over the baby. Blood seeped down the babies wounds and it opened its mouth to whimper.

"This baby could not live alone for the time these people have been dead," Matak said. I backed away from the grass while he carefully picked up the baby and retrieved his spear. We made our way back to the hut where the hyena had taken the child and looked inside. Again, the smell of decay blasted our noses. We held our breaths and stepped inside. As our eyes adjusted, we saw two bed nets and a wooden shelf. A red blanket covered a mat of grass on one side and tarps covered much of the dirt floor. Pushed up against the wall of at the edge of the red blanket, we saw a young woman who appeared to have curled into a ball as she lay on her side. Her ribs stuck out from her sides and we could barely make out the motions of her breathing.

"Woman," I spoke to her gently. "Woman, can you hear me."

She did not move but we could perceive the slight change in her breathing.

"Woman, we have your baby," I said.

We heard a whimper, and then slowly she unwound herself and turned slightly to look at us. She tried to speak but the words seemed to stick to her tongue.

"Give her some water," Matak said, still holding the baby.

I took my water gourd and held it to the woman's mouth. She parted her lips slightly and I poured water across them. She tried to rise, but I noted that her left arm was broken and angled abnormally below the elbow. I also saw the festering wound on her left thigh. She was so thin she appeared to be little more than thin skin draped over a girl's skeleton.

I held the water to her mouth again and this time she took great gulps. I stopped her before she drank too much, then helped her lean against the wall. Matak knelt before her and showed her the baby. The woman raised her good arm toward the child and stroked its cheek. We gave her food, but she could only swallow small bits of it. When she appeared a bit stronger, Matak laid the baby in her lap. It made a gesture to nurse from her but soon drifted off to sleep.

"When did the Laraap come and do this?" I asked the woman.

She shook her head. Matak and I looked at one another.

"Not Laraap," she said. "Dinka."

We could not believe our ears. Surely no Dinka would do this to another Dinka. We raid each other, steal cattle, food.

Sometimes we even take captive women for our own, but never in anyone's memory did we commit such an atrocity. Even against the Atuot we never wiped out entire villages.

"I do not believe Dinka warriors would do this," I told her,

"Believe what you will," she said in a soft whisper. "There were some Nuer, one or two Laraap, but most of the men who killed our clan were Dinka. Their scars told me so."

The woman reached out and drew the child close to her and stroked its bloody head. She rocked back and forth as we watched the child's breathing slow and then stop. She continued to hold it and whisper words of comfort.

We left her and went to see if there were more survivors hidden in the other huts. We found more women and children but none alive. We took the small amounts of food that remained. By the time we returned to the woman, she too was dead. We rolled her to her right side and tucked the child into her bosom facing west. When we did, we noted a bundle hidden beneath her cot. Matak picked it up and unwrapped it revealing a gun like the ones we saw the soldiers carry. It also contained a box of bullets. Neither of us knew how to use the gun, but we took it anyway.

We left the village and its stench and moved along a thin trail headed northward. When we had walked several hours we stopped by an open well near an abandoned groundnut field. Fresh cow tracks crossed the trail and a few goats busily stripped plants from the garden. It was as if all the people of the world had died and left the two of us alone. We slept again beneath a large tree near the well.

During the night we heard gunfire in the distance. Neither of us slept well and we wondered what we would find the next day. Surely every enemy of the Dinka people had gathered themselves into a great force that was sweeping the country and leaving death behind. It was as if my dream had taken life.

The next morning we ate flat bread that we had found in the last village, drank our fill of water from the well, and then headed again north. The trail wove back and forth but always moving us northward. The trees began to thin and by midday we found ourselves by the edge of a vast marshland. Large wading birds, some almost the height of a man stalked through the grass and looked down on us from bare trees.

"There is a lake across this marsh," Matak said. "People fish here, but the water is low now. We would have to cross miles of grasslands to get to it. We should stay along the edge of the wet grass. If there are people here, the cattle will come to water and we will see them."

We did as Matak said, but no cattle crossed our path. Here and there, deserted compounds lay fallow and a few goats wandered aimlessly about. When we came to a larger path, we turned west. I cannot say how we knew the way toward Rumbek. In Sudan, we Dinka can just think our way to a place.

The path grew wider as others joined it, making a pattern in the bush and grass like the convergence of rivers. We passed a well that was topped by cement, a rare thing in our area. In the center of the cement pad sat a metal pump. It seemed odd to find the well with its pump out in the bush with no homes nearby, until we tried it and found the well dry or the pump broken. We could not tell which. As we turned back to the patch, a flock of vultures rose from a dark form at the edge of the grass. We knew the stench of death and could see the vague outline of a body, now nearly stripped of flesh. Beside the body lay a green bag with shoulder straps similar to ones we had seen soldiers carry. I held my breath and ran to snatch the pack before I had to breathe the foul air. Even the pack smelled vaguely of decay, but I slung it over my shoulder and we continued down the path. Here and there, doubled tracks crossed our path indicating the passage of trucks. To our knowledge, only Laraap had trucks, and we began to move more cautiously. When we stopped to rest beneath a great fig tree, I opened the pack I had carried from the dead body.

We found papers of fine bold print, some written in what we believed to be Arabic and others in Dinka or English. Matak both read and spoke English, having learned the language from a Kawaja woman who visited the village and left materials with the elders and the few Christian men. He told me the papers were stories told of the great war and how the Laraap of Khartoum had sent many soldiers and great guns into the south. He read for a long time while I sat studying his face. The wounds of his forehead were almost healed and he now walked about without the leaf covering. I still wore mine, but was thinking that it was not necessary. As Matak read, the healing scars swept down into a deep frown.

"The Laraap still control Rumbek," Matak said after a while. "They are moving from town to town. Soldiers from the SPLA are coming here. Did you know that we live in the Upper Lake State?"

I did not. Men of the government had many names for the places we Dinka live. We used none of them ourselves.

Matak read some more of the news stories to me. We learned people all over the world were talking of Sudan. This confused me as I assumed that people everywhere knew of the Jieng and how we fought the Laraap from the north and that we were the best keepers of cattle anywhere. To hear for the first time that they were talking of us as if it was the first time they heard of us was a shock. Matak carefully folded the papers and returned them to the pack.

We also found small packets of salt and some wrapped bread and nuts. In a pocket on its side we found a round metal container. When we unscrewed the top we were greeted with stench of alcohol. We each tried a sip of the liquid and found it undrinkable so we poured it on the ground. The pack also contained a few items of clothing, six hundred Sudanese pounds, a photograph of a man in uniform, and two books. We found nothing to identify the dead person who had owned this pack. We took the money, food, and the container that had held the alcohol. We considered carrying the pack but decided that it would give the impression that we had killed or stolen it from its owner so we tossed it into the grass.

As we lay back against the tree, dozing and swatting the occasional fly, we again heard the distant sound of gunfire, this time south of us in the direction of where we had just been. But the sound was a long way off and we did not even discuss what it could mean. When we rose to continue walking the sun was almost to the treetops.

We had gone only an hour or so when were stopped by the sound of a bell. The ringing continued in a rhythm that would not be from a cow walking but by someone shaking the bell as some sort of signal. Since we were a good distance from Atuot territory, neither of us worried that the signal could be about us, so we took a small path that led toward the bell. After a short distance, the bell stopped to be replaced by the sounds of children laughing and shouting. When we came around a sharp bend of the trail we stepped into a clearing.

A man stood under a fig tree with the now silent bell in his hand. Behind him sat a wooden desk covered with paper and a few books. Groups of children walked away from the clearing down a web of trails.

"Kudwaal," I said to the man as we approached him. He nodded in reply, keeping an eye on the gun Matak carried slung across his shoulder.

"We are men of the Agar," Matak said.

"I am a man of the Aliab. This is my school," the man said waving his hand across toward the children. On the east side of the clearing, a grass and bamboo shelter stood leaning heavily to one side. A yellow tarp spread across part of the roof and a blackboard was propped against the far wall.

"An a chol, Thon," I replied. Matak also told the man his name and he introduced himself as Jima, which means "a man born on Friday." He said that this school was a Christian school and they taught children to read and write, do their numbers, and to believe in Jesus. He was the Headmaster of the school and there was another teacher who had not come to the school for almost one month. We told him we were moving toward Rumbek, hoping to find a man named Chol.

"Many families have lost children," he replied. "Chol, Compensation, is a common name here and there are many men around here named Chol," he said. "I know of none of the Agar by that name. Are you soldiers?"

We told him we were not, told him how we got the gun and about the village we saw yesterday where all the people had been killed.

"We know of this place," Jima said. "Some of my students live there and stay with family near here during school. We were on a short break last week and they went home. None have returned."

We both nodded. Jima invited us to come to his home and stay the night, as any honorable Dinka man would. As we walked to his home, he told us of how he went to Khartoum and then to Kenya to get his education. He told us he was a Christian man and that Christian people gave him books, paper, pencils and a little money to run his school. Children came from long distances to learn from him and the other teacher who is now missing.

When we arrived at his house, a few naked children came running to greet us. They took us by the hand and led us to a cleared area under a shea nut tree. Jima disappeared into one of the three huts and reappeared a few breaths later, now followed by a woman who looked slightly older than did he.

"These are men of the Agar," he told her, waving in our direction. "They will stay the night and eat with us."

As was proper, we declined the offer of food until Jima insisted. We then gratefully accepted. The woman's name was Achithiech, named for the fact that her mother had gone a long time without marrying. She wore a plain skirt about her thighs and waist as any proper married woman would do. Marriage beads of white and black swayed back and forth as she kneaded the sorghum dough on a flat, round board before laying it in a metal pan over the fire. She did not speak but looked at us repeatedly as if there was something that she wanted to know of us that she did not think proper to ask. We both noticed the glances and tried to bring up topics to her that would open the way.

"From what clan do you come?" I asked her. Dots of scars formed a series of lines across her forehead and I did not recognize the pattern. But women often make designs of the scars to their own liking and not to represent the clan as do men.

"I am of the Ajong Boma from Jobaar," she replied while working on the food.

"I have heard of them," I replied. "But I have not met anyone of them until today."

She nodded and continued working.

"Are you too a Christian like your husband?" Matak asked.

"I am not," she replied. "Neither is my husband."

Matak glanced at me.

"My husband has gone north some four years ago," she continued. "Jima is his younger brother."

Children gathered around her and watched. A dog with one ear shredded and large patches of missing fur slunk at the edge of the grass. A boy picked up a stick to throw but the dog, obviously used to being beaten, ran away before he could throw it.

"Are these all your children?" I asked, nodding toward the growing crowd of now eight children.

"I gave birth to all of them you can see," she replied. "The oldest twins and the two girls before my husband left."

"Why did you not go with your husband?" Matak asked. The question seemed too personal for me and I was surprised when she answered it, especially since Jima came to sit near us and could hear.

"At first, I thought my husband would be gone a short time," she replied as she continued to prepare the food. She did not look at us as she spoke and I was able to stare at her more closely without embarrassment. Her skin was lighter than most women of the Agar but just as smooth except for the scarred areas. She was missing the first finger of her right hand and I could see three parallel scars across her right calf as if a clawed beast had raked her from behind.

"He sent me a letter saying that he was employed by a group of British people giving injections to prevent some disease," she continued. "I do not read and I gave it to Jima to read for me. The letter also said that he would be gone for many more months and that I should come to him in Marial Bai. That is many weeks travel. I was taking care of the twins and carrying another girl near the time of birthing when I got the message. It was not possible for me to travel to him.

"My family sent for me and I went home. My father had prepared another man to marry me when my husband's family sent word that this should not be allowed as they had already paid a great number of cows for me."

When she referred to the cows a bit of pride crept into her voice. Jima nodded his agreement with the story.

"They said that I should be inherited by Jima and continue to bear children by him in the name of my husband. I did not know Jima and was not happy."

We both looked at Jima who did not seem the least insulted by this comment.

"I went to the cattle camp with my three children. My mother came to me and convinced me to come back here with Jima. She said that perhaps some of my children will die or turn out to be of bad character and then I would be as poor as a dog without a tail when I got old like her. Her words seemed good to me and I returned here."

"And you, Jima," I asked. "Do you also have a wife?"

"I have several women that I am now courting but my family has not yet chosen the right one for me," he replied. "It will be soon, I hope. These children are the children of my brother. I will have children in my own name. It may be soon."

"Yes, soon," Achithiech agreed. "We got word recently that my husband is coming back. Already, he has reached Rumbek. If the Laraap stopped their raids, he could walk here in less than two days."

"You will be reunited with the man you love," Matak said. Again it seemed too personal for me and I worried that he insulted Jima.

"I am a Dinka woman and have given no cause for anyone to doubt my good character," she replied. "I have loved Jima because we should not lay with a man we do not love. When my husband returns, I will love him instead. It will be a great day for all of us."

"Yes, a great day," said Jima, showing no signs of insult.

We continued to talk of the rains and crops, the fact that large game animals had recently been sighted nearby. We asked them about the airplane we saw earlier and were told that such sightings were common these days. As we spoke, a short man of great age and white hair walked into the camp. He moved hunched over and used short, shuffling steps. Jima immediately jumped to his feet and brought the old man a short wooden seat. We knew he was a Beny Bith from the fishing spear that he carried. He also wore a dark green robe with yellow cord sewn to the edges. His forehead was so wrinkled that I could not count the scar lines and therefore confirm his clan.

The man greeted Jima, nodded toward Achithiech, then introduced himself to us.

"I am Maciek," he said. "I knew of you coming."

Maciek meant "marked of God," a name given to a man who, like my mother, carried a defect of birth. I could see no defect on him and wondered if it was of his man parts.

We greeted him and introduced ourselves politely, as one should do with an elder. Maciek shook our hands and grinned a toothless grin as we told him our names, families, and our clan. We sat while Maciek and Jima spoke of the weather and some cows that were missing.

"Why do you travel this way?" he finally asked of us.

Matak told him the story of our search for Chol and my father. He left out the part where I had sworn by the spear that Chol was guilty of the murder.

"I have heard of men in Uganda using children for such evil things," Maciek said. "It is hard to believe that a Muonyjang would take up such a practice."

We all nodded and grunted agreement. We talked for a long period and learned many other things from Maciek. He confirmed that the Laraap held Rumbek still and that they were sending soldiers into the bush for raids against suspected sympathizers of the SPLA.

"My father's name is 'Koor'," I told him. "Have you known of an Agar man of that name?" Why my father had the name that meant "lion" I could not tell them. But it was a good name that told Maciek that my father was brave and to be feared.

"I have heard of one with that name," Maciek said.

I leaned forward, excited by this news.

"He fights with the SPLA with a unit not far from here," he said.

I heard again that the SPLA meant the Sudan People's Liberation Army, a great name for the men we only knew as soldiers. I asked him many more questions, but there was little else he could tell us except that my father's commander was known for winning battles and being ruthless with his men. Many deserted from his regiment, but those who stayed rose quickly in rank. This made me believe that my father would be a great general by now as he had been with the SPLA for almost three years, more if we counted the time before he came home for a few years.

"Also, the man who commands your father is known here for being a very bad man," Maciek said. "He comes here for more soldiers and even raids the school where Jima works. None of the children at the school are over twelve years old and yet he still takes the stronger ones. When parents refuse to answer truthfully about their children he beats them. Last month he put some men in a hut for two days without water or food and he had his men throw cow dung ashes into the hut. All because they would not tell him of the children that he would take for soldiers."

"My father would not do such things," I said proudly.

"Perhaps not," Maciek said. "But he protects those who do. It is his duty."

I had no answer to this, but Maciek continued with stories of how the SPLA appeared to have turned on some of their own people. They raided compounds and villages for food and even stole cattle. Some girls had relations with them by force, he told us.

"One man stuck a spear into the chest of a soldier who had beaten his wife," Maciek said. "The soldier had demanded food that the woman refused. When your father heard of it, his soldiers shot the woman's husband in the leg and put him in a hole alive. They then built a fire over him and laughed when he finally cried out in pain. They would not allow us to bury him for three days. If your father is the Koor who leads these men, then he is the one who did this thing. It will not be good for you to be found here as many men have taken vows of revenge against the soldiers. They would be just as happy to burn the son of one of them as to burn the soldier himself."

"I do not believe my father would do such a thing," I replied. "Perhaps his men did so without his knowledge, but he would not steal or kill without cause."

"Perhaps he believed he had cause," Maciek replied. "I cannot say. But the people here are looking for a compensation killing and you would be a fine target for them."

I nodded. Matak asked some more questions of Maciek, but I did not listen to them. I was filled with thoughts of the man perhaps my father had become. Perhaps he was now someone who could beat a woman not his own or burn a man alive. I have heard that war can make such men.

All became silent and I again noticed those around me. A few monkeys drifted at the edge of a distant field and eyed us cautiously. Grey kites swept down across the field and the monkeys scattered into the bush. I suddenly felt unsafe here.

"Did you hear, Thon?" Matak said.

I had not.

"Maciek has need of a new song to satisfy a jok living in the top of a tree near his house," Matak said. "He said that he will make a powerful prayer for us if I will sing him this song and let it become his. I have agreed."

I nodded and smiled, but it was the smile of one whose mind was elsewhere.

Matak began to sing. When he got to parts that I knew, I joined him, but mostly Matak sang alone. His voice was clear and wavered at just the right time in the story of the song, rose just enough to make us rise slightly from where we sat, and touched us somewhere in our chests where men hide secrets and try to kill their fears.

The song told of a monster of the river that came each month when the moon was hidden and the night was lit only by faint stars. The creature came from the banks and killed a child each night, leaving only a small bite mark on its head. Sometimes the monster took the child back to the river never to be seen again. Other times an anguished mother found the child, cold and dead at her side in the morning with the bites on its head. One such night a woman of great beauty slept with her father by the river, not knowing the monster lay in wait. When the monster crept upon them, the monster was overwhelmed by the woman's great beauty. He bit the woman's father and he died in his sleep. The beast then transformed into the shape of a man with smooth skin and long fingers. He then bewitched the woman with sly whispers and gentle strokes until the woman gave herself willingly to the creature, not knowing what it was.

When dawn came, the woman woke to find herself alone with her dead father. The woman buried her father by the river and walked home. On the way, not ten days from when she had lain with the monster, the woman suddenly went into labor and gave birth to a son not much larger than a hedgehog. She was not producing milk, so she fed the child juices of pumpkin and cow's milk. Within a year, the baby was the size of a man and greatly feared in the community. The woman fled with her son when talk started that he should be killed for fear that his strength would soon make him dangerous. They returned to the river and camped beside the grave of the woman's father. That night the creature of the river again came to the woman and had relations with her. But the woman's son did not recognize his father and killed it with a knife. Blood from the beast flowed into the ground over the woman's father and a great tree began to sprout. The woman and her son climbed into the tree as it grew and live there to this day. On some nights when the moon is hidden you can see them in the branches where they have taken the form of a bushbaby. Matak repeated some verses that described the beauty of the woman and the power of the beast, both combined in her son now living in the tree.

When he had finished the song, Maciek laughed long and hard.

"It is a good song and well worth my prayers," he said. "When we have eaten, I shall give them to you."

Achithiech brought a clay pot and poured water over our hands for us. She then brought us flat bread, goat meat, and ground nuts piled upon shallow pots. We ate quickly and noisily to show her our appreciation. Matak and I had not eaten so well in many days. During the meal, Jima assured us that he would allow no harm to come to us while we stayed at his home and he had sufficient standing in his community to keep us safe. We thanked him for his protection, though we all knew that it was expected of a Dinka man to do so.

Children gathered at the edges of the clearing and sat on their haunches while Achithiech brought smaller dishes of food for each of them. I counted eight children including two sets of twins, all of them resembling Achithiech more than Jima. Her husband would be very proud of her when he returns to find this many children being raised in his name.

The children chattered among themselves but kept their distance from us. As the sun fell to draw deep shadows across the compound, Maciek rose to his feet and took his fishing spear in one hand. He firmly planted the shaft of the spear into the ground and straightened himself. The feather he had tied to the base of the spear twirled gently in the evening breeze as he stood erect and looked at the sky. All the children instantly fell silent. A shaft of light hit his face and we saw that his eyes were closed and about him the air seemed to glow the yellow of the sun. When he raised his hands even the birds fell silent and the feather on his spear stopped moving as the breeze faltered. When he spoke, it was with a voice that seemed much younger than before.

"So be it. You of my ancestor, great father, Luol, and you of my ancestor Ayok, son of Luol, and you the jok of my father, I tell you what I have to say. And you, flesh of Pagong, I call you in my prayers, and you *awar*, grass of Pagong, I call you in my prayers, and you great hedgehog of Pagong, I call you in my prayers. I call you because we are your children and if a man calls on the jok of his father he must get something from it because he is its child. You, jok of my father, you will help. And now, evil has overtaken us. Hide us from that evil that we will not be tempted by it nor hurt by it."

Maciek hummed to himself for a few moments and swayed side to side. After a long moment, he continued to speak but I could not understand his words. Occasionally they seemed familiar and I almost caught their meaning but I was lost.

"He speaks in an ancient tongue," Jima whispered to me. "It is the secret song of his ancestors. It has a magic that keeps you from remembering the words even if you understood them now."

I nodded and kept listening as he fell back into the Dinka language that I could understand.

"I ask you to speak to the jok near you and ask them to speak to the jok near them that the land will be filled with spirits looking for this evil and the men who bring it. Guide these men to find the Chol that they have accused. Guide these men to find the father that they seek. Close the paths that are not for them."

Maciek continued to pray for every aspect of our journey. He prayed that our families would stay safe and our sisters would marry men with many cows. He asked Nhialic to bless us with good weather and that neither bullets nor spears could harm us. Evening fell and the shadows grew so dense that we could see him only in the light of the fire Only then, when darkness seemed complete did he stop praying and sit down heavily. He appeared exhausted as he turned to me and spoke.

"We have met before, I think," he said. I was surprised and shook my head. I was sure that we had not.

"Certainly we have. I came to you in a dream not one month ago," he said with a slight smile. "I was behind the cloud."

I recalled the dreams I had of an evil mist creeping across the land. Maciek read the recognition in my eyes.

"I warn you again in person," he said softly so that only I could hear. "There is an evil creeping upon the land. First the Laraap will sweep down on us from the north. Then brother will rise against brother, clan against clan. Famine will follow as fields lay wasted and women run to the bush carrying children."

Maciek spoke louder now and Matak and I leaned in to hear him.

"The prophesy is too powerful to be held by one man alone and Nhialic has sent it to many. Indeed, he has sent it to you and I was the one he used to send it."

I told the others of the dream and Maciek simply nodded.

"Can you foretell if we will be successful?" Matak asked.

" I can only invoke the blessings of the jok of my ancestors," Maciek replied. "It is men who form the evil you see as a mist in your dream. These men carry with them their own power. I cannot tell which is stronger. We Dinka have lost more battles than anyone can count. We have lost men, women, children. Before the British, the Laraap carried us away as *abeed*, slaves. They occupy our land for only a short time. But we always retake the land in the end. Before the British, the Turks came and ravaged the land, killed many. During that time and before, the Egyptians raided us. The slaves they take away are but flesh and blood that our strong Dinka women replace. The land has never been truly conquered and we Dinka have never lost a war. They always invade and we always fade away. We always return to the land and the invaders always leave. It is our curse and our blessing, this vast land. This is the way Nhialic protects us who live at the center of things where all life began."

We sat by a small fire that Achithiech fed with sticks of wood and spoke very little else that night. When the light completely failed, Maciek left without a word. Achithiech directed us into a hut where some of her children lay sleeping. We did not speak again until the next morning.

After we had eaten, Jima suggested that we take a trail that would avoid the others of this community as much as possible. As we walked with our backs to the rising sun, Matak complained that I did not tell him of my dream before this. I had no answer for him and he walked sullenly beside me for most of the morning.

We saw a dik-dik slip into the grass before us and hide itself in a clump of low bushes. We both noted the location and kept walking as if we would pass it. Matak stopped where a bush hid him from the beast and I kept walking as if to pass it. Dik-dik cannot count and the ruse worked. When I was a stone's throw away, Matak crept from his spot and speared the small creature where it lay hidden. Matak threw the animal over his shoulder and we continued walking, leaving behind spots of blood behind us that worried me.

Later that afternoon, we cleaned and cooked the dik-dik and packed the meat with our other belongings. We did not know how long before we encountered a woman who would cook for us and we did not wish the meat to spoil.

We slept that night beside the mud wall of a long abandoned hut that had no roof. Matak spent the night telling more stories and I drifted to sleep with his voice in my ears.

We traveled another two days and saw no one. We did see airplanes, some of them low enough in the sky that we could see letters painted on them. All of the planes seemed to be going in the direction we took. Every day we heard distant rumblings and the faintest sounds of gunfire. We could not tell the exact direction of the sounds and it appeared that they came from everywhere. On the third day we stopped to take water from an open well surrounded by empty and clean swept compounds with intact thatched roofs and unattended gardens. Using a thin rope Matak carried, I lowered the clay jar to the bottom of the well. Even before the jar came back, I could tell by the smell of the well that the water would not be good and we wondered if this was the reason the villagers had left. When the jar came into the sunlight, I was startled to find it full of worms squirming in brown, putrid water. I threw the worms back into the well and stepped away.

While I started a small fire, Matak gathered a bundle of dry grass. He lit the end of the grass and tossed it into the well. We watched it drop and land, not in water as we expected, but upon a lumpy mass. It took some time for our eyes to adjust and we had to hold our breaths against the smell. When we could see, we both started to gag. Covering the bottom of the well were small bodies that had to be children who should still be nursing. We staggered back and Matak leaned over and vomited in the dirt.

"Where are the adults?" he asked. I did not answer.

We quickly searched a few of the huts and found them abandoned and stripped of anything of worth. We found no other bodies, no weapons, expended bullets, or signs of a struggle. It was as if someone tossed all the village's infants into the well and the adults simply left. What sort of madness could this be, I wondered?

We quickly brushed away our tracks and tossed the ashes of our fire into the well. Then we took the first trail headed where we believed Rumbek should be and raced away from this place.

"There is something crazy happening here," Matak said when we slowed to a trot. "It was as if a spirit took all the people away and poisoned the well with the bodies of their children."

We stopped in a shaded area and caught our breath.

"I saw," I replied sharply. I did not feel this was the time for Matak to tell a story about things he knew no better than I knew.

"There has been rain here," I continued. "A large force of soldiers could have driven the people away and we could not see their tracks."

"But if they took the children, there would have been a fight," Matak replied. I knew he was right.

In the years that followed, I thought often of this village and what happened there. At the time, I had no idea of the importance that cursed place would have for me and for the history of our people.

The Evil Thing had come.

Chapter Thirteen

The next day we came upon a wide, hard packed road we knew led to Rumbek. We followed the road but kept near the edge so we could slip into the brush if needed. Twice, large trucks full of heavily armed soldiers passed us going in our direction, but no one saw us. We walked down a long straight section of road lined with giant mahogany trees. We both wondered who planted these trees as it takes generations for them to reach this size. Turks, British, Egyptians, Laraap— they all come here and leave something behind, some sign that they have at one time thought they owned this land of ours. We slept leaning against one of the great trees as gunfire of distant battles echoed through the forest and fields around us.

We woke to the sounds of hundreds of men singing and stomping. We just had time to hide in the bush when a group of soldiers passed us. They ran in time, their feet keeping perfect rhythm with the song. A man carrying a long switch and wearing a violet hat ran beside them. He sang a verse and the men repeated it as they ran. Some of the songs were in Dinka, some English, and some Arabic. The use of Arabic surprised me as you would not think the soldiers of the SPLA would use the language of the Laraap they fought. But many schools taught Dinka to read Arabic and become good Muslims and the SPLA had men of all tribes in its ranks. All of the men bore the marks of manhood. Some Nuer, some

Atuot, mostly Dinka. I saw marks that I did not recognize among the men who passed us chanting the songs of war.

When the soldiers were out of sight we ate the rest of the dik-dik meat and packed our things. Matak suggested that we wear the white jalabiyas we brought with us so we would not look as much like simple boys from the cattle camp. Mine was a little short for me and barely came to my knees while Matak's dangled to his ankles. We followed the dusty trail that the soldiers were taking. Even as we walked I wondered what we should do when we met the soldiers who were surely between us and Rumbek. If they knew of my father, perhaps we could use his name to gain safe passage. Of how to find Chol, I had no idea.

As we walked Matak began to sing again, his voice clear and sweet.

"Deng brings the rope of the finch,
That we may meet on the boundary
We and the moon and the jok
Give the rope of the finch
That we may meet on one
Boundary with the moon.
The finch Atoc Mayol cut the rope truly
The finch Atoc Mayol severed the rope on the right
The land was ruined in a single day
Alas, alas, alas."

"I do not know this song, Matak," I stated. The sun was behind us and we walked in our own shadows, something that I was told as a child was bad luck.

"I have put two songs together to make one," he replied. "I heard them from the Beny Bith of Yei one day while my father and I were selling goats in the market. Do you like it?"

"It is a good song. But I do not know of the finch or rope in the song," I replied.

"Ah," he said, taking an air of superiority that made me regret admitting my ignorance. "The song continues the story of creation and sin. I shall tell it to you.

"In the beginning, Nhialic created one man and one woman. He fashioned them from clay and baked them. They were very short, less than half our height. He named the man, Garang. He named the woman, Abuk. Abuk had large breasts and Garang was strong and swift despite his small size. At that time, the Rope of the Finch connected heaven and earth and it was possible to climb the rope and dance with Nhialic in heaven. Nhialic gave Abuk and Garang two commands. Other than these two rules, Abuk and Garang governed the whole earth. Even the beasts and birds obeyed them. One command was that they were to eat only a single grain of millet each day. The other command was that they should not flail about and dance on earth for to do so would disturb Nhialic in heaven. One day, Abuk was preparing to eat her grain of millet when she decided she wanted more. So she took more seeds and put them in a hollow log to pound into flour, intending to share her meal with Garang. While she was pounding, her movements disturbed Nhialic in heaven. When he saw what Abuk was doing, Nhialic grew angry with them and he cut the Rope of the Finch and forever, man has sought to return to heaven, but there is no way to do so. This song is about the finch and the rope. If you do not know this story you could not understand the song."

"Sing another one," I pleaded with him. Matak was easy to convince as we walked down the straight road covered with lines of giant trees as the dew dried from our skins and the sun warmed our backs. It was a great day and for most of the morning, the seriousness of our journey did not enter my mind.

We stopped by another open well and took water and a bit of food. Matak found some nuts nearby and we ate as many as our stomachs could hold and packed away more for later. It was after midday before we realized that we were not hearing the sounds of gunfire.

The road bent to the north and south a bit, but always westward to where we knew Rumbek and, I hoped, my father's unit lay. We saw more airplanes, but no traffic on the road. All of the huts we passed were empty except for a few chickens and one sickly brown and white sheep.

As we came around a bend, we could see a great distance and ahead of us, not a hundred paces away, a log lay across the road. We eased ourselves out of sight and crept to the edge of the bush where we could see the log again. Deep in the bush, just past where the log lay, I saw puffs of smoke rise from the tangle of leaves. Matak saw it too. Someone was waiting there, smoking a pipe to pass the time. We whispered to one another, trying to decide if we should talk to the man or try to sneak around him. Sooner or later, we would have to talk to a soldier in order to find my father, so we decided to go ahead and do so now.

We took our packs, but Matak hid the gun in the bushes. He made a small sign of stones that no one else would recognize in order to mark the spot. We then eased onto the road, but kept on the same side of the man smoking in the bush. Matak hid behind a tree while I stood on the road and called out to him.

"This is a man of the Agar coming here," I said loudly. "Am I welcome?"

The bushes moved slightly and the smoke stopped rising. I repeated my greeting.

A man in a green uniform stepped onto the road next to the log.

"What is your business here, man of the Agar?" he shouted to me.

"I am looking for another man of the Agar," I replied. "I have a message from his family."

"And why do you think this man is down this particular road?" asked the soldier.

We talked back and forth from a distance that required us to keep shouting toward one another. The man glanced several times into the bush across the road from him. I signaled Matak with my eyes and he signaled back that he saw the gesture.

"Dinka men who support the SPLA have no need to fear," he finally shouted. I looked toward Matak and he seemed to agree, so he stepped on the road beside me. We walked cautiously toward the soldier who simply stared at us. As we stepped to the log on the road, two men carrying guns came out of the bush and stood behind us.

"Show us what you carry," the first soldier ordered us. There was no hint of friendliness in his voice and his tone told us he expected to be obeyed without protest.

We lay our spears and clubs on the ground and opened the rolls of cloth to show him the food and water. Without a word, the soldier took the food and tossed it to the men behind us. Matak started to say something but I shot him a warning look and he stood silent.

"We have a truck here," the soldier told us. "Pack your things and we will take you to our base at the edge of Rumbek town." Again his tone spoke of a command and not a request. We followed him a short distance down the road while the other soldiers melted again into the bush. He took us to a white truck with an open bed on the back which was cleverly hidden in the bush. "Get in the back," he ordered us.

Neither of us had ever ridden in a vehicle before. When he finally started down the road, the soldier pushed the vehicle to speeds we never thought possible. In spite of the danger of being in the hands of a soldier of unknown intent, we smiled at one another as the wind whipped across our faces and we clutched the sides of the truck.

After a long ride that would have taken us the rest of the day, the soldier slowed as we passed more soldiers with guns moving in the opposite direction. We came upon four men who waved at him for a ride. The driver skid to a stop and waved the men toward the back of the truck. They eyed us suspiciously as they piled in with us. All of them seemed thin and frail as they hugged their guns and looked somberly at us. No one spoke as the truck again lurched to great speed. Beneath their caps I noted the scars of Rek on one man and those of the Bor on the others. I knew of no enmity between us and I tried to speak to them. The Rek man replied to me in Arabic and I could not understand. The other laughed at whatever he said so I kept quiet with one hand on my spear and the other on my club. One of the men motioned toward my spear with his gun and said something to the others that caused them to laugh again.

After another long drive, the driver pulled over by a great tree under which milled more soldiers. Across a bare field, more soldiers stood in lines while important looking men walked up and down their ranks. Our passengers got out here and spoke briefly to the driver before we started moving again. We went only a short way when he pulled the truck by a cement block building with a metal roof that reflected the sun so strongly we could not look at it. The driver ordered us out. When we reached back to get our spears, he told us to leave them.

Matak protested, but the soldier put his hand on a pistol at his waist and said in a harsh tone that there was no need of weapons here and that nothing is stolen in a soldier's camp. I thought of the food he had just that day taken from us, but I knew it was foolish to contend with this man. A man without a uniform but carrying one of their guns came forward from the building. The driver spoke to him in English. Matak translated for me in whispers.

"He said that we are men of the Agar and he thought the Commander should talk to us about conditions near the river," Matak told me. The other man looked at us and motioned us to follow him.

We entered the building and were directed to sit on a flat bench against a wall. The insides of the building were painted white and green and most of the open spaces had been covered with posters and pictures of politicians and soldiers. Matak read the posters to me but I recognized only one name—John Garang, a man said to be uniting the Dinka tribes against the Laraap of the north, a man named for the first man that Nhialic had created. Someone educated in the west and wise in the ways of foreigners and Sudanese. I saw his face smiling down at me above a listing of the months and days of the year.

The insides of the building were much hotter than the outside and we dripped sweat while our Jalabiyas clung to our skin. I saw through the open door that a breeze swayed the tall grass by the road but none of this made it into the building. We heard voices in the other room speaking in hushed tones that made us skittish to leave.

Finally, another door opened and the soldier who had driven us there motioned us to enter. The doorway was so low that even Matak had to duck to enter the room which was dim and smelled of old cloth.

Behind a large desk covered with papers sat another soldier with many decorations on a stiff uniform. His face was round and puffy, so much it seemed he had to fight to keep his eyes from closing. He had sparse grey hair and fingers so short that I do not think he could even wrap them around the shaft of a spear. He did not look up at us as we entered but continued to write something on a yellow pad of paper in front of him.

In one corner, another man in uniform sat in a chair that appeared to be made of metal. He stared at us but did not speak. After a few minutes of tense silence the man behind the desk put down his pencil and looked at us. He smiled slightly, but I did not know how to interpret the look on his face any way except that it was the same smile that my uncle gave me when I arrived at his house unannounced. Welcoming indifference, is the closest I can describe it.

"You have not been men for long, I see," the man behind the desk said, motioning to the fresh scars on our faces.

"A little more than a month," I replied.

The man nodded and appeared to be remembering something that he did not share with us.

"I am Commander Daniel Awet. I am in charge of all the soldiers in the Upper Lake State. Tell me, did you come from south of the Bahr Naam?" he asked.

"Yes, Monydit," I replied, hoping that he appreciated the courtesy.

He smiled again, but I did not see pleasure in the smile and his eyes spoke of something else.

"Did you see soldiers there?" Awet asked.

"We saw some after the river, but none south of it," I replied.

He looked at Matak who nodded in agreement.

"Do the people there support the SPLA?" Awet said. His eyes seemed to recede into deep folds of skin and I saw only a dark slit where they should be.

"I think the people support those who fight for them," I replied. I wondered if it was a good time to ask him of my father.

"And what do you think of the SPLA?" Awet asked, this time looking at Matak.

"I think my father's father has told us stories of how the Laraap ride horses from the north during the dry season and steal women, children, and cows. It has been so for as long as anyone remembers," Matak replied. "I pray to all the divinities of the Dinka that the SPLA can drive them from the land and make them dust to be blown into the desert."

The soldiers all laughed.

"That was a good answer," the man in the corner said. He had a slight accent that I could not place, but his Dinka was like that of the eastern tribes.

"I would have you go with my men to the river," Commander Awet said. "We need people who know this area. Would you be willing?"

Matak glanced at me, knowing that this was not a real request but an order.

"Monydit," I replied. "I have a task that was given to me by the chiefs of our village. I would ask that you allow us to complete this task. Then we will go with your men and lend them any aid we are able to give."

Commander Awet frowned, obviously used to hearing only a "yes" to any of his questions.

"And what is this task?" he asked.

I explained to him the murder that we believe Chol to have committed. Awet glanced at the man in the corner when we told him we believed he would continue to kill children and use them for the evil rituals he had learned while in Uganda.

"And I am looking for my father," I said without thinking. "He is a soldier who has fought with the SPLA for a long time. I would find him and greet him with news of our family."

"Your father?" he replied. "What is his name?"

"Koor," I replied.

Again the soldiers exchanged glances.

"Do you know him?" I asked. I think they saw me note the recognition in their eyes.

"Yes, we know him," the man in the corner replied. "You have his look about you."

It took all of my strength to stand in front of Commander Awet rather than leap across the desk and demand he tell me where my father was.

"It would be best if you came back another time to meet with him," Awet said.

"I have not seen him for three years and we have traveled far and endured many hardships. I would like to see him immediately," I replied. This time I was the one whose voice spoke of urgency and demand. Awet smiled with only half of his lips. Again I did not know what such a look meant.

"Then you shall see him today," Awet said. He then spoke in Arabic to the man in the corner and we were motioned to leave the room. The man who drove us here waved for us to return to the truck.

"It was not wise to speak to the Commander in such a way, foolish one," the driver said. "My name is Cagai. I too know your father."

Cagai, named as one born when others are dying around them. Born during a famine or a plague. It is a harsh name and all the people I know who bear it are harsh people.

"Can you take me to him?" I asked.

"I have been commanded to do so," he replied. "But it would have better if you had done as the Commander suggested and waited."

We got back in the truck and were relieved that our weapons and belongings were untouched. Cagai drove us back to where the soldiers had been lined up. He stopped the truck under a tree and we walked to the edge of the clearing while soldiers in straight lines marched back and forth around the field. At the end closest to us sat two thick, upright posts in the ground that would, in other times, serve as goals for football games. I thought that before the soldiers came here that this must have been a school.

A dense knot of soldiers at the opposite end of the field moved toward us and the ranks of soldiers parted to let them pass. In the middle of the soldiers, a man walked with his hands tied behind his back and wearing only pants but no shirt or shoes. He kept his head down and a soldier behind him occasionally prodded him with his gun to move faster. When they got to the goal posts, the soldiers untied his hands and retied them to a spike driven into the top of the post. The soldier now stood on his toes with his bare back to the others. I felt my stomach tighten and my heart raced as I realize what they were preparing to do to him. Just then he raised his head and turned his face toward me. From less than fifty paces away, for the first time in three years I looked into the eyes of my father. For the first time ever, I regretted it.

Chapter Fourteen

Koor lay on his stomach in the shade of a strangling fig tree. Ragged breaths escaped his lips as the army doctor, or whatever he called himself, cleaned the deep wounds of his back, and then applied a white salve. As while he was being flogged, he uttered no sounds of pain.

"Do not wear a shirt until these have scabbed over," the doctor instructed him. "I will care for them twice per day for as long as you and I both stay here or until you are healed." Then he leaned in to whisper into his ear, "All of the men know you acted as a man of honor, Koor."

The doctor then packed his supplies into a cloth bag and left us. I sat within reach of my father but Matak stayed away, barely within hearing of us as he leaned against the base of the tree. Koor's eyes were closed and he breathed deeply, asleep or unconscious for all I could tell.

"You have the marks," he said without opening his eyes.

"Yes," I replied. "And so does Matak."

His head moved in a barely perceptible nod.

"Is your mother well?" he asked after a long wait.

"She is well."

"Your brothers and sisters?"

"They also are well."

Again a long silence. Then he struggled to force himself to rise. I started to help him but he waved me away. The movement opened his wounds and a trickle of blood ran down and disappeared within the waistband of his trousers. He brushed the dirt from his chest and face, and then turned to face me. He sat directly on the ground, which is not something a Dinka man would usually do. I wondered what other improprieties army life had forced into him.

We spoke for a long while as he asked about the village, friends and family, how the crops were doing and if the cattle were well and safe. He asked about several of the cows by name. I answered his questions and held back my own.

Several soldiers came by while we spoke. They avoided his eyes, but spoke to him with respect and affection. Some left him food and water while one brought him a green pack that apparently held Koor's belongings. Sweat mixed with the blood that drained from his body. He stood to change his pants and when I saw his naked body I was startled to see the many scars on his legs and noted the ones on his chest that I had not seen before. He put on sandals and clean pants, and then sat on a protruding root from the fig vine.

It was then that I told him of Chol and our quest to find him, told him of the Beny Bith's visit to me in the dreams, and of the death and violence we had seen visited upon the surrounding villages.

"The Laraap come first, asking for information about the SPLA and forcing the villages to give them food and some men to carry things for them," Koor told us. "After that, we SPLA go in and do the same. I am not sure who is harder on the people, them or us. But we do not, will not, kill the villagers..." His speech faded and he looked down at his hands that lay folded in his lap. "We fight for the people, not against them."

I was about to ask him why they flogged him when he told me on his own.

"I was leading a patrol probing the defenses around Rumbek when we came upon a small village. We had not known the village even existed, it was so well hidden in the bush. Already some SPLA soldiers under the direct command of ..." He hesitated, then continued, "a high ranking officer were in the village. All of the adults, almost fifty of them, were lined up and had their hands tied behind their backs while long ropes held them together by their necks. Some of the women cried, but most of them simply gazed straight ahead, a hopeless look about them. It was just as the elders described the way Laraap and Turks carried away slaves in the old days. But these were fellow Sudanese doing this to Dinka men and women. We asked the highest ranking person we could find why this was being done. He told us the villagers had refused to support the SPLA and were suspected of giving food and shelter to some Laraap. I doubted the Laraap from Rumbek could even find the village and told him that. He shouted at me to leave the village at once. This soldier outranked me, so I turned to leave when one of my soldiers ran up to me and begged me to follow him. The commander of the other unit continued to shout at me to leave while I went to see what my soldiers had found."

Koor rested for a long while again, and then continued.

"We came upon some of the other soldiers in a newly ploughed field. They had thirty, maybe twenty children of all ages with them. Most of them were already dead. Others were screaming, some just crouched and cried silently. A soldier I did not know appeared to be examining a young girl as I walked up to them. His back was to me as he turned the girl around and looked her up and down like he was buying a sheep. Then, as quick as a snake, he whipped out a knife and sliced off one of her ears. Before the girl could even cry out, he plunged the knife into her chest and twisted it about."

Again, Koor rested for a bit before continuing.

"I shot him on the spot," he continued. "But not before noticing the pile of human body parts he had laying on a tarp by his side. His soldiers raised their weapons to me but did not fire. My own soldiers also raised their weapons. I called for everyone to be calm. I called for one of the strange soldiers to come forward. He then told me that his commander, the man I left in the village, had instructed them to cooperate with the dead man and not to interfere. He was examining the children to see if there were any defects in them. If they were defective in any way, a scar, sore, anything, they were left alone. If they were perfect, the dead man chose one part of the child's body and cut it off with a knife, and then he killed the child. The tone of the man's voice told me that he was disgusted by what he saw and was glad that I had killed him. His comrades appeared also relieved and all of us lowered our guns. Most of the remaining children had run away when I shot the man and we chased off the remaining. Older children carried with them the smaller ones and they fled into the bush."

Matak had moved closer to us and we held our breaths at this news. Could such an evil thing be practiced among the Dinka? We could not believe so.

"We left before the commander of the other soldiers could find us," Koor continued. "When I got back, they put me on trial. It turns out that the man I killed was not a soldier at all or they would have executed me. I still don't know who he was. They took my rank away and had me flogged. I think they would have killed me except that they feared my men would have revolted if they had."

"What was he doing with the children?" Matak asked. My suspicions were so horrible that I dared not ask myself.

"Some of the men have been to Uganda. A man claiming to be a prophet of God, a man named Joseph Kony, commands men there to do great evil. They teach that charms can be made of body parts of children, but only children without blemish. These charms are supposed to protect you during war and bring blessings of many children and great fortunes."

"Just like Chol is doing," I said.

Matak and Koor both nodded.

"Some of the higher ranking men here were educated in Uganda. They learned of this evil thing there. Some have fallen in with Kony. Others came here but brought the practice with them. John Garang himself is aware of it and is trying to purge it from the SPLA. This is another reason why I was not executed."

"But there are men here who follow this belief?" I asked.

Koor nodded. The bleeding from his back had stopped. I waved my hand across it to keep the flies from landing. I knew that there would be a few maggots that would hatch in the exposed flesh, despite my best efforts.

"Daniel Awet, I think, is one of them," Koor said. "Never repeat this."

Matak and I both swore that we would not.

We spent the rest of the day beneath the tree while Koor recovered. His men kept stopping by to offer words of comfort and a great deal of food. Two of them stationed themselves nearby with their guns at the ready. I got the impression that they would not let another thing happened to Koor, obviously a much beloved leader.

We set up nets under the tree and spent a restless night listening to the sounds of gunfire in the distance, most of it coming from Rumbek. The next morning, the doctor came and treated Koor's wounds. At Koor's insistence, he applied a light dressing that allowed Koor to wear a shirt. When he was dressed and wearing the hat bearing the purple color of his division, Koor looked like the man I remembered—strong and tall, fierce eyes that sat above high cheekbones. He had a long neck and arms, giant hands, and a stride that spoke of great strength despite the wounds his shirt covered.

"This man has saved my life more than once," he said, patting the doctor on the shoulder.

"And this man has given me much practice at taking care of battle wounds," the doctor replied with a laugh.

We walked to another clearing where small tarps and many mosquito nets lay strung about on sticks driven into the ground. A red flag marked a spot a hundred paces away. Koor told us that the flag marked the distance you should go to relieve yourself.

"If you do a short call closer, the men will chide you a little," he said. But if they catch you taking a long call closer than the flag, they will be greatly offended. It is not a good idea to offend my men."

Matak and I nodded and grunted to indicate we understood.

Men gathered around Koor as he strode through the camp. Some slapped him on the back before realizing their mistake. Koor grimaced but did not cry out. I did not think anything could make him cry out. He was the greatest Dinka man I had ever known. Enduring the knife to get my scars seemed petty in comparison to the hardships of his life. I was proud of him and desperate to make him proud of me.

We shared food with some of the men under a great tree. Women served us, always bringing Koor the first portion. I could tell by the way they looked at him that they would have given themselves to him at any time. One particular woman brought him food and then stood close to him while he ate. She wore no marriage beads, only a simple skirt. Once she leaned across him to gather some pots and let her bare breasts graze across Koor's arm. He did not seem to notice her touch or the way she looked at him. The other men noticed and whispered among themselves when she left.

A man came running up, saluted and stamped his foot, then handed Koor a piece of paper. Koor read it, signed it with a pen the man offered him, then handed the paper back.

"That paper confirmed I have lost my rank, but not my position as leader of these men," Koor said. His men all shouted for joy. "It appears that somehow John Garang became aware of my charges and intervened," he continued. "That is good, for we are planning a great surprise for the Laraap in Rumbek."

His men pressed him for details but he ignored them. They continued joking and eating while the camp women swarmed about them bringing and taking pots of food. When we had finished the meal, they took away all of the dishes and except for two armed guards who sat on either side of Koor's tent, the men left us alone again. I told him that the Commander wanted us to guide their troops back south. Koor did not seem surprised.

"Do as he asked," he told me. "You will be part of a great enterprise of which many songs shall be sung. You will see."

Again, he refused to give us more details. Despite the doctor's advice, he wore a complete uniform when we left their camp. We walked to the Commander's headquarters, a much longer journey without the truck. The sun was almost straight up in the sky when we arrived. Men saluted Koor and some spoke to him in whispers about the way he was treated. All of them seemed to respect him. When he approached the building, a guard slipped inside for a moment, then motioned him to enter. Matak and I hesitated, and then at his urging, we entered as well.

Commander Awet sat with a cluster of other soldiers pointing and commenting on a map spread across his desk. The other men acknowledged Koor with a slight lifting of their chins, and then they looked at Matak and me.

"They are with me," Koor said. Awet did not seem pleased to see either Koor or us, but after throwing us a brief but threatening glare, he turned again to the map. I could not understand most of what was discussed, but they repeatedly spoke the name of the Bahr Naam River.

"You and your friend will go with Cagai," Awet told me.

I nodded. Koor stood looking at the map over the shoulder of another man. When we did not move, Awet turned and spoke in a harsh voice.

"Go now!"

We hastened outside and found Cagai leaning against his truck with six other men. A large gun had been mounted on a rack on the back of the truck and a large, angry appearing man stood holding the handles and looking toward the sky. I looked upward, wondering what he was watching, but remembered the stories of the airplanes dropping bombs. Almost as if in response to my thoughts, a white plane flew over, barely visible in the bright sky. I waited and wondered how long it took for a bomb to reach the ground from such a height and how they could possibly hit anything from so high. None of the soldiers appeared worried.

Matak and I got in the back of the truck with the gunner and three others while two rode up front with Cagai. None of the soldiers seemed interested in talking to us and we held tight to its metal sides as the truck sped along the open road to the south.

"We are headed toward home," Matak said over the noise of the road. I smiled and nodded in reply.

When we reached the place where Koor had been flogged, we passed row after row of soldiers walking south with us. Only a few had uniforms, the rest a patchwork of old pants and ragged shirts. All of them wore green hats, that and the guns slung over their shoulders the only signs that told us they were soldiers. They chanted as they marched. The sound of their voices rose above the din of the road, strong and confident, the kind of voice that made your heart race and called you to fight with your brothers. I thought that perhaps Matak and I should join this group of men defending our home from the hated Laraap. Then I remembered the sight of Koor's flogging and the feeling left me. I sat low in the truck and held a cloth to my face against the dust as we sped south for a purpose unknown to us.

Chapter Fifteen

I have crossed over the Bahr Naam many times on foot and always felt the bridge sway slightly beneath my feet in time to my steps. Sitting on the back of the truck as we eased our way across the single lane, I felt sure we would all crash into the muddy waters below and be crushed by the steel structure. But we slowly rolled across and stopped while some of the troops that had left earlier in the day crossed as well. Women washed clothes and children downstream of us and some men of the cattle camps watered their cows on the other side. They shouted greetings and news of families to one another.

We camped on the south side of the river amid a tangle of low brush. Before we settled, Cagai had the men cut brush and cover most of the truck, leaving exposed only the large gun pointed at the sky. Matak and I sat against an acacia tree as the sun dropped to the tree line. Large, grey wading birds flew from the marshy areas over us to their roosts. Some had heads the shape of a Laraap's sword. We saw them drop into nests of sticks that seemed large enough to hold the Cagai's truck. Flocks of ibis and herons passed over us and at several distant points across the marsh downstream of the bridge large flocks of vultures circled a great distance marking death to our northeast. It was late into the night before the main body of the SPLA forces had crossed the river. At one time a plane swept low over us, circled for another look, then headed north again.

Camp followers lit cooking fires and we heard the last choked bleating of several goats that would later be eaten. Smoke drifted slowly through the bush and melded with a light fog rising from the river. Some women, different from the ones before, brought us large metal plates of rice and meat, sorghum mush, and a sort of sweet drink from a glass bottle that neither Matak nor I had ever before tasted. We ate our fill, and then set up our mosquito nets near the truck. Late into the night, another truck pulled in next to ours and I heard Koor's commanding voice in the darkness. I stayed in my tent and marked the direction of where I thought he had set up his own net.

The sun had not risen yet but the eastern sky glowed with a deepening red when I heard the sounds of airplanes. I lay under my net and blanket listening to them over the sounds of frogs and insects of the dawn. The sound grew louder and soon I heard others moving quickly around the camp. Matak rose from his net and stood looking at the sky while a man jumped into the truck and swung the great gun around in the direction of the airplanes.

They came in low and fast, a blurred roar over the trees that was followed by a sound so loud I thought it was the earth splitting. The first bomb hit a group of men clustered at the edge of the river grass. Men and equipment flew into the air amid a shower of shattered ground that flattened the grass around them. Another bomb landed near us and sent splinters of wood flying into our midst. Matak went down when a piece of jagged wood struck him in the back. The sound of the mounted gun pounded my ears as I ran toward Matak who lay moaning on the ground. He did not reply at first, but looked at me as if we were strangers. The wood did not penetrate very deeply in his back and I pulled it out with ease. I spent the next few minutes removing smaller fragments, then pushed the blanket over the wound and yelled at him to stay where he lay.

He looked at me with eyes so wide I could see the whites around his dark pupils, a look that I saw in animals resisting the slaughter. I tried to reassure him with calm words but I could not be certain that he heard me over the roar of the planes and guns. A trickle of blood ran from his left ear.

I ran to where I thought Koor's bed would be and found an empty net and blanket. Just then, another plane flew over, this time at a much greater height. I heard a strange whistling sound followed by another explosion across the road. I did not see where it hit, but the men were camped so tightly that I thought some had surely died. Eight more bombs fell near enough for us to hear them before the planes stopped appearing. Each flight after the first one was higher than the last and I thought that they had been frightened by the terrible gun on Cagai's truck.

When the bombing stopped, I went to find Koor and the doctor. I stepped from the bush to where I could barely see the bridge over the Bahr Naam in the distance. As I watched, I saw a figure dart across the bridge and disappear into the bush on my side of the river. The man carried a long stick and wore a dark, green Jalabiya and there was something familiar about him I could not quite recall. It was very unseemly for a Dinka man to run and, though he dressed like one of us, my first thought was that this was an outsider. I had no time to follow him, so I turned and walked quickly down the road.

I found Koor directing men to a clearing in the dense bush where the doctor had set up medical supplies. He wore a thin grey shirt without buttons that was soaked through its back with blood. Several mangled bodies lay in neat rows to one side and men lay about on blankets while he and six others tended their wounds. Bright light now poured through the bush and made dense shadows on the men. None of them made the sounds of pain as befitted men of the Jeeng and again I felt a closeness to them that I could not explain.

I stood near Koor while he commanded those who came and went, again noting how those who heard him responded instantly and always with a crisp salute.

"These planes will come back," he said to a soldier who had given him a report of the wounded. He looked at me also as he said this. "They have returned to the airfield in Rumbek to get fuel and more bombs. Keep the wounded hidden here. But we must move the mass of our troops further south. Keep to the plan."

The man saluted and trotted back toward the road. Others came and went as the early morning gave way to a bright, windless day. Koor told me to go back to Cagai and stay with him. I wanted to salute him in reply but was afraid that the gesture was not seemly for someone who was not a soldier, so I turned and ran back to our camp site.

Matak seemed to have recovered adequately and had already packed both of our nets and other belongings and put them in the back of Cagai's truck. Men darted in and out of the bush and shouted to one another. Despite the confusion, Cagai leaned against the side of his truck and casually lit a wooden pipe decorated with brass rings. He acknowledged me by raising his eyebrows and chin slightly, then turned away to puff on his pipe and watch the sky.

The sun had not reached its noon peak when we again loaded into Cagai's truck and slowly rumbled south away from Rumbek and toward our homes. We raced ahead in the truck, then waited for the troops who were footing behind us to catch up. I was astonished at the distance so many men could cover, especially loaded with weapons and supplies as most of them were. Several times Cagai stopped the truck and asked us about the next village. Were they friendly to the SPLA? Did they contain Muslims? Are there wells nearby?

Before and after each village we passed, dozens of men fell out of their formations and melted into the bush. I sometimes could see them cutting brush and creating clever hiding places for themselves and their weapons. Each of these groups carried at least two evil appearing weapons that Cagai told me were rocket propelled grenades. There were no Dinka words for this weapon and he used a mixture of English and Arabic to describe it to us. Matak understood first and suggested that it was this weapon that made the strange swishing sound followed by an explosion that we had heard days earlier. I did not want to see the use of this thing that could destroy an entire house.

Most of the villages we passed were completely empty except for some old men and women who had refused to leave. Many appeared too feeble to flee to the bush, though they would have had much experience in doing so. Their families had left them food and water before taking the livestock, women, and children along well-worn paths to secret places in the bush where only a local such as me or Matak could find them.

At one place, I showed Cagai where the patches of high ground in a large, now dry, floodplain connected. Men followed my directions and marked the places where they could, if necessary, flee from attackers who held the road. When we returned to the truck, Cagai told one of the men riding up front to go to the back and he had me ride beside him. I had to keep moving my legs out of the way as he manipulated the gearshift of the truck. It was my first time inside a vehicle of any kind and it made me feel important.

"I suppose you can guess what we are doing," Cagai said as he drove.

"You are guarding the road," I replied. "That much is clear. Past that, I do not know."

"Not exactly guarding," Cagai said with a chuckle. He held the steering wheel in place with his knees and used both hands to light his pipe again. The sweet smell of the tobacco filled the truck.

"We know the Laraap are planning to push south from Rumbek as far as they can. They believe we, the SPLA, hold the villages with only a few men and they want to claim the entire Upper Lakes Statel is under their complete control. We learned this from some men whom we captured while they were raiding villages north of the river."

He took a few deep puffs from his pipe and exhaled smoke from his nostrils. I saw that the scars he bore were of the Dinka Rek. He held the pipe with teeth that seemed so full of holes and decay that I thought surely they would fall out at any moment. As I looked at him he smiled at some inner joke and showed me his few other teeth.

"They will come down this road and we will let them," he said, chuckling again. "An entire division of Laraap, mostly in trucks, some covered with armor. Big guns, airplanes. We will let them come. They will pass by our men we are leaving on the road. They will not see us, but we will see them. We will let them get all the way, almost to your home, before we stop them. The road here is narrow and a force as large as the one assembled in Rumbek cannot change directions easily in such a place. We will pour fire on them from one side of the road at one place, then another side of the road as they flee. We will keep killing them as they stumble over each other to flee.

"These men who fight for Khartoum are not the Dinka of this area. They are not defending their families as we do and their allegiance to the government is weak. We have seen many times that they will not stand and fight. They raid villages, kill men, women, and children. They do terrible things to the girls. Sometimes to the boys as well. Then they kill them or take them to the north where we never see them again. We cannot count the numbers that are slaves to the

Laraap even now. It is this kind of war that they wage against us. When we fight as one, fight as Dinka warriors, they flee from us.

"They will turn the vehicles that can turn around and try to drive back toward Rumbek, but our men will be waiting for them. None will make it over the Bahr Naam alive."

Cagai chuckled again. "Brilliant plan," he said to himself and then laughed again. "Brilliant."

Now knowing what the SPLA planned for the Laraap, I told him several times to stop as we grew closer to the places where Matak and I grazed the cattle frequently. We knew of places where many men could hide and places where a few could stay close to the road without being seen. We showed these to Cagai and he sent men to them. Late in the afternoon, a truck painted the colors of grass roared up to us and skidded to a halt. Koor stepped out and greeted us with a wave. He and Cagai spoke briefly, then Koor jumped back in his truck and his driver again sped southward.

"Koor himself will lead the initial attack," Cagai told me when we were again driving south also. "Daniel Awet saves himself for the finish."

"What is the finish?" I asked.

Cagai thought for a long while, and then said, "The finish is when all of Sudan is free and prosperous. That will be the finish."

The two men crammed in beside me nodded in agreement. I did not understand what he meant at the time. Surely there are no men alive who are more free than we Dinka, I thought. We come and go as we please. We go to bed when we want, we fish or hunt when and where we want. I did not know what we needed freeing from or from whom. I saw only the few Laraap traders who made it to our village and I had not love nor hatred of them until now. What I saw in the villages around Rumbek made me hate them, though I was more than a little unsure how much of the destruction was from the Laraap and how much came from other Dinkas.

Shadows covered the road when we finally stopped and made camp. I never saw the women travel with us during the day, but somehow they managed to appear at our camp and they lit fires for us. By the time we had set up our nets for the night, the women had prepared food and brought us large gourds filled with milk and some water. We ate again, better than we did at home, and then went to sleep with a watchful eye on the skies.

I again had the dream about the mist covering the land and taking the form of a man's face. This time I heard the Beny Bith's voice from the mist. It called a warning to us, or at least that is the way I recalled it. I could not make out the words, but the feel of them thudded in my brain and I awoke with a gasp. The night was silent. A few men sang songs in sluggish voices very far from us. I could picture them drinking the sorghum beer as they sang. Night birds called. From a few bed nets I heard the sounds that men and women make when they lay together. It took a long while for me to drift again into a dreamless sleep.

The next morning, I stayed under my net and watched as the eastern sky began to glow red, then yellow. Birds called and I heard hyena in the distance. Somewhere to the west of us I barely caught the sounds of cows mooing. I could tell that there were at least twelve or more cows in the herd, though the way sound travels in our flat land they could be many miles from us. I knew of a small cattle camp near here and wondered if some people had moved their cows there ahead of the coming battle. Scouts from the camp would have heard our vehicles and guessed that soldiers were about. The herders would not wait to see if they would be left in peace, but in the early morning would push their prized cattle further west. Laraap and SPLA alike took cows from those foolish enough to leave them nearby. I worried some over the cattle I had left. It then struck me that Koor had not asked about the cattle of his name, though as head of the household, they were more his than anyone else's.

I heard stifled giggles and rhythmic movements coming from where Cagai had set up his netting. After a time, I barely could make out the girlish figure that slipped away from him toward the dense brush.

Matak had barely spoken to me the previous night and I worried that he was offended by not being invited to ride in the front of the truck. But he did not seem offended so much as troubled by deep thoughts. His net was only a few paces from my own, so I called his name softly. He immediately replied, obviously already awake.

"One of the soldiers riding in the back of the truck with me is a distant relative," Matak told me. "He told me of the attack the SPLA is planning on the Laraap."

I was relieved not have to tell him of this, not sure if I was allowed.

"They will let the Laraap come very close to our village," he said. "Should we try to warn the people there?"

"I do not know how we can," I replied. "Perhaps Koor will tell them to hide. He could be there now."

Matak lay in silence.

"When the soldiers are hidden, they will have no further need of us," I said. "Maybe then we could go home and warn the people. Or, perhaps we should stand and fight with the SPLA, protect our people and their property."

"These men have guns," Matak replied. "I hid our gun near the road as you know. We cannot fight guns with spears and clubs."

"We cannot run either," I replied. Matak reached to touch the scars on his foreheads and as he nodded.

We again lay in silence until Cagai began to rouse the troops around us. We bundled our belongings again and climbed into the truck.

"We will not wait for the Laraap planes to catch us again sitting still," Cagai said. "Another thing. When the fighting starts, if you wish to fight with us you must dress like us. Otherwise our men may shoot you. Would you fight with us?"

Matak said "yes" to this before I even understood the question. I nodded in agreement.

"Here," he said as he pushed a bundle of clothes toward me. "Wear these clothes. Put on your feet whatever you find but do not go barefooted. In a battle, there may be a great deal of sharp metal or wood on the ground and you may have to move fast. You have no rank on your uniforms so people will think that you are a private or a civilian who is doing work for us on contract."

Cagai saw the bewilderment in our eyes, and then stated, "A private is the lowest rank of any soldier. You should salute everyone who has any symbols on the collar of their uniform."

He spent a short while showing us how to salute and telling us how to recognize ranks. "Your father, Koor, was a first lieutenant before they punished him. Of the people in our division, only Commander Awet was of higher rank. Avoid the Commander as much as possible. He may not like you wearing the uniforms."

"Will we get guns?" Matak asked after he had donned the uniform.

"We do not have extras," Cagai said. "But watch during the battle. If someone is killed or hurt so that he cannot fight, take his gun and ammunition. Also, sometimes even the courage of a Dinka man can fail him and at almost every battle one or two run away when the fighting starts. They will often throw away their weapon when they flee. If you see one, take the gun and shoot the coward. It will save us the trouble of tracking him down ourselves."

We loaded the truck and resumed our slow ride south. Deep pits scarred the road and Cagai told us they were made by the bombs the Laraap dropped from the air. When we had cleared the roughest area, Cagai sped up until he was out of sight of the men on foot. When he came to a section of deep forest, he pulled the truck to the side.

"You must learn to shoot," he said. "Later, we can give you more detailed lessons, but now I have only a short while."

He borrowed a weapon from one of the men riding with us and handed it to Matak. He then handed me his own. He showed us how to hold the weapon and look down the barrel through the notched piece of metal and line up the sight. He then showed us the latch that allowed the gun to be fired and how to pull the trigger. We stood a few paces from a teak tree and took turns shooting at it. I was surprised when the gun hit my shoulder and seemed to rise in the air as if someone was pushing it to shoot at the sky.

"This gun was designed by a Russian man, or someone working for them," Cagai said. "It is very reliable and easy to shoot. But the gun always angles up from the recoil of each shot. Keep that in mind if you must shoot many times quickly. Always aim lower with your first shot."

He showed us how to make the gun shoot one bullet at a time and how to flip a switch so that it sprayed bullets. When I pulled the trigger after flipping the switch, bullets made a line up the surface of the teak tree and shattered several small branches. Matak let out a whooping call and laughed at me.

We got back in the truck and Cagai drove us to a shaded area where we could watch the roads but the planes could not see us. We saw them flying high back and forth along the road. Several times we heard deep, booming explosions and knew that they were pouring death onto the main body of the troops. One plane flew directly over us and later we heard the sound of more bombs falling in the distant south. I worried that they were attacking our village.

By midday, the troops we had left behind caught up with us. Some of the men were wounded and being helped along by their comrades. Cagai arranged a resting place for the wounded and left them water and food for a few days. He then urged the rest of the men to move quickly. They formed parallel lines and began to trot south again, their officers chanting songs of battle and courage while the men echoed the words. When I heard them chant and heard the sounds of their boots pounding the hard ground in time, I felt a surge in my chest and again I wanted to be one of them, to join them in their proud march and sing songs that spoke of great battles and men of valor. Cagai called us to the truck and we drove alongside the chanting men. They all looked straight ahead, faces determined and hard with a fierceness in their eyes that surely would turn aside any enemy.

We stopped four more times and sent men into ambush sites before Koor drove up again. He stood in the back of a truck before a large gun similar to the one in Cagai's truck. He stood, facing forward and called to the men as he passed, many of them by name. They raised their guns over their heads and cheered as he passed. Koor was a man that men would follow into hell, I thought. He passed us and acknowledged me with a nod. As befitting a man of the Jeeng, he showed no sign of pain or weakness, despite the wounds I knew festered beneath his uniform.

When we reached Atiaba, around fifty men were left of the hundreds that started the journey south, the others behind us in concealment along the road. The Laraap would have to pass dozens of ambush sites both coming and going. The road was death for them.

I watched from a distance while groups of men set up metal tubes at least a thousand paces from the road.

"Mortars," Cagai told me when I looked questioningly at him. "They send small bombs over the heads of our men and into the ranks of the enemy."

Through a series of signalmen, Koor directed the men to fire their weapons and make small adjustments until the bombs landed in the center of the road and blasted pits in the hard dirt. The men left their mortars in position and began piling grass and branches around themselves so that even the most suspicious eyes would not notice them. He also had the men fill the holes the mortars had made, leaving no sign that the road had been so targeted.

Koor had men remove the great gun from his truck before sending the driver to hide it in the bushes. Four men carried the gun to the outside of a curve in the road where they could see down a long, straight stretch but was deep in the shadows and tall grass. Men with axes felled trees and quickly built a wall of wood around the gun. Forward of the large gun, they dug pits and laid brush and sticks over them. Koor walked up and down the road, directing the work and urging the men to work faster.

He then had the men dig a trench across the road within a stone's throw of the great gun. Twelve of them attacked the ground with metal tools and dirt flew from the road in large clumps, forming a pile on either side of the trench. When the men were waist deep within the trench, Koor directed them to throw the dirt far to the side of the road. Then they put thin sticks and leaves across the trench, slightly deeper than the surface of the road. On these they spread some dirt, then brushed the whole area with branches. Only the closest inspection would reveal the deep trench that lay below the dirt and branches.

While this work progressed, other men dug shallow holes into the road into which they carefully placed square packets of material. They inserted a short rod with wires coming from them into the packets, carefully covered the holes, and ran the wires into the bushes. We guessed that these were explosive devices and Cagai confirmed it for us. Twice more in the afternoon planes flew over our position. When we heard them, the men scattered into the bush and lay still, but no bombs fell and we had no indication that we had been seen. The sun was almost set when the men finished the work. They sat to the side of the road drinking water from metal containers and eating what food they had. I sat on a log next to Koor while Cagai showed Matak how to disassemble and clean a gun.

"This will be the killing field," Koor told me. "It is a great thing that you are here with me for this time."

I fought to control the tears that welled up in my eyes and looked into the darkness to hide my face from him. This was a moment that I could only have dreamed of before and it did not seem real. I was sitting with my father preparing to fight for my people. He wanted me here.

"Cagai told me he showed you how to shoot the guns," he continued. "If you get one, find a place where you can see a small part the road and do not concern yourself with the rest of the battle. Wait for someone to step within your sight, and then kill him. Shoot one bullet at a time. Resist the temptation to set the gun to fire repeatedly. You will hit nothing like this, but the sounds of your shooting will draw attention to your position."

I nodded, hoping that he could see my reply in the failing light. Koor allowed no one to light a fire and the camp women were nowhere to be seen.

"Whatever happens, do not let them capture you," Koor said from the darkness. I had not considered the possibility that we would lose the fight and the idea hit me like a fist in the chest. Koor did not explain, but I knew enough of the ways of the Laraap to understand what he meant.

"Sleep while you can," he said as he stood. "Tomorrow, you will stay by my side as long as possible. Do what I say without question or hesitation. If any of my men tell you something, treat their words as if they were mine." He walked away in the darkness.

I set up my net while visions of the pending battle flew through my head. As I lay down, I realized how tired I was. Sleep came easier to me than I expected and I did not hear Matak setting up his net beside me.

Chapter Sixteen

I rose before dawn and carefully packed my belongings. Matak did the same, and then followed me to find Koor. Around us the men began to rise from hidden campsites and move slowly to their positions.

We found Koor already walking among the men giving instructions and encouragement. Cagai joined us as we followed him. He had the men position small sticks to the left and right of themselves, indicating the area into which they were to fire. He instructed them not to fire until the enemy was visible between these sticks. He walked the entire length of the ambush several times, having the men raise their hands when he was within their field of fire. When he found a gap where no one raised their hands, he repositioned the men. By the time he was satisfied with their arrangements he could walk the road and at least one man or group have their hands raised at every point on the road.

"These men have been with your father for a long time and through many battles," Cagai said to us as we walked. "They have killed many Laraap and have lost many men to them as well. These are the best men the SPLA has to offer. We will hold the day."

He laughed quietly. "The Laraap of Rumbek do not know it, but they are walking into the teeth of a lion. Your father came up with the idea almost a year ago. We began to harass the Laraap troops in Rumbek, but not confront them.

When they came at us, we ran away. When they turned back to their bases, we attacked. They have as many troops as we do and with many more weapons and much more ammunition. We could not confront them in open battle, so we kept picking at them until they were enraged. Some Laraap officers even executed their own men for being cowards, accusing them of not trying to find us. But they did try. We were just too clever for them."

We paused when Koor stopped to study a configuration of trees that I knew hid some of the soldiers. After a minute, he resumed walking.

"We wanted them to think that we could not mass a large scale attack on them," Cagai continued. "We wanted them to think that we were leaderless bandits and not an organized army. Koor thought of it all and now the time has come. This day, the Laraap will learn what their forefathers before them learned. Sudan has suffered many invasions, British, Turks, Egyptians, some that no history has even recorded. These Laraap make the same mistakes that those who came before them make. They do not know us, do not know the heart of the Dinka and what makes us Muonyjang. Their arrogance and their ignorance will be their undoing."

Cagai laughed around the clenched teeth that held his pipe. Some of the men close enough to hear him laughed as well.

A red dawn cast ghostly light upon the road as Koor walked back and forth along its length. Far away down the road we saw a baboon almost as tall a man stride cautiously out of the bush. He sat and looked toward us. Other smaller baboons crossed under his watch. Within seconds, they all crossed and the great male followed them.

Koor approached Cagai.

"Tell the men on this side of the great bend to gather along the road," he said. "I would speak to them."

Cagai nodded, then trotted to relay the message along the line. In minutes, dark masses of men emerged from the trees and grass, many more than I believed could have been hidden from me. Cagai barked a few orders and the men quickly assembled in straight rows that stretched across a grassy meadow. They stood straight and tall, each with a weapon held proudly by his side. None spoke and all of them kept their sharp eyes looking ahead. A gentle breeze swayed the grass around them and crows called in the distance. A grey kite swooped down and snatched a rat as it tried to cross the road and elude the trampling boots.

Koor stepped before the men and seemed to grow even taller. Almost as if on cue, the wind died and silence fell across the land. Koor's voice lifted over us, the deep bellowing sound of an angry lion.

"Invaders from the north brought this war they call the Anyanya to us, a war we have fought for longer than most of us have breathed the breath of life," he began. "All of us have lost much to it, land and cattle, family and friends. But we are still here, still strong, still standing against those who would kill and enslave us. Today we meet the Laraap in the greatest battle of this war."

Koor paused, looked at the sky, down at the grass, then at the men. He spread his hands as if making supplication to Nhialic.

"The Laraap have many great guns of which we have none," he said. His voice growing louder as he bellowed. "I say let them come!"

"Let them come!" the men shouted in reply in a roar that hurt my ears and caused my tense nerves almost to snap.

"They tell old women and children that they can rain fire from the sky and wipe us from our own lands as if we were insects. I say let them come."

Again the men answered, "Let them come."

"Their steel battles against our courage, we who have never tasted defeat. Again I say, let them come."

"Let them come."

"Today we will remind them of why their ancestors feared us. Today we will remind them of what it is to fight Men of the Jeeng in the land of our birth, men who defend their women and children, uncles and fathers, mothers and sisters. I say, let them come."

"Let them come."

Koor paused and wiped the sweat from his forehead with the back of his hand. He gazed up and down the ranks of the men and smiled.

"SPLA," someone shouted and the chant rippled across the land. "SPLA, SPLA, SPLA."

Koor raised his hand and again silence fell.

"The story of this day will be repeated for generations both among our people and the Laraap. They will tremble when they speak of it while we rejoice. Today we will teach them fear, teach them to tremble, for today we teach them yet again the meaning of Muonyjang."

The men cheered and waved their guns in the air as Koor abruptly turned and walked away. Cagai shouted a few commands and the men returned to their positions leaving a field of flattened grass and echoes of their pride in my ears. In minutes I could see none of them as if they had melted into the landscape.

Cagai sent six men to watch the road to the north as Koor walked the road again and again while carrying a leafy branch. He brushed a place here and there, wiped out footprints and moved fresh cut branches so that they did not appear out of order. Then he sat on a log and looked at the road. No one approached him. Matak and I joined Cagai under a teak tree. All was silent.

"Koor can see a battle before it happens," Cagai told me. "He can see where men will fire, where the enemy will come from, how they will run, where they can see. He can see it all in his mind. The men know this. We have experienced it many times."

Sunlight poured through the trees onto the road by the time Koor stood. He walked again the long, straight stretch of road and looked for even the slightest indication of a trap that would warn the enemy of our presence. He made sure that the men on either side of the road were not positioned so that they would shoot each other, but that their angle of fire was away from each other. He made sure that the men carrying the rocket propelled grenades were secured within hidden pits that held a good view of the road. When at last he returned to the great gun, he again moved a few branches around and directed men to tie bundles of tall grass to the logs. He then leaned several bundles of grass against the front of the wooden wall, completely hiding the gun. The bundles would fall away at the slightest nudging, allowing the gunner a full view of the road.

When he seemed satisfied, he nodded to a soldier beside him. This man raised his gun over his head with both hands and signaled the man at the distant bend in the road. This man acknowledged the signal, then turned and signaled another soldier further up the road. Cagai told me that six men would relay signals to us when the Laraap were coming, giving us plenty of time to prepare. He said that they had a few radios but that they could not be sure that the Laraap could not hear them.

Cagai then pulled Matak aside and showed him where the spare ammunition was stored. He told him to take note of all of the men's positions. If the battle went longer than expected, some of the men would run low on ammunition. Matak was to carry them boxes of bullets when Cagai directed him. I was told to stay with Koor. I followed behind him, feeling out of place and useless. Koor at last sat on a short bench of logs well into the bush behind the great gun. A gap in the brush allowed him to see the far bend in the road where the soldier who would signal the Laraap's approach lay hidden. I stood until he motioned me to join him. I did not speak for fear of disturbing his thoughts.

"We are as ready as we can make ourselves," Koor said. "Pray now that Nhialic will bless our efforts and protect us in the battle to come. I do not think we will wait long. The Laraap planes have watched us all day yesterday and they want badly to finish us. They will come quickly. I am counting on it."

He swatted a tse tse fly that had landed on his neck, leaving a smear of blood where it had already bitten him.

"Let them come," I said softly to him. He looked at me and smiled. It was the best moment of my life. Nodding, he then turned again to look down the road.

I did not speak again, but sat twirling my spear between my fingers and feeling foolish with it amid so many guns.

"My only worry is the planes. They have a kind that can hover like a kingfisher and fire down on us. We have reports that the Russians have given them four such planes and that two of them are near here. We can fire our grenades and the large machinegun at them, but if they stay high in the air, it is not likely we will hit them."

He spoke while looking into the distance and I could not tell if he was saying the words to me or to himself. Cagai came and sat with us, puffing his pipe calmly.

My stomach rumbled from hunger, but I ignored it. I knew that I was sitting with great men at a great moment in Dinka history and did not want the moment to end. Hornbills lit in the trees over us and called loudly to one another. A line of geese flew over us toward the river, the leader emitting a rhythmic squawk as they flew. I watched a lizard twice as long as my foot carefully stalk an earwig that clung to the side of a tree. The lizard's body was the grey of bark, but its head was orange and yellow. When it was close to the earwig, it lunged to it and gulped it down. The pinchers of the earwig stuck out of its mouth until the lizard convulsed and swallowed a second time.

"Tell the men to eat well and drink water," Koor told Cagai who continued to puff his pipe. "It will be a long day for us."

Cagai tapped his pipe on the bench, then stood and walked away. I realized that he was the only man here who did not salute Koor every time he came or went. Instead, they acted as longtime friends with one another, though clearly Koor was the dominant one.

Koor asked me again of our family and again I told him of the children, my mother, and all of the relatives that he had not seen in the years since he went to war. We were close to home now, within half a day's walk at the most. I knew the nearness of his family and my mother tormented him.

I told him about the cattle camp, of who won the Fat Man Contest, and about the boys who got the mark and became men. None of us were killed for cowardice that day, I told him. He nodded. I told him of the songs and dances I had heard and seen. I even told him of the young girl who caught my eye while I was getting the marks. He smiled to himself. My stories appeared to calm him so I continued. I talked to him about the Atuot man, Jurkuc, and how he killed the great crocodile and that others said that I had killed it. I told him of meeting Jurkuc's son and that the son was looking for his father.

"The Atuot are great fighters," he said at last. "They are organized and fight as a unit. I worked with my men for years to get them to act as one—something the Atuot seem to do naturally. I have been told that they are so good with the bow and arrow and with poisons that even the British army did not dare go into their territory. They left the Atuot to themselves."

He then asked me to tell him more, so I told him about meeting John Deng and how he told us that there was a book about God written in the Dinka language. I told him about how the girl of the cattle camp was murdered and that I had sworn on the Chief's Spear that what I said about Chol was true. When I said this, I recalled the figure I had seen slipping across the river, but of this I said nothing.

I spoke as the land grew hot and the sun baked us. No wind stirred. Sweat trickled down my face and dripped onto my legs. The land was silent, not even the sounds of birds coming to us. I heard the faint sounds of a plane in the distance. Koor tilted his head slightly and sat straight, but the sound grew fainter and then disappeared. The air was silent and I could not find more stories for Koor, so we sat together and waited. My back hurt from sitting on the log bench for so long, but Koor just sat as if he was himself made from the same wood. He closed his eyes and I heard his breathing, steady and deep as if he was sleeping. He opened his eyes for a moment when the sounds of another plane filtered through the trees to us, but closed them as it also grew fainter and fainter and eventually faded away.

We heard men coming and the occasional thud of a blow followed by a grunting sound. Two men approached us dragging a small, naked man with them. His hands were tied in front of him and he swayed as he was forced to stand before Koor.

"This man came to us from the north," one of the soldiers said. "He says that he is looking for one of his cows. He says that someone stole it from him and that he has tracked the thief to this road."

The man looked at Koor, showing no emotions. He had scraggly hair and was covered with white ashes. The soldiers held a spear and goatskin bag that was surely his possessions.

"He tried to run when we stopped him," the other soldier said.

"Why did you run?" Koor asked him.

The man did not answer until one of the soldiers struck him across the back with his own spear. He flinched slightly and cast an angry look toward the soldier. Then he turned to Koor.

"Men with guns come out of the bushes on the side of this road and you wonder why I ran?" he said. The soldier raised the spear again but Koor waved him off.

"What is your name?" he asked.

"I am Cigut," he replied. I cringed when I heard this name which means that "my world has ended and all my parents have died." It is a name given to a cursed man whose name will no longer be spoken—one doomed to become a troublesome spirit when he died.

"You bear the marks of the Misseriya, Cigut," Koor continued. "You are a long way from home."

Cigut nodded but offered no further explanation. Koor cocked his head as if pondering a great thought. Then he looked past the man toward the road again for a long moment, so long that I began to wonder if he had forgotten about the prisoner.

"Take him to the road leading south from us and let him go," Koor finally continued. The soldiers appeared ready to protest, but a sharp look from Koor stopped them. "Give him his belongings and watch him until he is well away from us. If he turns off of the road or does not do as you say, shoot him."

They pulled Cigut away and disappeared.

"Could not this man have been a spy?" I asked.

"Perhaps," Koor replied. But there it is a great distance to go around us to the north from where the men are sending him. He cannot warn the Laraap of anything important. We must not be harsh to the people we fight to free, Thon. Besides, the Misseriya are a small group that live way to the north as far as Abyei. They move from place to place and do not have land of their own. He is just as likely looking for cows to take back with him as he is looking for a cow that was stolen from him. I do not think he has any interests in either side of this war."

We resumed our long wait. Koor and I moved to the great gun and leaned against a tree where Koor could more easily see down the road to the first signalman. We had barely settled when the man at the end of the road stood and raised his gun over his head. One of the gunners signaled him back.

The Laraap were here.

Chapter Seventeen

Koor stood slowly and deliberately, and then walked casually around the gun to the road for one more look around. When he was again satisfied, he took a position to the left of the great gun. Without a word, four men with very serious looks about them positioned themselves around him. They all carried guns and grenades with extra ammunition strapped about their chests. I had not seen these men before. I sat behind a tree within an arm's length of Koor. One of the guards gave me an angry look that I took as a warning to stay out of the way.

Another plane buzzed overhead, this time much closer, but continued south. We heard a deep boom from where it had gone. Moments later, we heard what I thought was likely the same plane as it flew back toward Rumbek. A ground squirrel ran onto the road and briefly dug around the trench close to us, then stood as if to look around at all of us before he ran into the grass and disappeared. Nothing else moved.

I felt the earth rumble before I heard any sound. Koor's guards flattened themselves to the ground but Koor stood motionless, only a few sticks of bush hiding him from the road. I moved closer to the tree and peaked around it to the road. Over the tops of the bush in the distance I saw a cloud of dust rising as if from a great herd of cattle. The earth continued to rumble and I could now hear the squeaking and belching of the machines of war the Laraap brought to kill us. I had never heard such a thing and I am not proud to say it, but my heart froze at the sound of it. If Koor had not been with me, I would have fled into the bush.

At the distant bend in the road, I saw a truck many times the size of Cagai's rumble into view. It had wheels in the front like a normal truck but its back was supported by a flat, metal track that tore into the road and scattered dust and dirt in its wake. Men stood in an open space in the back and pointed their guns nervously into the bush. When the vehicle had turned to face down the long straight, it stopped suddenly. Other trucks of similar design rolled to a stop behind it in a line that disappeared behind the bush as the road curved away from us. A man stood in the back and put something to his eyes. He appeared to be looking through the device at the road ahead. After a minute, he slapped his hand on the roof over the driver and the vehicle lumbered forward. The others followed.

Koor knelt behind a bundle of grass in a smooth motion that could have been a big cat beginning its stalk. He stayed motionless as the vehicles came closer and closer. The sound of them was a mix of metal screeching across metal and the rumble of engines as black fumes puffed into the dry, still air. The vehicles moved only slightly faster than a man could walk and it took a few terrifying minutes for the first of them to cross the straight section of road. The lead vehicle was so close that I could see the eyes of the men in the truck and felt that surely they were looking straight at me as they came. All of the men wore uniforms of green and grey. Most looked like Dinka men, but some were lighter skinned. They all looked both angry and anxious as they scanned the bush about them.

I was about to run away from them when the front wheel of the lead vehicle dropped into the trench Koor's men had dug and thudded to a halt. Men spilled forward over the roof and tumbled in a heap on the ground as the front bumper of the vehicle dug into the earth sending up a cloud of dust and debris. Instantly, the great gun before us opened fire and raked the Laraap troops both in and out of the vehicle. A heartbeat later, mortar bombs began to fall along the road, filling the air with smoke and flying debris. Already, wounded Laraap screamed for help and blood splattered the dusty road. The truck behind the one that had fallen into the trench slid to a halt a few steps away and men piled out of it, shooting wildly into the bush. I heard a few bullets crash through the brush over my head. The sound of the great gun raining death upon the Laraap shook me to my chest.

From their hiding places, Koor's men fired into the men and trucks as the Laraap fell by the score. I heard the swish of a rocket followed by a deafening explosion. The second vehicle burst into flames. Then, as if they were thrown by the earth itself, three of the vehicles rose into the air and shattered as Koor's men set off the charges that they had buried in the road beneath them. Mortars continued to drop into the line of vehicles and men, shattering both into bloody shards.

A constant cloud of rockets poured into the line of vehicles and I watched as hundreds of Laraap dropped to the ground. Many fled down the road away from us but were cut down by Koor's men who the Laraap had still not seen when they had passed. One of the trucks had a giant gun mounted on its rear. The gunners were protected by a metal plate. These men turned the weapon to the great gun near Koor. It roared to life and an instant later the ground in front of Koor's gun exploded, sending dirt and debris raining over me. I saw the Laraap gun rise slightly, and then fire again. This time, the entire log shelter holding the gun in front of me exploded. Pieces of men and wood flew in the air around me. Koor sprang to his feet and jumped into the pit left by the explosion. His guards followed him. I watched them pull the dead gunners away, then turn the gun upright. Koor got behind the gun and leveled it at the machine that had just fired at him. Almost as one, three rocket propelled grenades converged on the truck and it exploded in a cloud of smoke.

Laraap soldiers continued to fire from behind the trucks, but found themselves receiving fire from behind them no matter where they tried to hide. More and more of them ran northward and a few made it around the bend in the road. Most lay dead or dying on the road and I heard men moaning in pain as the shooting slowly died away.

Koor signaled a man behind him who relayed a message to another. Within seconds, the mortars stopped, but gunfire and grenades continued. When it seemed that the last of the Laraap were dead, Koor grabbed a gun from the embrace of a dead man and raced up the road after the fleeing soldiers. I found a gun and a packet of bullets lying beside a headless Laraap and took it. Men poured from the bush and we all rushed up the road after the enemy. My heart pounded in my chest and my ears rang like a cow bell.

When we got to the bend in the road, Koor slowed, then crept around to peek up the road. I stood beside him. We watched as hundreds of Laraap ran away from us, leaving most of their vehicles empty and smoldering. A few of the trucks at the end of the long line were maneuvering back and forth trying to turn around, running over fleeing men as they did. At least six of the trucks were able to turn around and we saw their dust as they ploughed through their own soldiers crowded on the road in flight. Koor's men roared like lions and fired into the backs of the fleeing enemy.

From the north we heard the sudden eruption of dense firing as the Laraap ran into one ambush after another. Koor and his men walked calmly down the line of vehicles shooting the wounded and collecting weapons. When we heard a plane approaching, we all ran to hide in the bush. One plane swooped low over us and as it passed the men stood up and unleashed a barrage of fire upon it. I saw pieces of metal fly off the plane and heard its motor sputter a few times, then die. We watched and cheered when it disappeared and fell to the earth behind a line of trees sending up a great plume of fire. I still had not fired my gun. I walked to a burning truck draped with dead Laraap.

Were these men, I wondered? They did not seem to be. When one of them appeared to move slightly, I pointed my gun at his head and pulled the trigger. The gun pounded my shoulder as the man's head exploded. As I turned, I saw Matak watching me. He too had a gun. He turned and walked into a cloud of smoke.

Koor and his men worked their way up the line of Laraap trucks and tracked vehicles. Already, women of the camps had come from the bush and were busily stripping the dead of any possessions. Koor sent word to warn all the people that only the SPLA could recover weapons or ammunition. The engines of a few of the trucks still ran. After they were loaded with guns and ammunition, Koor ordered soldiers to drive them south.

Koor's drivre came to us and we all got into the back of his truck. We passed ambush site after ambush site as we drove northward, each marked with the bodies of the enemy— so many that I could not believe any survived. Cagai drove behind us. We came upon one area where the SPLA had chosen its ambush site poorly and the Laraap had overrun them. Koor looked at the bodies of his men for only a moment before ordering their burial.

"The sun will not set before any of our soldiers who have died here are properly returned to the earth," he said.

We continued to drive past patches of the enemy dead, sometimes piled upon one another as if they had cowered behind their comrades. Many of the light skinned Laraap wore leather packets around their necks held by strings.

"I have seen many of these," Koor said as he plucked one off of the body of a Laraap. "They contain folded paper on which an Imam has written verses of the Koran. They claim that any man wearing these things cannot be killed in battle."

He laughed, and then tossed the charm into the burning wreckage of a nearby truck.

"They are wrong," he said. Some of the men near him laughed as well.

We loaded back into the truck and continued north. As we approached the Bahr Naam River, we heard sporadic gunfire. Koor sent some of his men ahead of us on foot while we waited in a patch of acacia trees. The sun was dipping to the horizon and the shadows grew long before a man came running back to us.

"None of them made it across the river," the man said between breaths. "We have a few of them trapped behind their trucks near the riverbed. The unit leader is trying to talk them into surrendering."

"I gave orders that we would take no prisoners," Koor replied sharply.

"I do not think they are looking for prisoners," the man said.

Koor ordered his driver forward and we rode within sight of the bridge. Off to our left in a patch of thorny trees sat three trucks. We could see men crouching behind the trucks and hear the shouts of the SPLA soldiers taunting them. Koor had just gotten out of the truck when the enemy soldiers stood, holding their guns by the barrels in surrender. They filed out and formed a line against the trucks. SPLA soldiers swarmed over them, took their guns and forced them to their knees. They then tied the men's hands behind them.

"Take their boots," Koor ordered. Men quickly complied. I saw that the boots were black and shiny.

The captives spoke in Arabic and Koor answered them in Arabic. I could not understand what he told them, but they shook with fear from it. He ordered men to walk the captives to the bridge. He made them line up at the edge of the bridge facing downstream.

I wondered why he did not just let these men go home. When the Laraap were things seen from a distance, I did not think of them as men with blood that would flow from their wounds or families who would mourn their deaths. They were things that threatened us and threw fearful weapons and bombs at us. Now that I could see them, smell their sweat and fear, hear their breathing, they were men like us. I hoped that Koor would scare and humiliate them and then release them. It was not to be.

I started to step backwards away from the others when I noticed Koor watching me. The dim light made his face to be only a shadow, but I could tell he watched me closely. I walked slowly to stand by his side.

"The Bahr Naam flows a great distance to the White Nile," Koor told me. "These waters meet those from Ethiopia and flow past Khartoum. Perhaps the bellies of the crocodiles will be full by the time these men float by and we can send them all the way back to their masters."

He pulled a pistol from his waist and quickly shot the first two men in the head. They fell backwards into the river and were whisked out of sight. One of the men tried to run but another soldier shot him in the back and rolled his body into the waters below us. I felt my bowels turn to water and struggled to suppress the tremor within. I remembered the marks of manhood on my forehead, a reminder that I was a Man of Men and the new scars on my forehead felt hot and raw. I knew what Koor was doing and why he wanted me on the bridge with him.

The other three Laraap shook and pleaded with Koor. One appeared to be praying. I was grateful that the light was so dim that I could not see their eyes for I believe that I would have carried the sight with me to my grave. Koor looked into my eyes.

"Shoot them," he ordered.

I still carried the rifle, but I did not move.

"Shoot them, Thon," Koor again ordered.

Even in the faint light I felt the eyes of the men and the soldier upon me. I had felt the child in me die on the day I got the marks, but somehow that evening I felt a last cry of desperation from it in my heart, a cry that I could not, would not admit to my father or the other warriors who stood watching me. Every muscle in my body tensed and I had to fight to control myself. I felt thankful that the bright light of day had passed so that no one would see my inner struggle. I had felt bones break at my hand during wrestling matches. I had felt and heard metal slice through the flesh of living animals, smelled the warmth of fresh blood that poured onto the ground. These things and all of the training and teaching of my childhood had prepared me for this moment and yet I hesitated for just the briefest of a moment before I suppressed my dread of making this one last step into manhood.

Before Koor could command me again, I walked to the first one, raised my gun, released the safety latch as Cagai had shown me, then I pulled the trigger. The gun clicked in my hand but did not fire. The man screamed, then crumpled and fell into the river. I did not see him rise again. I took the clip off the gun and refilled it from the box I had found. I then pulled back on the chamber and worked a bullet into position. This time when I pulled the trigger I was rewarded by a loud sound and the sight of the Larap falling backwards into the river. I then stepped sideways to stand before another. The last man did not shy away from me but stood tall and straight. I could see that the white showed all the way around his eyes, from terror or from anger, I could not tell. He spit Arabic words at me that I am sure were a curse. He was still shouting at me when I sent a bullet into his chest and he too went into the river.

By this time, the Bahr Naam was a ribbon of blackness and I could barely see those standing on the bridge around me. Koor spoke a word and the men turned from the bridge. I heard the faint sounds of movement in the water downstream and stood for a long while listening. When I did not hear it again, I too went to find camp for the night.

It was a different Thon that slept that night. I should have been kept awake for the bloodshed I had seen and made that day. Something, some inner law in me protested the thing I had done on the bridge and what I had become. It was, however, only a weak and insubstantial voice and the man that I was forced it into oblivion. I, Thon Bol, killer of the enemies of my people, slept well.

Chapter Eighteen

With so many soldiers around, he had taken a great chance crossing openness of the bridge. He was sure that someone had seen him, but in the growing darkness he would be nothing but a rustling of grass and shadow. He followed them, these men of the Jeeng. He could hear them breathing, could feel the way the mass of men disturbed the scent and feel of the night air and he could tell without sight where they lay at night and where they had walked. It was so strong an assault to his senses that he wondered why the Laraap could not sense them as well. He could tell that the Dinka were luring the Laraap into a trap, one so obvious that he thought the devastation it caused was deserved. Men so foolish as these deserved to die, needed to die so the strong could live.

When he made it to the river grass on the south side of the bridge, he slipped into the brush and found a thin trail that followed the Bahr Naam. Hours later, when he was confident that no one was near, he stopped and made camp. He allowed himself the luxury of a small fire and used it to warm himself and the small strip of smoked goat meat he carried. As he chewed the meat he thought of the trap that the Laraap were walking into, and again he wondered why they could not see it. He did not care for the Laraap or the rebel soldiers, had no concern for who would win this battle or the next. He only cared that the fighting continued so that he could ply his trade and gain that which only war can bring.

He thought of his time in Uganda and how Joseph Kony himself had taken an interest in him. He thought that perhaps he would join them, the Lord's Resistance Army, when they moved into Sudan. He knew that the Uganda Peoples Defense Force was looking for them and Kony had pledged to keep fighting. Kony was, after all, a prophet, chosen of the One True God to bring wrath upon the people of the earth. He thought with satisfaction of how he was used for that wrath and thanked God for allowing him to profit in pain.

He huddled next to the fire and fondled his treasures. These were the talismans of good fortune that he had learned from the master of such arts. Kony carried them and they had protected him from the thousands of soldiers the governments of many nations had foolishly set against him.

"Look for women who entered as a bat fluttering against the window," Kony had said. "Those that care for the children born of their own womb watch them too closely. Those that enter a household by the window instead of the front door are prone to hate the children of the wives before them. These are the easy ones, those brought by the woman of the household."

Kony's words had proven true as women brought their stepchildren by the scores to him for sacrifice, often asking no more for them than they would a small goat or plate of maize. In Uganda, children were easy to come by. In Sudan, where centuries of slave trading had made the people hard and secretive of their broods, finding victims had been harder. Until the war started again and soldiers came to his assistance, he had been forced to slip into small towns and steal the children he needed. It had been risky in those days. Now he had all of the tools he needed. Soon, he thought. Soon, they will all know and fear his person as they now fear his spirit. Soon, he knew, he would have all his heart desired—revenge, fame, power, and a position to pass to his heirs. Girls would come to him for no other reason than that he chose them. Women would quake in his presence and men would take his word as law.

He reached into a large pouch and pulled from it the head of a young boy. The foolish child had stumbled across his camp as he rested near where the river entered the great lake. He was surprised that such a young and inexperienced boy could get so close to him without being noticed and he had killed the boy before he could even think to question him. The boy had with him a small bag of groundnuts and a knife that carried marks made by the Atuot. He had washed and searched the body for defects and found only a small worm coming from his ankle, not enough to devalue his body.

This was a powerful talisman sent to him from heaven, he had thought as he removed the boy's head from his body. He could make great magic from it and sell many charms from it. He had taken a finger and the head from the body and then moved further into the bush. He knew the body would be found by hyenas or jackals, knew that the flocks of vultures would bring men to the site where they would find the remains. He had confidence in his skills such that no one would see signs that he had been present and it amused him to think of the spirits and jok that would be blamed for the boy's death.

He gently took the severed head to the stream and again washed it of dust and grime. He carried it gently and with reverence he would never have shown the child when he was alive. Then by the light of the fire, he used his knife to carve charms from it. As he worked into the night he trembled as an unaccustomed feeling crept over him. He knew as only creatures of the night can know that somewhere in the darkness something came for him. He could sense a presence on his trail and he welcomed the hunt.

Chapter Nineteen

We woke to the sounds of bombs dropping. Up and down the road, the airplanes dropped bombs along the line of disabled enemy trucks. Several of them exploded and many burned. The air was filled with the smell of their fires and the sounds of fuel and weapons exploding.

We waited in hiding until the bombing seemed over then slowly crept from the bush. All of us assembled by the road at the edge of a floodplain. Koor had large guns arranged around the area pointing into the sky, but by midday, no more planes appeared. The men stood in loose formations, laughing and sharing food with one another in elation over the victory. Koor and Cagai moved about them, returning salutes and handshakes, slapping them on the shoulder and congratulating them for surviving. I again saw how the men responded to him and looked affectionately at him. My father had brought his soldiers through another great battle and his legend would grow even more, I knew.

Hours later as the sun began to move to the western sky, three trucks raced up the road toward the collection of men. At the lead, Commander Awet rode in a truck decorated with a red flag. The trucks slid to a stop and kicked dust in the air around us. All of the nearby soldiers came to attention when he got out of the truck and the officers saluted him smartly. Koor also saluted as Awet walked up to him, all smiles and congratulations. No one would have guessed that a few short days ago this man had ordered Koor to be flogged.

One of Awet's aids spread a map on the front of his car and Koor and Awet spoke while pointing and tracing lines on it. After a short time, Koor stepped back, saluted and stamped his right boot on the ground, then spun on his heals toward us. He walked stiffly with his arms straight as if marching in a parade. He went to Cagai and spoke for a moment. Cagai saluted him, the first salute I have seen him make, then in turn went to other officers who had collected nearer the assembled soldiers. I stood to the side partially hidden in the grass. Until he spoke, I did not notice him, but Matak came to stand beside me while the officers conferred.

"You are now a soldier?" he asked while continuing to watch men saluting one another.

"I am a man of the Agar only," I replied. "I have not forgotten Chol."

He seemed satisfied and slipped away silently. By early afternoon the soldiers had all gone into the bush or back to their bases. I stood with Cagai and Koor watching as the last one, including Koor's truck and driver, hurried away. The wreckage of the Laraap trucks and other vehicles still smoldered and great flocks of vultures had found their dead. The familiar stench of death mingled with the acrid smoke of burning tires making me feel as if I would vomit. I welcomed the smell of Cagai's pipe when he and Koor came to stand beside me.

I still carried the gun I had used to shoot the Laraap prisoners. My spear and leec lay with my other possessions near Cagai's truck. After seeing the battle and the power of the weapons both sides employed, I again felt foolish looking at the spear and club. One man with the gun I now carried could stop a wave of men carrying spears and I wondered if they would allow me to keep the gun. As if aware of my unspoken question, Koor walked to me and handed me several metal clips full of bullets.

"Join us on a short trip," Koor said to me. I was not sure if it was an invitation or a command, but I would obey either.

Matak joined me in the back of the truck while Cagai and Koor rode up front. Cagai drove south for a long distance, and then turned to the west along a road barely wide enough for the truck. People were beginning to return to the area and we passed long lines of men herding cattle and women carrying children and supplies. I did not know where we were going and did not ask.

When we had gone a long distance into the woods, we came to the marshy grasslands bordering a lake. Scattered huts with smoldering fires covered the edge of the grassland and I saw children and women working in the gardens. We stopped next to a hut where an old man sat on a low stool in the shade. An old woman, missing her right eye, knelt in the ground and pulled weeds from a garden. Cagai went to speak to the old man while Koor motioned for me and Matak to follow him.

"This is Cagai's father and his father's first wife," Koor told us as we walked. "I do not know why, but Cagai believes that he will not live out the year. He asked for this time that he might see his parents one last time. They do not know that Cagai expects to die, so say nothing to them about it."

We could hear them greeting one another enthusiastically as we walked down the narrow trail. We found a circle of wooden rail benches under a mahogany tree that surrounded a raised mud platform. Someone had nailed a wooden cross to the tree. Koor enticed Matak into telling him stories of our village while we sat. By the time darkness fell, Matak had almost run out of stories, something that I had never seen happen. We returned to the truck and were beckoned by Cagai to enter the compound. The old woman and some girls had prepared large metal platters of goat meat, paper food, flat sorghum bread and crushed pumpkin leaves. We ate until we thought our stomachs would burst while the girls skirted about and laughed at us. Cagai teased them and called to them by name. We all slept on raised cots in a nearby hut.

The next morning, the girls again brought us food, water, and a large gourd filled with milk. We ate and drank again until we could hold nothing else. Cagai's father asked us to sit with him for a while before we left. After more polite greetings and thanks, he furrowed his brow and spoke seriously to us.

"I once met the great Nuer prophet, Ngundeng," he said to us. "I saw him do many miraculous things, proving to us that he was to be believed. Ngundeng was born in the time that my grandfather was yet a child. He was born in a place called Waat in Upper Nile region."

We all sat close and listened for I could tell in the way the old man was speaking that there was something important in the word he wished us to hear. All around, adults, children, even the birds and animals seemed to grow silent as he continued.

"The people believed that Ngundeng was born with God," the old man said to us. "When he was about twelve years, he started performing miracles. He had books in his hands that carried words of God. He did not go to school. He invited people to come to him to learn what was in his books. No one knew where he got those books. When people heard about him, they ignored him and said. 'How can a child teach adult people? How can the black writing in his books be important?' Ngundeng did not give up. He kept talking about strange things. Few people started to come to him. He performed his first miracle of the spears.

"'I need one very long fishing spear and one spear,' Ngundeng asked the people.

"'Look at this false leader. How can we give a very long spear to a child? Just give him a very short spear of about five inches,' they said. He was given two spears. He invited people to witness the miracle. The crowd gathered around him. He first put the fishing spear in his hands and rubbed it. The fishing spear turned into a bullet. He put it down. He rubbed another spear and turned it into a gun. There was a gazelle which stood on the ant hill. He loaded the gun and shot the gazelle from a far distance. He told them to go and see the gazelle. When people saw the gazelle, there was a bullet shot at its chest and it had died. People came back and he asked them, 'What have you seen about the gazelle?'

"'The gazelle is dead,' they answered.

"'In some years to come, the animals will fear humans. They will see people and run away. The people will get them by the means of the gun,' Ngundeng prophesied.

"People started to believe him as a result of this miracle. 'What will happen to us in the future, Ngundeng?' they would ask of him.

"'You black people will fight with brown people in the North,' he answered. 'There will be a left-handed, bald and short man with one testicle who will come. This man is not born yet. I saw people walking in line and this man is in the last part of that line. When he reaches you, he will lead you to the war with brown people.' He prophesied this.

"When many people heard about Ngundeng, Ethiopians under the rule of Menelik came to him to get the power of victory over any enemy. 'Your country will not be defeated by any nation,' he said. 'I will give you a red bull which signifies your forever power in Ethiopia. Take this red bull with you to your place and slaughter it in your land.'

"This, the Ethiopian heard and then he left. After a while Ngundeng called his people and said, 'You follow the Ethiopians. When you get them, cut the tail off of the red bull and come back with it,' he told them. They did it as they were told. They came back with the tail and brought it to Ngundeng.

"'Now you have got the power too. In some years to come, you will go to Ethiopia and that is where you will get your power,' he told them. 'You Nuer tribe, in the future when you come here you will offer a sacrifice. When you have done this sacrifice, there will come a man called Ajokkok, meaning 'the crow.' He will come and ask you for the hump of a bull you have sacrificed. You will ask him his names. He will tell you, 'I am Ajokkok.' When you ask where he comes from, he will not tell you but you will give him the hump.' He prophesied this. Some years after this, the Nuer had the sacrifice and Ajokkok came. They gave him the hump and he did not tell them where he came from. In a few years, Anyanya One broke out and they could eat meat with people and they did not tell them where they came from."

Cagai's father stopped for a long while and we sat listening to the sounds of the forest. Cagai asked him to tell us of another story regarding Ngundeng and his father seemed happy to do so. I was not sure why Cagai wanted us to hear this story, but years later I recalled how people said that the Nuer betrayed the Bor and how this led to a great slaughter. Cagai's father spoke again as the children and women gathered close about us. I could tell that he had told them the story before and that it was one of their favorites.

"About the day Ngundeng cursed Bor? There was a man called Bor who was Ngundeng's foodstuff keeper. Ngundeng only used to eat from the seed a certain tree called 'thou' in Dinka language. The people crack the hard part of the seed pod and removed the seed. Bor kept them for Ngundeng. One day Bor ate the seed. When Ngundeng became very hungry, he came to Bor to ask him for his food.

"'Bor, I am now very hungry, bring my seed to eat,' he told Bor.

"'My master, your seeds were stolen,'" Bor said, lying to Ngundeng to cheat him.

"'No, Bor, my seeds of my thou plant that you garden for me were not stolen, but you have eaten them,' he told Bor.

"'Yes, master, I have eaten them when I was very hungry,' he confessed. 'I know I have committed a crime to eat the seeds of your thou. Please forgive me,'

"'With which tooth did you eat them? Is it this tooth?' he pointed to one tooth.

"He had pointed to one of the incisors in the middle. His four fingers except middle finger were bent toward his chest. The tooth immediately fell down. It became the curse of all of the Bor tribe. Most of the Bor people do not have one of the middle incisors to this day. When two people fight, the tooth will fall off. When two people play, the tooth will fall off. Or when they wrestle, the tooth will fall off."

The old man continued, "Of his death, Ngundeng told people, 'When I die, my grave will be beside a hill and a pond. In that pond will grow sea papyrus, lily, and some water animals like hippopotamus, and crocodile will dwell in it. My grave will be a fence of ivory. The people will bring sacrifices to my grave year after year. There will be many women married to my ghost. These women will be inherited by all people in the South. Any man who visits my grave with his wives shall produce many children. These will be Dinka men and Nuer men. I will still talk to people from the grave in the form of a ghost. There will be times when my tomb will melt to oil and you will remember the miracles that I produced among you."

The old man took a deep breath and looked for a long while at all of us before saying, "All of these had been fulfilled."

The old man took a stick and began cleaning his teeth. He spit twice, and then started to speak again.

"He was a normal man before Deng possessed him and gave him that name. I stood in a crowd once when he prophesized of this war in which you now fight. He said that others would take of our land for a time and that war would cloud all of our futures but in the end, the people will win and drive the foreigners away. He said many things and I am old enough to have seen them come to pass. Cagai told me of the great victory you had over the Laraap. 'The Battle of Bahr Naam,' it will be called. We will make songs about it and your grandchildren will sing of when you brought the prophesies of Ngundeng to pass."

Matak and I looked at each other, then back to the old man. Already he seemed to have shrunk back into himself and I knew that we would hear no more stories from him that day. We both leaned upon our rife barrels and seeing Matak with his reminded me of how quickly we had become accustomed to them, carried and leaned on them as easily as we had our spears.

Koor thanked him for these words and we loaded into the truck again. We returned to the main road from Rumbek to Akot where Cagai stopped the truck. Children came from the bush and swarmed around us. Koor took no notice of them. A woman called to the children and they ran to her. When they had left, Koor told us to go home.

"This war is my life now," he said to us. "It is all I know. I do not think I can return to herding cattle or selling goats. This is not a good life, no family, no roots. But it is what has been thrust upon me and it is now who I am. It is not who you are."

Matak did not reply, but I remembered the feeling of belonging and oneness I experienced when the men marched and sang and we stood as one to cheer the victory. I wanted to stay with him, fight alongside of him and I told him so.

"No, Thon," he said. "You have great courage, I can see that. You have the marks of the Muonyjang on your forehead. But I saw the look in your eyes when you killed the Laraap on the bridge. Killing does not come to you as it did me. It is not an honor or a shame to kill in war. It is just what you have to do. But you are now the head of our household. You must speak for us with the clan and protect your mother, your sisters, your brothers. You must do what I cannot do."

I hung my head with these words. I could not imagine returning to herd cattle while I knew the soldiers like Koor fought for us. But he was my father and I would obey. He patted my shoulder firmly and shook my hand before we left. I stood and watched them drive away.

We then started the long walk home, past villages with silly children and old men who talked about things of no consequence. The sun beat down on us and made the metal of our guns painful to touch. They seemed heavier now, more of a burden than they had when we were with other armed men. Matak and I still carried our guns in the open. As when we walked past the people, they hushed their speaking and watched us pass. We walked long into the night before making camp.

The next morning we were packing our belongings when I saw a familiar figure pass us headed north where we had just come. I called to him and Gum ran to us.

"I almost passed you by," he said breathlessly. I made him sit to catch his breath.

"Mother sent me to find you and warn you," he said.

"Of what?" Matak and I spoke as one.

"Chol has returned to Akot," Gum said. "He sits with the Dungoor Bai and tells lies about you. He claims that you have stolen cattle from him and that you took them to the Laraap in Rumbek to sell. He says you spy for the Laraap."

"We have only just now fought in a great battle against the Laraap," Matak said.

"We already know of how the SPLA gained a great victory over the Laraap," Gum said. "Daniel Awet has gained great honor for it."

I almost choked when I heard this. No mention of the honor due to our father, Koor.

"Chol claims that you went to Rumbek and told the Laraap that the people of Akot were all fighting for the SPLA and that you urged them to attack us," he continued. "He says that Daniel Awet saved us from the attack that you tried to arrange. He says you did it for promises of wealth and an appointment as Payam Administrator."

"Surely no one listens to him," I replied. "He is a liar and a murderer of children."

"He says that you are the one who killed the girl in the cattle camp and that he has a witness," Gum replied. "The witness has taken the oath of the spear, just as did you."

"Who is this witness?" I asked.

"It is Matur, Chol's uncle," Gum said. "Mother says you should not return now as the Dungoor Bai has instructed all of the men to capture you if you are seen."

"Where does she think I should go?" I asked.

"She did not say. She just says that she fears that the Dungoor Bai is siding with Chol against you and that you should stay away."

We sat and discussed the situation as the morning gave way to the burning heat of noon. I sent Gum home with a message to my mother that I am well and that I have met up with Koor. I told him to tell her that I would return to Akot to clear my name of the charges against me.

When he had gone, Matak and I discussed the possibility of finding Koor again but we had no idea of where he would be now. It was likely that he and his troops would stay hidden for a few months before engaging the Laraap again and there was no real hope of finding him. We considered returning to Cagai's family also. In the end, we both wanted to go home and face Chol. We were now men who had seen battle and killed enemies. We both carried guns and, while Matak may hesitate, I knew I could kill Chol at the first opportunity with no remorse. We sat through the day and thought of what we should do and spent a restless night without any clear ideas.

In the morning, we packed our belongings again and started home. If we walked fast we could be in my compound by noon and we hurried to get there. We walked up to the compound and were surprised that no one greeted us. The dogs and children were gone and my mother's pounding stick lay on the ground by a pile of millet seeds being eaten by a small goat. We chased the goat away, then sat and waited for most of the afternoon thinking that someone would return. Evening came and we were still alone. We slept in my old hut fearful of what my family's absence could mean.

In the morning, we took our guns and extra ammunition and walked into the market area. People milled around and stared at us as we walked by. I understood their looks. A few short months ago, we were boys herding sheep and catching pigeons. Now we walked down the middle of the market with healed scars of manhood and carrying the weapons of soldiers. No one, even those of our own age set, approached us or spoke to us. A few of the younger children waved and called our names, but they were quickly hushed by their mothers and whisked away.

We walked to the gate of the Dungoor Bai's compound. The same crowd of old men sat under a tree, many of them smoking pipes. Four of them played a card game, slapping the cards down on a wooden table and laughing. None of them took note of us as we stepped inside the gate.

A dog growled at us from beside the fence and the men as one turned to look at us. No one moved. Neither Chol nor the Dungoor Bai was with them. We walked to them with our fingers on the triggers but being careful not to point our guns at the elders.

"You come looking for Chol," one of them said. The old man puffed his pipe and sent clouds of smoke into the air around him. His eyes squinted at us and he appeared amused by our appearance.

"They are gone to the cattle camp to take some of your family's cattle in payment for your crimes," he said eying the guns. "The Dungoor Bai declared you guilty. He ordered that your mother and all of her children be taken prisoner until you were captured or turned yourself into to him."

"Where is she?" I demanded.

The old man took a puff from his pipe, then pointed with its stem toward the hut at the far end of the compound. I ran to it while Matak stayed with the elders.

I called Athen's name as I ran but got no reply. The door of the hut was latched from the outside and I ripped it from its leather hinges as I jerked it open. I stepped inside to be greeted by all of my mother's children except Gum. My mother sat naked against the wall with wire wrapped around her wrists and ankles. I could see where the children had tried unsuccessfully to unwind the wire which cut into her flesh. Her lower lip and right eye were were swollen and dried blood covered her chin and chest. I knelt before her and worked carefully to unwind the wire. She flinched only slightly as I eased it from the cuts in her wrists.

The children cried and clung to me as I worked, but neither Athen nor I spoke. I could imagine what they had done to her, how they had stripped her and bound her hands. How they made her walk through the market naked and bleeding while her children cried around her and begged them to release her. I could see in her eyes the pain and humiliation she felt and I hated them for it. When I had released her, I told her to stay inside. I then went to the elders and without asking any of them, I jerked a blanket from around the closest one. I returned to the hut and gave it to my mother who wrapped it around herself and tied it in a knot at her shoulder. I then stood aside as she stepped carefully into the light. From behind her I could see where they had lashed her back and I swore under my breath that I would avenge her pain.

Athen herded the children out the gate, pausing long enough to spit at the ground and cast a wicked look at the elders. I then went to stand beside Matak.

"Tell me why I should not kill you all where you sit," I said angrily. It took all of my self control to keep from putting the weapon to repeat and spraying them all with bullets.

The elder who spoke to me first replied. "We did not harm your mother, Thon. The Dungoor Bai and Chol did this to her. What did you expect of us?"

"I expected you to protect the women and children of your clan," I spat at them. "I expected you to be men, not slaves."

"You expect a great deal of old men," the elder said. The others sat motionless and stared at us. "We complained to the chief that this was not fair, but Chol's family had already bribed him. We told the Dungoor Bai that you or your father would come for revenge on this injustice, but he laughed. I believe it is what he sought."

I heard Matak switch off the safety of his gun.

"I do not think that we will miss the elders that would let this happen," Matak said. Before I could reply he sprayed bullets into the air above them. Most of them dropped to the ground and covered their ears. The old man who spoke to us calmly puffed his pipe and gave us an amused look.

"We deserve your vengeance," he said when Matak stopped firing. "But I would save your bullets for those who mean you harm. You will find that Chol's family has many supporters and that fear of the Dungoor Bai runs deep. You will not scare them as you would defenseless old men, Thon, son of Koor."

Matak cursed at them and I pulled him away before he had a chance to shoot them all. When we walked back through the market, there were no people in sight. A few dogs barked at us and we saw movement from behind curtains and doors, but the people had heard the shooting and would not challenge us.

We walked back to my compound where my mother was cleaning her wounds. The children were eating as if they had never eaten before as she carefully washed her own wounds and spread a salve on them. I could not look at her eyes, but she pulled me to her and put her arms around me. For the first time in my life, my mother cried. Great sobs burst from her and I felt her tears flow down the back of my neck and shoulder. I held my gun in one hand but put the other around her as the children stopped eating and they too cried. It was a long while before she controlled herself and stepped away from me.

"They did this to trick you," she said to me. "They want you to do something foolish. Did you shoot any of the elders?"

I shook my head, no.

"Good. Koor can deal with them later," she said. "Chol has gathered the warriors of his family at the cattle camp by the eastern marsh. They wait for you there."

I had not seen Matak leave and he likely slipped away to avoid adding to my mother's sense of shame when she started crying. I knew he would be with his family to assure that they were well. Matak also was the oldest of his family and we could expect no help from them. His father would come with us if we wished, but I knew Matak would not risk losing him and leaving his family without a leader. We were on our own.

That night I did what no Dinka man would do. I walked to the well to gather water for my family. As I approached the well, women stared in disbelief. They had never seen a man carrying a water container before and they parted to give me a place next to well. I put the large clay pot on the ground and lowered the communal bucket into the well. I pulled the rope against logs at the edge of the well that had deep grooves where thousands of others had also dragged their ropes before me. When I brought it up it was heavy with clear water. I turned to empty it and almost upset the water pot. One of the girls rushed to steady it and she held it carefully while I filled it with water. She averted her eyes from mine as she held the pot. I recognized her as the girl I watched dance on the day we got the mark.

"What is your name?" I asked her.

"I am called Akol," she replied shyly. It is a name that means she was born in the light of the sun. It was a good name for a girl so beautiful as this one, born when we could see her and appreciate her face and form.

"I am Thon," I replied.

"I know who you are," she replied. "Everyone knows who you are. You are the one whose father fights in the war and whose mother was mistreated by Chol and the Dungoor Bai."

I nodded. Other women eased closer to listen to us.

"You will find the ones responsible for your mother's pain?" she asked.

I nodded.

"We all knew you would," she said. "But we did not expect you to return as armed soldiers. Neither would the Dungoor Bai or your enemy, Chol."

The other women nodded in agreement.

"They will wait for you on the trail to the cattle camp," she said. "I overheard them saying so. Be on your guard for some of them are not at the camp as the old men think."

I nodded again that I understood.

"Kill them," she said. I could hardly believe my ears.

"Kill them for us as well as your mother," she said. "Chol has infected the Dungoor Bai with an evil way. I lost a sister to them, I am sure. Others have lost children as well. They make up crazy stories about demons that hide in the bush and carry them away, but we know that it is Chol and the Dungoor Bai who do these things. We know what you swore on the spear and we ask you now to kill them for us."

"I will kill them," I said.

Akol looked the other girls and they smiled at her and nodded toward me, the kind of thing girls do when they have some unspoken agreement among them.

"When you return, you can have your choice of wives among us," she said turning her eyes to the ground. "Any of us."

I took her meaning. I thanked the women for the information and assisting with the water. Two of them went with me and carried the pot for me. They explained that they did not want me to be called the man who works like a woman. Athen thanked them when they deposited the pot by her side and they hustled away into the darkness.

I slept that night with my back laying against the warmth of my mother's spine. I heard her sob a few times before her breathing eased and she fell asleep. My siblings lay strewn across the floor, all of us sharing the same hut. I still had not seen Gum.

The next morning, Athen rose as if nothing had happened to her. She prepared food for us to take with us and for the early meal. As I finished eating, Matak arrived. He had replaced his uniform with a green robe of light cloth and he wore leather sandals. He still carried the army pack and gun. I also changed to a Jalabiya and picked up my gun. The flowing robe would hide my gun if needed. Before we left, Athen put a hand on my shoulder and pressed her forehead into my chest. She stayed that way for a brief moment, and then turned to walk to her garden. The children followed her as if they were afraid to let her leave their sight.

As we walked, I told Matak of the conversation with the women at the well. He did not seem surprised and gripped his gun even tighter to his chest. We moved quickly at first, wanting to eat the trail as fast as we could so that we could spend the night close to the cattle camp and where we believed the Dungoor Bai and Chol lay in ambush. We wondered how many men he would have with him and if they were armed with guns or spears. When we were close to the stream, we diverted to the south and took a trail that few knew. It circled around the main approach to the camp through thick brush and high grass that hid our approach. By the late afternoon, we could hear the cattle bellowing in the distance. We saw no one but still we crouched and slipped from cover to cover, all the while watching for our enemies. After the great Battle of the Bahr Naam, this enemy seemed small and insignificant, more like a deadly snake in the grass than an enemy of men.

As we crept slowly through a section of grass, we saw two men. They were facing away from us and hiding from being seen by anyone taking the main trail. Matak and I took long knives from our packs, then lay the packs under a dense bush. We strapped our guns across our backs and began crawling slowly toward the men. Once, we had to stop as two other men came from the direction of the camp. They went to the two men we were stalking and spoke in hushed whispers. They looked around them as if they suspected we were there, then turned and watched the trail again. We lay in the grass considering what we should do. To take all four of them, we would have to use our guns. If we did that, Chol and the others would know where we were. While we lay whispering to each other, two of the men left the other two and returned to camp. We continued to crawl through the grass, moving as silently as a fox. We stopped almost within a spear's length from them and lay still behind a clump of thin grass. We listened to them speaking in whispers to one another.

"Chol is a crazy man," the one on the right said. "He is mad with hatred and so is his uncle."

"Yes, I know," the other replied. "But I married the uncle's daughter with a promise of cows that I do not have. If I refuse to help him, they will take her back."

They continued to look intently at the trail that they believed we would take. Each of them had a spear in his right hand and another spear sticking from the ground in front of them. Apparently Chol had not told them that we may have guns or perhaps he did not care if these men died as long as he was warned of our approach.

I looked at Matak who made a slashing sign across his own neck. He wanted to kill them. I shook my head, remembering the words of Koor as he let the Misseriya man go free before the great battle.

I carefully lay my knife on the ground and lifted the gun from across my back. Matak did the same. As one, we silently rose from behind the men.

"If you run, we will shoot you," I said in a clear voice that sounded in my head like Koor's.

The men jumped, and then turned quickly to face us. They lowered their spears to the ground when they saw our guns pointed at them.

"We have no quarrel with you," I said. "If you leave your spears and go away from the cattle camp, we will not kill you."

They looked at each other then at our guns. Neither of them spoke.

"Go now," I said, motioning with the barrel of my gun to the trail away from the cattle camp.

The men backed away from me slowly, and then turned. Just as they started to walk away, Matak told them to stop.

"Who waits for us in the camp?" he asked.

The men exchanged glances. "Tell me," Matak demanded as he raised his gun and pointed it directly into the face of the man closest to him.

"The Dungoor Bai has twelve men with spears arrayed against you. He himself carries a pistol I think Chol gave to him," one of them said. "They wait further up the trail for you. We were told to give an alarm when we saw you."

"And Chol?" I asked.

"Chol has only his uncle," the other said. "His uncle has a gun like the one you carry. Chol also has a pistol."

"Does the Beny Wut support them?" I asked. The Master of the Cattle Camp would not normally involve himself in fights between families, but he would be expected to side with the Dungoor Bai.

"The Beny Wut does not," he replied. "They have threatened him and even beaten one of his wives, but he would not support them."

"Leave now," Matak said. "Do not return to the cattle camp. If you do I will shoot you."

The men turned and hurried down the trail as the light began to fail. They had gone a short distance when one of the men turned back to us. He ran to us with his palms raised.

"Chol has your brother, Gum," he said to me when he was close. "Also, you should know that a great Atuot warrior stalks this camp. He kills the men who venture out alone. We are told that he seeks vengeance for his son that Chol killed. His son was not even a man."

I thanked the man for the information and he hurried to catch up with his companion. We could not be sure that they did not turn back to the camp to warn Chol and the Dungoor Bai, but I believe that they had had enough of this fight.

We took their spears and moved back into the bush to a hiding place where we could watch the spot where the sentries had been waiting. We took turns sleeping and watching the trail as the night grew long and cold. No one else appeared from the camp.

While I was on watch, a great owl flew overhead and landed in a nearby tree. I could see its eyes shimmering in the moonlight. I was glad that Matak slept as he would take the owl's presence as a bad omen. A distant hyena called and others answered it. A flock of fruit bats fluttered overhead, filling the sky by the thousands before disappearing over the horizon. I worried for Gum, who finally got to come to the cattle camp. Tomorrow I would free him from Chol even if I died in the effort.

The words I spoke while getting the marks came back to me.

"I will fight for the people, Babba Dia." I had said.

"Will you die for the people?" the elder had asked and I replied.

"If the Beny Bith sees it, it will be as you say. If Nhialic wills that I should be protected, it will not be as you say. I will fight for the people when the people need me to fight."

I would die for my brother, I knew. The words I spoke had not been false.

A grey dawn crept over the land and clouds hid the morning sun. Dew covered us and sent chills down our backs as we ate the food that Athen had prepared for us and discussed what we should do. Twelve men could be managed with two guns as long as we could see all of them. But Chol would surely hide behind Gum. His uncle's gun and his pistol presented the greatest challenge.

We decided to creep into the cattle camp and look around. As we gathered our things, we saw two men come from the camp and walk to where the sentries should have been. When they were not there, the men hurried back to camp. Perhaps they would think the men just went home, I thought, though I knew that our presence would now likely be expected.

"We should have shot them," Matak said and I knew he was right, but we could not know who among the men who fought the Dungoor Bai and Chol did so out of loyalty to them or because they were forced to do so as the two sentries had been.

We circled the camp and stood in the trees where the Nuer raiders had hidden on the night of their aborted raid on us. We could see into the camp as women built fires and young men released the tethered cattle in order to take them to graze. There were less than half the cattle that should have been there and the men who drove them looked skittish as they moved the cattle from the camp. We eased deeper into the trees as the light grew and we watched patiently for signs of where our enemies lay.

We saw the Beny Wut emerge from his grass hut and sit by a fire. He took food from a woman and ate alone. Then we noticed him glance back into his hut and we saw movement within it. Matak replied to my unspoken comment by lifting his chin slightly.

Then we saw movement in the grass between the trees in which we stood and the clearing of the cattle camp. Just a slight bend of the grass that made no sense. Gradually as the light grew brighter I could see the outline of a man lying in the grass. He was looking to our right. Soon we could barely see the figures of other men in the grass around him. They lay where Matak and I had lain when the Nuer raiders had threatened the cattle camp.

Matak signaled me to stay where I was. He slipped away without explanation, though I had an idea of what he had planned. I waited a long time and as noon came, I heard a commotion from the trail on which the sentries had been posted. Matak walked straight into the camp carrying a spear but no gun. The men in the grass rose slightly in order to see. As they did I counted nine of them. I took the gun from my back and brought it to my shoulder.

Matak found himself with a man with a spear on each side of him, herding him toward the Beny Wut's hut. He went with them but did not relinquish his spear to them as their gestures suggested to me they were demanding. Just then, the Dungoor Bai stepped from the Beny Wut's hut with his pistol raised. I almost fired toward him but knew I would have no chance of hitting him from this distance, even if I was more experienced with the gun than I was. He advanced toward Matak shouting as he walked. I could not make out most of the words but could hear my name being called.

The Dungoor Bai stopped a dozen paces from Matak and scanned the area before turning again to Matak. As he did, Matak raise his spear and before anyone could react, he threw it. The spear lodged in the Dungoor Bai's fat stomach and he fired his pistol as he bent over. I began firing at the men in the grass who stood and looked at me foolishly. One by one I killed them as I walked through the grass. They appeared unable to run from me and I felt no remorse as they were dropped dead by my gun.

I shot what I thought was the last of them and had to reload the gun. While I was doing so I heard a commotion behind me and the sound of a spear cutting through flesh. I turned to see a man with a raised spear in his hand and a bloody point sticking out from his chest. He fell on the spear and its shaft wobbled back and forth for a few seconds. Behind him stood a man with the scars of the Atuot. Jurkuc, the man who killed the crocodile by this very river stood smiling back at me. He motioned me to proceed into the camp as he pulled his spear from the man's back and seemed to melt into the tall grass.

The men guarding Matak had fled at the sound of gunfire and were nowhere to be seen. Matak had run back into the bush to retrieve his gun and when he returned, we met to stand over the Dungoor Bai. The spear pulsed and swayed as it stuck out from his great belly. He had dropped his pistol and Matak retrieved it. The Dungoor Bai's beady eyes glared hate at us and he groaned in pain. Matak pulled his spear roughly from his belly and wiped the tip on the Dungoor Bai's jalabiya. He then spit on the man's face and turned away. I stood looking down on him, the hated man of supposedly mystical powers. The one set up to judge over us, himself but a criminal and enemy of the people. I considered shooting him but felt joy from the grunts of pain he emitted and I did not want it to end. His jalabiya had risen over his legs and I could see that he had opened his bowels and lay now in his own filth.

The Beny Wut came to stand beside me and also looked down at the dying man.

"You can never return here," he said to me while looking up at me.

"I know," I replied. "Where are Gum and Chol?"

"Chol has taken Gum to the river," the Beny Wut replied. "I think they have a canoe there. You should hurry if you want to catch them."

Matak and I ran toward the river as fast as we could. We crashed through the bush and found the trail, the same one that we had taken many times before with our cattle. When we were within sight of the river a shot rang out and a tree splintered near my head. We dove behind some bushes and looked for the shooter but could not see anything. From the river I heard Gum's voice cry out before being muffled. I rose slightly and another bullet sliced through the grass near me. This time I saw the shooter as he ducked down behind the bank of the river. I told Matak what I saw. He ran in a crouch to the right and I ran to the left as another shot echoed across the riverbed. As I ran I saw Chol drag Gum into a dugout canoe and push away from the shore.

I saw Matak running toward the river but did not think he could see Chol and Gum. I kept running through the grass and brush as more shots followed me. At last the shooter rose to fire but nothing happened. He disappeared behind the bank to reload as I jumped down the bank beside him. Chol's uncle worked furiously to reload his gun as I walked to within arm's length of him. When he saw that it was futile, he dropped the gun and raised his hands over his head. I shot him in the chest, and then leapt over him to pursue Chol and Gum.

I could see them as the canoe was caught in the current and swung downstream. Matak ran to the edge of the bank looking toward me. I cried out a warning to him and he finally turned to see the canoe that floated silently beside him. I watched helplessly as Chol raised his pistol and shot Matak. Matak fell backwards over the bank and out of sight. I raced along the river, jumping ridges and gullies as I ran. The canoe picked up speed as the river flowed into dense brush into which I could not follow. I watched Chol paddle away. Before they disappeared around the bend he looked back at me. While I watched, he turned and struck Gum across his face with the pistol and Gum dropped to the floor of the canoe. I screamed at him as he disappeared from view.

I found Matak lying on his side rolling back and forth in pain. Blood seeped between his legs. I tore his robe around the wound and looked at it. Blood spurted from his man parts and where his testicles should hang, there was only a mass of pulp. I made a bundle from strips of his robe and pressed it into the wound. I felt his blood, hot and sticky, pour through my fingers and Matak cried out in pain.

I helped him to his feet and we walked back to the cattle camp as people began to emerge from the forest. One woman told me that she was related to Matak's mother and she offered to help us. After only a few steps, Matak collapsed and I carried him to her hut. Once inside, we laid him on a blanket. She wrapped cloth around his waist and legs to hold the dressing tightly in place. Almost immediately the bleeding stopped as Matak appeared to have fainted. The woman put her hand to his chest for a moment, then looked at me.

"He will live," she proclaimed when she straightened.

I stepped outside and found the Beny Wut.

"I expect him to be cared for and protected," I said sternly to the Beny Wut. It seemed strange to me to speak thusly to one of his position, but the Beny Wut did not seem offended. He simply nodded. This man was not my enemy, I reminded myself.

The Dungoor Bai still lived but no one came to his aid. He hurled threats and curses to anyone who moved within his sight, but he appeared unable to move his legs. I walked up and looked down at him. He called me a dog, son of a dog, and other insults. He promised to curse my life and all of my family. I knelt beside him and listened to him rant. When he stopped to breathe, I spoke to him.

"Where will Chol take my brother?" I asked him. He replied by spitting at me and renewed his curses. He tried to grab at me but I knelt out of his reach. He rolled back as his limp legs flopped about and smeared his filth mixed with blood into a muddy pool.

"Tell me where Chol is going and I will ease your passing," I said softly. He replied with more curses.

I looked at him and for a moment almost felt sorry for him. Then I remembered the sound and feel of my mother's grief and saw in my mind the wires that had cut into her wrists and ankles. I pushed the dangerous rage down into my chest and forced my face and voice to be calm. Slowly I rose to my feet and stood at his head. I then lifted my robe and pissed in his face. He screamed and flailed his arms about in a mindless rage. I looked about and only a few older boys stood at a distance and watched me. The Beny Wut sat on the log by his fire and did not look toward us. I then walked to the Dungoor Bai's side and again knelt, leaning against my rifle.

"The dogs will eat you while you still live," I said to him. "They will shit your body in piles across the land and no one will even know you ever existed. Tell me what I need to know and I will kill you quickly and give you a burial fit for a Dinka man."

The Dungoor Bai tried to roll toward me and slapped at me again. I easily blocked his weak blows. When he stopped I heard gurgling and saw bloody bubbles coming from the wound in his belly. Already a great swarm of flies had gathered to his smell and I knew that within a day they would fill his body with maggots. He stared at me for a long while and then spoke.

"Bring the Beny Wut to me and make your oath so he can hear it," he said in a raspy voice.

I walked toward the fire where the Beny Wut sat and told him what the Dungoor Bai had said. He came to stand beside me and we held our noses at the smell of him. I repeated my vow to kill him quickly and bury him if he told me where Chol had taken Gum.

"Will you hold him to this vow?" he asked of the Beny Wut.

The old man nodded in reply.

The Dungoor Bai sent curses flying at no one in particular, then looked at me. I could feel the hate in his eyes as he whispered to me.

"There is a village near the lake which is west of Rumbek," he said. "Chol has been there before. The Laraap killed all of the adults and threw them into the lake. They are crocodile dung now. The children they gave to Chol. He used them to make his charms."

I asked a few more questions until I was sure that this was the village that Matak and I had found where the well was filled with dead children. He confirmed my suspicions. The stream here ran to the lake and by canoe Chol could be there in less than a day.

The Beny Wut returned to his fire and left me with the Dungoor Bai. He lay there eyeing my gun and waiting for death.

I knelt beside him and leaned on my gun. I looked about to confirm that no one could hear me. A few women glanced at me as they tended their fires while others dug graves for the Dungoor Bai's men that I had killed. I leaned forward so the Dungoor Bai could hear my words.

"I am Thon, son of the great warrior Koor," I said to him. "He is son of Mayol, son of Matur, son of Kau. My brother's name is Gum which you know means 'suffering.' I owe no honor to a worm like you. You will rot in the sun. What the dogs do not eat, vultures will strip away until only your skeleton remains. Even then you will have no rest. My ancestors will chase you in the afterlife and the jok of my clan will curse you forever. You will wander the earth a restless spirit suffering the pain you feel. Now die in disgrace. No one here will help you."

The Dungoor Bai tried to scream at me but the sound caught in his throat and he coughed and gagged on his own saliva. I left him gasping and cursing and returned to the Beny Wut.

"You will not assist him or allow anyone else to help him," I said coldly. The old man nodded as if he expected nothing else. "When he is dead, have his body dragged into the field and leave it there. When I return I expect to see his flesh rotting from his bones."

Again, the Beny Wut nodded. "We have no love for this dog or his minions," he said, and then he turned again to the fire and puffed on his pipe.

Chapter Twenty

Moving as fast as I could it still took me the rest of the day and night to reach the trail to the lake. Somewhere ahead, Chol had my younger brother. I already knew what he did to children and I pushed the thought of it from my head. I rested only briefly and ran through the night.

As dawn crept across the sky, I paused to eat the little food I still carried. I then left everything I carried except a skin of water, my gun, and ammunition and hurried up the trail, gaining speed as the light improved. My legs grew heavy and cramped, but I pushed myself forward.

When I thought I was near the village where I believed Chol waited, I slowed to a fast walk and scanned the bush. Nothing seemed out of the ordinary and I pressed on. I stopped at the edge of a clearing nearest the well and peered into the empty village. I saw nothing move. Somewhere toward the lake I heard a muffled cry. Again, I smelled the stench of death coming from the village, unabated since I had been there before.

I worked my way toward the sound of the cry expecting Chol to spring out at any time. I felt as if ghosts watched me from the empty village. I heard another cry from toward the lake and hastened to find it. At the edge of the village I saw a compound surrounded by a high, bamboo fence. Smoke drifted up from inside the fence and I saw new tracks going into the closed gate.

I crept silently to the gate and edged it open. The gate creaked loudly in the silence of the morning and I knew if he was inside, Chol could hear it. I waited for a few breaths to see if he would show himself. When I saw no one, I slipped inside the gate and scanned the compound. Two round huts lay in the corner of the compound and a larger square hut dominated the center. A fire smoldered in the center of the compound. As I crept to the larger hut, I heard again the muffled cry. It came from behind one of the smaller huts. I then made a mistake.

I turned toward the sound and put my back to the larger hut. As I did, I felt the jolt of a blow to my head and the world turned black.

As I recovered consciousness, I first heard sounds, and then I felt pain. My head pounded as if my skull had been crushed. It took me a few minutes to understand why my shoulders hurt until I realized that I was suspended from a log by my arms and my joints were almost pulled out of their sockets. I tried to open my eyes but they seemed to be glued shut. I took a deep breath and found that my mouth was filled with some material held in place by a cloth around my head. My legs were tied together and did not touch the ground. As I worked my eyelids to try to see around me, I heard again the muffled cry that had brought me to this side of the village. I also heard someone humming to himself and smelled tobacco smoke.

When at last I was able to force my eyes open, sunlight poured in and I could see only a blurred brightness. I blinked several times and gradually the forms took shape. Across from me, his body bound to a post with his hands tied to another post in front of him, was my brother, Gum. Someone had stuffed his mouth with rags and tied them around his head just as they had done to me. I struggled against my bonds when I saw him but only succeeded in causing more pain in my shoulders. It also seemed that my efforts actually tightened the knots on my wrists. As I looked at Gum, I noted blood running down the post where his hands were tied and that someone had cut off two fingers of his left hand. He stirred weakly in his bonds and raised his head to stare at me. I saw him throw his eyes to my right as if to point to something or someone.

"I believe that you have killed the Dungoor Bai," came a voice barely out of my field of vision. I knew who spoke. "Did you know that I was his favorite nephew?"

Chol stepped around to face me. He was naked except for a small leather pouch hung around his neck by a string. He had painted white lines of dung ash across his forehead and made circles on his cheeks. Black circles of charcoal surrounded his eyes which stared at me showing too much white, giving him a crazed and demonic appearance. I struggled again against my bonds.

"I will return to Akot and take his place," Chol said with a laugh. "It will be you who put me there. Your own family will have to bring their cases before me and ask me for justice. Your mother will have to ask me for justice." Chol laughed again. "Your mother, a woman that I now know very well."

I roared against the gag in my mouth and struggled. I looked around me for any hope of escape or help and saw only Chol. On a wooden table to my right lay a large knife. Next to it, two small fingers that I assumed belonged to Gum had already been strung on a wire.

"Do you like my work?" Chol asked. "I learned the trade from my uncle. He trades with the Ugandans near the border. They pay him well for any amulets he can bring them. When word of his work spread, he enlisted me to help him. We must use the parts of virgin children. Of course, after I have from them what I need there is no need for them to stay a virgin." He laughed again showing yellow teeth, some of which had been filed to a point.

Gum began to struggle and cry out. Chol walked to him and slapped him across his face with the back of his hand. "Do not interrupt me," he spit at Gum who hung his head and was quiet. Chol then returned to stand in front of me.

"Soon, a few of the SPLA who had been to school in Uganda began to come to us requesting our amulets," he continued. "You met our best customer just recently. Commander Daniel Awet."

The man who had my father flogged for interfering with the torture of the children, I thought. Many things came back to me. The way Awet looked around when I had mentioned Chol's name, the story of soldiers being forced to protect a civilian who killed the children. Even this village, now fit into an evil puzzle .

"He was a simple soldier before he began to wear our charms," Chol said. "Now look at him. Commander in charge of thousands of troops and hero of the Battle of the Bahr Naam River. He gives my uncle and me all the credit, at least in private it is what he says. He has no gift for making these charms for himself."

My hands grew numb as the ropes bit into them, but still I tried to lunge at Chol. Despite my bonds, he stepped back a pace, then laughed at me again.

"I am afraid that there is no market for Dinka men who have the marks," he said. "It is this thing about being flawless."

"Gum, however, is a different story," he turned to my brother who raised his head when he heard his name, his eyes wide with terror. "I thought you should live to see this," he said over his shoulder to me.

Chol walked to the table and took his knife. He then walked casually to Gum and grabbed his left ear. Gum struggled but could not shake his grip. Chol then carefully sliced off most of Gum's ear as a hoarse cry exploded from

Gum's gagged mouth. I cried out as well and renewed my struggle against my bonds. I almost lost consciousness again as I struggled. When I looked again, Gum lay sagging in his bonds. I could not see that he still breathed.

Chol had turned his back to me and stood at the table, carefully wiping blood from Gum's ear. While I watched him he stopped working and raised his head as if listening for something. A moment later he resumed cleaning Gum's ear.

Something moved at the periphery of my vision and I both heard and saw what appeared to be a very small spear imbed itself in Chol's right thigh. Chol cried in pain and plucked it from his leg. I now could see the fletching of a small arrow. He flung the arrow to the ground and reached under the table to retrieve a pistol. When he turned around to look for his attacker, his movements were sluggish and his knees seemed about the buckle. He fired two shots into the bush, but I did not believe that he saw anyone and was shooting to frighten someone. He raised his pistol again but seemed to be having difficulty holding it steady. He looked at me and then pointed the weapon at my face. I watched as the gun wavered. He fired a shot at me that grazed my cheek and left my right face numb. When I looked up at him again, he had collapsed into a heap and upended the table.

As I looked about, a clump of grass rose from the ground and took the shape of a man holding a bow. The man walked to Chol and nudged him with a bare foot. He then took out his knife and went over to Gum. I tried to scream at him until I saw that he was cutting away Gum's bonds. He then came to me. While he was freeing me, I again recognized the scars of the Atuot on the face of Jurkuc. This was the second time in as many days that the warrior had saved my life.

By the time he had freed my hands, Gum had wrapped me in an embrace. Jurkuc had to shove him aside in order to cut the bonds that held my ankles in place. We stared at one another for a moment, then Jurkuc gave me a barely perceptible nod of his head. I nodded in reply and we both felt satisfied that enough had been said between us.

Jurkuc walked to Chol and again nudged him with his foot, this time rolling him onto his back. Wide, glassy eyes stared back at us.

"He is not dead," Jurkuc said. "The poison of my arrow will make him unable to move or speak for a time, perhaps an hour or less. He is very strong. If we leave him on his own, he may recover."

Gum had wrapped his hand in a strip of cloth and stood fighting back tears. The place of his severed ear still dripped blood down the side of his head. With his good hand, he leaned down, took a fistful of dirt, and drizzled it slowly over Chol's face and open eyes. He looked around, I believe hoping to find a club or spear.

"You will not kill him now," Jurkuc said. "He has mutilated and killed my son. My son's name was Matueny. When I found his body, I tracked down the killer and found him to be this man, Chol. I also backtracked Matueny's path and saw that two of you encountered him by the river near the cattle camp, the one you just left."

I nodded understanding. I had heard of trackers with great skills like this before and knew again that this was a warrior of note.

"If you leave him to me, I will avenge my son's death and he will suffer a great deal more from me alone than he would from a quick death at your hands," Jurkuc said. "I have earned this."

Again, I nodded. Gum came to stand beside me. As he pressed his body to mine I felt him trembling. I looked about and retrieved my gun and other belongings before taking Gum down the trail that would lead us to the road and on to home. We walked slowly. Just before we left sight of Jurkuc, I turned one final time and looked in his direction. He knelt working on the body of Chol. At this distance, I would have thought that he was cleaning a dead goat or cow. Jurkuc looked up at us and raised the hand that held a knife. I called out to him.

"You are a great warrior and a worthy friend," I said as loudly as my voice allowed. "There will be peace between your people and mine. There is no river between us."

Jurkuc waved his knife in acknowledgement. We turned and started the long walk home as the afternoon sun moved slowly through the trees.

A dream came to him as he lay on the wooden cot inside his spacious tent. Around him, thousands of soldiers slept or stood guard. He had dreamt many such dreams, but they all predicted victory and glory. These he had shared with his men and his family. In this dream, a great warrior as those of old called out for a child, called with the voice of a father for his son. Anguish and rage poured from him as he searched the forest and grasslands alone. In his dream, the man crouched within the tall grass from fear of the warrior. The warrior passed him by, still calling for his son, calling a name he could not quite make out. When the warrior was out of sight, the man turned to run in the opposite direction and stumbled over a something lying in the grass. As he struggled to stand, he looked and saw blood covering the grass around him. He looked down at himself and saw blood on his body and hands. When he got to his feet, he froze. A lion stood staring at him with deep, yellow eyes and sniffed the air. A low growl rumbled from its throat.

He ran in his dream, trying to get away from the blood and the warrior, but most of all, from the lion. He knew it was futile to run from a lion and he knew it would smell of blood he tracked through the grass. As he ran he could hear the sounds of padded feet and growls behind him. He stumbled and fell across the dry ground just as the lion leapt.

He awoke sweating and panting with the sound of the lion's roar still in his ears. He threw back the netting that covered his cot and sat up. In the distance, he heard music playing over a cheap radio as men laughed and talked. He saw the faint glow of a cigarette where one of his guards stood. The air in his tent was heavy and still. He pulled on his pants and threw back the flaps of his tent. Two men jumped to their feet and saluted him, barely visible in the light of a smoldering fire. Nearby, a woman stepped from a hut of woven grass. The bright orange skirt, the only thing she wore, seemed to glow. She stood looking at the man, watching for a hint of what he wished of her, ready to meet his need. He walked back into his tent and left the flaps open, her signal to come to him.

Later that night, she bathed his hot and sweating body with water she dipped from a shallow, clay dish. She felt him tremble and fight the sleep that crept over him.

Chapter Twenty-One

Under the care of the woman from the cattle camps Matak recovered well from his wounds and we continued as best friends and agemates. On our return to Akot, he created elaborate stories of how the spear of the Dungoor Bai killed Chol and his accomplices for swearing on it to a lie. People grew more afraid of the spear and it was eventually given to Matak.

During the next rainy season, against his wishes, his family picked out a girl for him and he married his name to her. Since his injury, he had no interest in girls and he gave the honor of impregnating his wife in his name to one of his half brothers who lived nearby. Matak's chaste life and secrecy added to his reputation and his fame and people came from long distances to ask his advice or to pay him for rituals. Matak shared his wealth, as any honorable Dinka man would. My mother continued to hope that he would take my oldest sister as another wife later, but I knew that Matak would not do so. No one in the village other than our own Beny Bith and I knew of Matak's injuries and of her prophecy about him—a prophecy that she told him even before we got the marks. Like the Beny Bith that he was gradually replacing, Matak's legacy would live on, not in his bloodline but in name alone, which for a Dinka is enough.

Within the same year in which Matak married, I began to formally court the girl, Akol. She remained as beautiful as the day I secretly watched her while I took my marks. At her urging, and because the community now considered me of high character, her family and mine negotiated only a short while. They then arrived at a price of cows that is so low that I do not think that I should tell anyone of it. Akol is the sun to me, as her name implies, and I love her dearly.

Before our engagement, Akol had started following the teaching of a Catholic priest from a country called Mexico and she went to their gatherings every week. On occasion I went with her, but I remained confused as to the meaning of the words and rituals. Koor had still not returned to us and my uncles lived a great distance away. Athen did not object to Akol's new religion and spoke openly of her great joy to have a daughter-in-law of such high character. Akol's family agreed to let us marry as Catholics, so I learned enough of the words to recite the things the priest told me. He sprinkled water on me and on that day, so it seems, I became a Catholic. The next month, the priest did a ceremony for us and we were husband and wife. For the sake of honor, my family still insisted that we pay them the cows and goats we had agreed upon and that we get the blessings of the Beny Bith, so we did this as well. Akol did not hide her distaste as the old woman danced about and sacrificed a chicken to call blessing down upon us. Matak watched from a distance, and though he was not the Beny Bith my family had chosen to perform this ceremony, I saw him dancing and lifting his hands in what I knew would be a prayer for our safety and fertility.

Just before our wedding, I went in secret to the cattle camp to be certain that my demands about the Dungoor Bai's body had been obeyed. I found his bones scattered across a dry, mudflat, some of them already having been ground into hyena dung. In the darkness I slipped unseen into the camp and spoke briefly with the Beny Wut. He gave me his blessings but warned me not to come to his camp again. Chol's family still kept their cattle at his camp and he wanted no more trouble. I agreed to stay away and thanked him for the warning.

Three months after I had taken Akol as a wife and in the rainy season where tracking was difficult, I went into the Atuot territories looking for Jurkuc. I found him in their market selling the hides of several gazelle he had snared. He told me that he had recovered the parts of his son's body that Chol had stolen and that he was now properly buried. He also introduced me to his wife and some other of his relatives. I think he saw that I had grown nervous about being among so many Atuot so he led me to a place on his compound where we could be alone. When no one else could hear us, I made my request. I had one thing I needed to learn from him and he was more than willing to teach me.

Matak and I had discussed what I must do for many months and I dissuaded him from coming with me with great difficulty. I left Akol when our first crop of groundnuts was ready, assuring that she would have plenty of food for the season. I also had gained a pledge from Matak to provide for her needs, a pledge he gladly gave. I gave my spear to Akol's father for safe keeping. Wearing the uniform Koor had given me and carrying my gun, I walked north for several weeks. I went from village to village looking for any SPLA that knew of my father's whereabouts. Months later, when the dry season had come upon us and the nights chilled me to my bones, I finally found a soldier at home on furlough from the SPLA who knew Koor and where his troops now stayed. The distance dismayed me. They were all the way north in Abyei guarding the border of Darfur.

I began walking north as the nights grew cold and the days dusty and dry. I passed villages where the Laraap had burned all of the huts and the people worked to rebuild them. Some contained craters that I knew were made by bombs dropped from airplanes. Now that I had seen their work up close, I could imagine the devastation that they had brought.

The people stared at me but did not offer conversation unless I stopped. Even then, many of them hurried away, as afraid of the SPLA as they were of the Laraap. When I stopped for the night, they followed the ancient Dinka custom of providing shelter and food to travelers, but I could see them hurrying their children away from me. I learned that the SPLA recruited young men and even older boys to fight with them. If they refused, the soldiers would often retaliate by beating the parents, so they became accustomed to denying they had children. The old men told me Laraap slave traders did the same in generations past. Some had told me that in the past years, children had disappeared into the night without a trace and it reminded me of Chol's evil deeds. I did not tell the parents of my suspicions as it was kinder to leave them thinking that an animal had taken the children than to suggest the horrors that Chol would have done to them.

Some villages lay untouched by the war, or so it seemed as I passed them. They had wells with new metal pumps, small buildings where a man gave out medicines, and even some motorized grinders where a woman's entire crop of sorghum or millet could be turned into flour in less than an hour. Most of the men complained that the flour did not taste as good as it did when the women ground with their sticks, but I could not tell the difference.

On a few days, I was lucky enough to wave down a passing truck and I covered in hours what would have taken me days of footing. Most of the trucks that would stop belonged to merchants trading goods with the few shops that had sprouted in the villages.

One day, a white truck driven by an old, white-haired kawaja skidded to a stop behind me as I walked along a long straight stretch of road. He beckoned me to join him in the cab of his truck. Red dust covered the truck but I could see letters beneath the dirt that spelled "SPLA". I could not have read the other letters, even if they had not been covered with dirt. The back of his truck was filled with books and he listened to a radio station in English as we drove. He spoke only a few words of Dinka, just enough to learn my name and to tell me that he was called "Billy." He gave me a Dinka name for himself as well but I did not believe it was truly his.

The old man let me ride with him for two days more. He slept upright in his truck while I slept on the ground. He took me all the way to Abyei, letting me out by an SPLA camp surrounded by barbed wire. As he sped away I waved to him and he waved back over his shoulder.

I spoke to a man standing guard at the gate and he told me that there was no man there named Koor. He motioned other soldiers over. One of them knew Koor and told me that he was in a camp with the officers a few miles away. I started to walk in the direction he indicated when he told me to wait. Within minutes, a truck came to the gate and the soldier arranged for me to ride to Koor's camp.

As I rode, the man asked me many questions; where I lived, was I a soldier, if I was not a soldier, why was I carrying gun and wearing a uniform? I told him that I had worked for the SPLA, in truth this was what I had done at the Bahr Naam. He seemed satisfied with my answers.

"Why are you looking for Koor?" he asked. He drove fast and the truck skidded around curves in the dusty road. I clung to the door handle and tried not to appear afraid.

"Koor is my father," I replied.

"Koor is a great soldier," he replied. "It is good that you come to visit him. I would be happy if any of my sons came to visit me."

He talked of the war and how a country called America was working to force the Laraap into making peace with the

SPLA. He told me of a plan by the Laraap to steal water from the White Nile and leave us southerners dry. He said that the SPLA had destroyed the machines that dug trenches to steal the water. He talked of so many things that I did not have to say another word until we reached the camp. A guard stood by a log which lay across the road. When he saw the truck, he waved familiarly to the driver and dragged the log to the side. We drove through a line of dense trees into a vast collection of grass huts and tents. Many civilians worked in dry gardens and groups of boys watched a small herd of goats.

The driver took me to a fired brick building with a shiny metal roof. A metal pole sporting the flag of South Sudan and the SPLA rose over the building and the flags swung slowly back and forth in the hot breeze. Men with guns, most in uniform but some in short pants and thin shirts, lounged about in the shade of the roof's overhang.

I got out and the driver sped away, leaving me staring at the men. They looked back at me but did not offer to greet me as would be proper. I walked to the door of the building, but one of the soldiers rose to block my way.

"I am here to see Koor," I said to him.

"Who are you?" he asked, not politely at all.

"I am Thon," I replied. "Koor is my father."

The man stepped back and looked toward the other men. They rose and greeted me, this time with the politeness befitting a Dinka man. They led me to a room and told me to wait. The room smelled of dust and stale air. Paper posters with the image of John Garang covered the walls. After only a few minutes, Koor entered.

We greeted each other warmly and Koor told me to sit on a chair covered with soft cloth. When I sat down, the chair leaned backwards and I almost fell. Koor laughed, then sat across from me.

"You have come a long way," he said.

I nodded.

"Why are you here?"

Koor and I spoke for a long while. Once, a soldier came into the room and apologized for interrupting us and he asked Koor a few questions. Koor answered him curtly and the man left. We continued talking for hours as a plan began to take shape. As the afternoon became early evening, Koor and I left for his hut. I was surprised that he lived in a simple hut of woven grass covered with sheets of thin blue material. A woman brought us food and we ate alone. Two days later, I was ready. Koor arranged for a driver to take me almost to Rumbek with some of his soldiers who had been reassigned.

Chapter Twenty-Two

Commander Awet awoke to a stabbing sensation in his right arm. He rose, pulled back his mosquito net, and looked around the dark room in which he slept. He could see nothing, but believed he heard someone, maybe two people, breathing in the dark. Across the room, someone lit a match and touched it to a candle. In the faint ring of light he saw Koor's face. Behind him, he could see but not identify another person.

"Koor. What is it?" he demanded. Even then his voice seemed sluggish and forced.

Koor lit two more candles and the hut filled with a warm, orange and yellow glow. Koor stood beside Awet but did not speak.

"Koor," Awet said again, this time with more difficulty. "I asked you a question. You will answer."

At this time he noticed me standing in the corner holding a sharp piece of metal shaped like the head of an arrow. I carefully wrapped the object in leather, placed it in my pack, and then came to stand beside Koor.

Awet tried to speak again, but could make only rasping sounds. When he tried to stand, he fell backward into his cot pulling the mosquito net into a heap on top of him. Koor gently raised his feet to the cot, put a pillow under his head, and straightened the net.

"I found the amulets that you purchased from Chol," Koor said softly.

Awet's eyes grew wide and a gurgling sound came from his throat.

"I know of the abomination you have brought to us," Koor said. His voice was cold and caused a shiver to run up my spine.

"You have claimed to have had eight dreams, some bad and some good, and that all of them came true. Tonight I give you a ninth dream, and it is not a good dream for you. Tonight you will die in your bed," Koor said. His voice was steady and calm, giving no indication of the hatred carried in his words. Awet tried to speak but made no sound as his mouth moved to open and close like a dying fish.

"No one will know how you have died," Koor continued. "Perhaps they will suspect a poison, but you ate what the other men ate, drank what they drank. No one will notice the small prick in your arm. They will think your heart gave out and that you died in your sleep. As you are dying, let this be your last dream. Your wives will become my wives. Your children will become my children and these children will say that they are the sons of Koor. Your name will not be spoken and it will be as if you had never lived. You will join Chol as a spirit without power and without rest. This I pledge to you now. Let this be the last words you hear before Nhialic expends his wrath on your dark soul."

Awet's eyes stared at the ceiling without blinking. Koor put his hands over his Commander's mouth and nose while I blew out the candles.

Chapter Twenty-Three

The next day, I refused the offer of a ride to Rumbek in one of the army trucks. Koor tried to persuade me to return home, but I had made up my mind. Later that day I met with a man who wrote my name in a large book. He gave me a pair of boots and a bit of money. Koor himself drove me to a place where other new soldiers walked in formation and chanted. Just as Koor had taught me, I saluted the officer who met us, then stood at attention while he and Koor talked for awhile. I still stood at attention when he drove away, leaving me with the officer and the band of new soldiers.

I have fought in many campaigns since that day, the day I became a soldier. Our leaders are very careful of where we engage with this enemy, melting away when we cannot hold the field and killing the Laraap to the man when we can, teaching them that they cannot win this war but can only lengthen it. We of South Sudan have fought invaders in this manner for so many generations that we do not remember peace and war is what we know, what we are.

I did not see Akol for two more years after I enlisted. By then, she had born me a strong son. We named him Manyol, which means "One Who Can Delay For The Future." It is what I want for my son, to live for the future when we are free of this war, free of the Laraap and the other invaders. It is for that future that I left the cattle and family that I love. Under Matak's protection, our cattle continued to multiply and Akol's gardens grew thick. I spent enough time at home to assure that we would have another child, and then I hurried back to the war. I would rather have stayed with Akol and the rest of my family but that is something that will wait for another time, a time that may never come.

Something drives invaders to die on our soil. Ottomans, British, Egyptians, Kawaja, and Laraap alike expend themselves in futile wars to make us, the Dinka people, bow to them. They steal our children, take what our lands can give them, and convince themselves that they can own what Nhialic has given to us. It is why blood so deeply stains our land and why our wives make so many children that never grow old. Perhaps the others also know that we lie at the center of all things, a place others covet. Nhialic gives them green lands, and they want ours. Nhialic gives them many children so that they cover the rest of the earth, and they want ours. He gives them clear water from great rivers, and yet their armies return to camp by ours. We fight with the hope that one day, all of the outsiders will leave and not return. Leave us so we can live as free people. It is what I hope for and fight for, to live in peace with my family and my cattle-- to sit by the river and watch my children play, to grow old and wise, to give advice to my clan, and to honor Nhialic. Perhaps someday it will be come to pass. For now, the War of the Anyanya still rumbles across the earth like the sin of man and I must take my place against it.

It is my duty to fight in this war, for I am Thon, son of Koor, son of Mayol, son of Matur, son of Kau. I am a warrior of a people who have never been conquered. I bear the marks of a Man of Men, Husband and Father, Protector and Guide to the People. I live in the great land without stone that lies at the center of the world.

I am Muonyjang.

THE END

Author Notes

While performing anthropological research, I commonly utilize a somewhat labor-intensive tool which produced the vast majority of the materials for this book. As I learn about the people I am studying, I will take some specific ritual or belief and write a fictionalized account where local people practice or execute this specific event. This exercise always reveals severe deficiencies in my understanding of their practices and what it means to them. Put in anthropological terms, what I learn from the etic perspective (view from the outside) I try to express in the emic perspective (view from the inside). I never get it completely right and expect that I never will. I am content, however, with what noted anthropologist Nancy Scheper Hughes calls "good enough ethnography". This is not a call to mediocrity, but rather recognition that a lack of perfect representation should not preclude a respectful attempt at some sort of representation. My ethnography of the Dinka Agar, published by Markoulakis Publications under the title, *A Land At the Center of the World* is full of details and analysis that one would expect from an academic work. I have found, however, that the fiction can be a much more textured tool for communicating reality than is nonfiction. They both have their functions, but fiction is a tool that allows a writer to draw the reader into a story and feel what the characters feel-- see, hear, and smell the world with them.

This work was originally just such an exercise, a humble attempt to fuse the etic and the emic of my experiences in South Sudan where I worked intermittently for six years as both an anthropologist and a physician. As the story grew, I became drawn into it myself and, as work on the academic text drew to a close, I felt compelled to complete the novel. I wanted to see where it led.

Hoping this fiction would not only entertain, but serve also as an anthropological tool, I have stayed true to Dinka practices as much as possible but took poetic license on rare occasion. The *Dungoor Bai*, for instance, is not a proper name for an individual, as used in this story, but a political position. In case it was not obvious or that the reader assumed it was a typo, *Laraap* (*Larap* in the singular) means "Arabs" in the Dinka dialect spoken in the areas near Rumbek. *Dheeng* is the closest Dinka equivalent to the word, "beautiful," though in the song the word is used as a noun such that the closest rendering of the word would be "the beautiful thing." Also, *abeed* is an Arabic derogatory term sometimes by the Northern Sudanese to describe South Sudanese as ones fit only to be a slave. The term is, according to some Dinka scholars, still used with unfortunate frequency. The closest American equivalent would be a similar racial slur which is fortunately rapidly disappearing from our vocabulary but carries emotional and historical baggage sufficient to communicate the level of affront this term would carry to a Dinka. Also, of course, there is stone in Sudan. In fact, large areas of the north and also surrounding Juba hold small mountains of stone. It is not so in the land in which most of my work was done. Since I am a bit of an amateur rock collector, I was struck that for many miles around my tent camp there was not a single stone that had not been trucked into the area for construction purposes. Geologically speaking, there was simply nothing to study except for clay and sand. People in our region tended to speak of their area as representative of the rest of Sudan in such ways, an extreme example of colloquial thinking.

Several other credits are needed, especially for some of the songs. Godfrey Lienhardt's classic ethnography, *Divinity and Experience: The Religion of the Dinka* (Oxford Press, 1961), is the source of several of these songs. Francis Mading Deng's work, The *Dinka of Sudan* (Waveland Press, 1972) is the source for some others. While the many Dinka myths and rituals are described from personal experience, their interpretations are significantly influenced by these two authors.

I drew most heavily from the guidance and suggestions from my many Dinka friends, especially Gordon Mayom Makueng Ruai Kuany—here being a rare place where either of us ever use his complete name. Mayom is one of my heroes, a man who has endured untold hardships, guided and protected me and my family, and is the kind of man that speaks of great hope for South Sudan. The legend of Ngundeng, while described in many other places, comes from a recorded interview with him. Many references place Ngundeng's death at around 1906. Other friends that provided advice and logistical support include Edward Awuziamvi of the Norwegian People's Aid, Abraham Maper (who spent many hours and days walking with me explaining "the Dinka way of life" and who baptized three of my children in the Bahr Naam River within view of the great battle site), Billy White (who makes a cameo appearance as a lone kawaja who gave our protagonist a random ride, something he is apt to do), Benjamin Mathiang Meen Matak Agai (who I almost drowned in a dugout canoe while crossing the Sabot River), Isaac Bol (who brought us lifesaving water once when my son and I were stranded at a cattle camp), Kuwat and Rose Malual (Rose for feeding us and Kuwat for just being the best of friends), and other friends that I know only by their common names. These include Chadrak, Santino, Joseph, and James. Missionaries Mark and Cathy Kissee also introduced me to these remarkable people and provided valuable support and advice on numerous occasions. Guy and Betty Beatty funded the vast majority of the medical work we did while in Sudan and I must again thank them for their generosity.

In order to obtain supplies for the medical clinic in which my wife and I worked, I drove from Akot to Rumbek many times and in doing so crossed the Bahr Naam River. I have seen and photographed the remnants of the Battle of the Bahr Naam River that lies along this road. I also interviewed dozens of participants and witnesses to the battle but can find no other historical references to it. While in this novel, I purposefully leave the dates of this storyline uncertain, this specific battle occurred in 1985, during a time that the Anyanya Two was in one of its most intense phases. Though some are composites of actual historical figures, the people are fictional characters and do not represent individuals any individual, living or dead. As told in this story, Daniel Awet was the heroic commander of the SPLA forces during this battle but there is no evidence linking him to specific atrocities or child sacrifices. While I was working in the area, Mr. Awet held the office of Governor of the Upper Lakes State and most recently was elected as a representative in the newly formed government of South Sudan, now based in Juba. He is also, as of this writing, alive and well.

The borders of Sudan set in 1956 made it, by area, the largest country in Africa. Northern Sudan, which includes the states of Darfur, has come under increasing Muslim influence while states in the southern regions have resisted such changes. Prior to the 2011 referendum on independence, the regime in Khartoum was recognized by the United Nations, the African Union and the United States as the only legitimate government. It is also led by the only sitting head of state to be indicted by the World Court for crimes against humanity and to have an outstanding arrest warrant still in effect.

Since obtaining independence the northern central government and rebel forces in the south of Sudan have maintained separate legislative bodies, armed forces, cultural identities, and economies. Sudan, therefore, has functioned in effect as two separate nation-states whose interactions have been characterized primarily by conflict and not cooperation for the good of its citizens. The result is the longest running civil war in modern times. Anyanya One and Anyanya Two are what the Sudanese call two phases of what is, in reality, one prolonged conflict. In January of 2011, the most significant single event in Sudanese history took place when citizens of the South voted in a referendum on whether to stay a part of a greater Sudan or to secede from the union. As expected, the vote was overwhelmingly for independence. We must wait and pray that there is no Anyanya Three.

South Sudan continues to be a country of extremes within extremes. Inhabiting these extremes are highly marginalized people who deserve recognition and a voice. They are not, as I have heard them described, 'a primitive people,' in any way except that they lack most modern technologies. They possess intricate relationships, a rich and complex culture, history and sophisticated philosophies — in many ways more so than those found in Western urban cultures. In a word, they are humans whose similarities with the rest of us far outweigh their differences and whose worth is equal to our own. I am blessed to have known them during my time with them and I hope you enjoyed meeting them here.

Hen agoor ba meeth leech pan Aköt. Nhialic abi thieei.

J.L. Deal, Majok-Bar Akiim

Other books by Jeffery Deal

A Land At the Centre of the World, revised edition

The Second Coming

Toccoa

Time Drive